Praise for Marilynn Griffith's writing:

"Marilynn Griffith is a fresh voice in Christian fiction. Her funny, breezy style is sure to take the market by storm!"

Tracey Bateman, author, *Leave It to Clare*

"From beginning to end, you can't help but see the hand of God ministering through Marilynn Griffith's work."

Vanessa Davis Griggs, author, *Promises Beyond Jordan* and *Wings of Grace*

"Marilynn Griffith digs deep inside to write a novel about everyday people who love the Lord."

LaShaunda C. Hoffman, editor, *Shades of Romance* magazine

"With poetic description and compelling storytelling, Marilynn Griffith delights readers with every sentence."

Stephanie Perry Moore, author, *A Lova' Like No Otha'*, Payton Sky series, and Carmen Browne series

"Looking for a sassy, engaging read that keeps you turning pages and recalling your faith? Look no further. Marilynn Griffith won't disappoint."

Stacy Hawkins Adams, author, *Speak to My Heart*

"Marilynn Griffith's writing makes the five senses come alive. Her writing makes you taste color, smell love, hear hearts, see purpose, and touch God's truth in every word and phrase. She is a master storyteller!"

Gail M. Hayes, author, Daughters of the King

jAde

jAde

Marilynn Griffith

R Revell
Grand Rapids, Michigan

Published by Fleming H. Revell
a division of Baker Publishing Group
P.O. Box 6287, Grand Rapids, MI 49516-6287
www.revellbooks.com

Printed in the United States of America

Library of Congress Cataloging-in-Publication Data
Griffith, Marilynn.
    Jade / Marilynn Griffith.
        p.   cm. — (Shades of style ; bk. 2)
    ISBN 10: 0-8007-3041-0 (pbk.)
    ISBN 978-0-8007-3041-3 (pbk.)
    1. Women fashion designers—Fiction. 2. Wedding costume—Fiction.
    I. Title
    PS3607.R54885J34 2006
    813'.6—dc22   2005037995

For Ben, my little man.

Do not conform any longer to the pattern of this world, but be transformed by the renewing of your mind. Then you will be able to test and approve what God's will is—his good, pleasing and perfect will.

Romans 12:2

Where there is disease, make us instruments of healing
Where there is brokenness, make us the tie that binds
Where there is pain, have us bring relief
Where there is death, let us bring assurance of life in
   Thee.

May we receive the sick with compassion
May we treat the sick with competence
And so reflect the Master Physician
That they go with Thanksgiving and a new understand-
   ing of Our Savior's Mission.
This prayer is offered in the Name of the Divine Physi-
   cian who heals us all.

Amen.

Episcopal Medical Missions Foundation prayer

Prologue

The envelope held Lily Chau's future. She held a letter opener, running the tip under her nails for the remnants of her past. Skimming under the nail of her ring finger, she snagged what she'd been going for—a hunk of prunes caught under her nail during the chop-and-puree fest once known as her mother's breakfast. A breakfast her mother had returned as quickly as Lily had spooned it all in, leaving Lily standing in a puddle in her best shoes.

Lily had tried to wait, but her mother hadn't been in a waiting mood. The guilt over leaving her with their neighbor had sent Lily into a chopping, blending frenzy that ended as such things usually did, prunes seeping into her shoes and staining her best pants. But that was okay. She'd put a barrette in her mother's hair and fed her breakfast. Where God chose to store that breakfast was up to him.

Two weeks ago her mother had made her own prunes three days in a row. Toasted a scone even. But today was today, with prune stains on her favorite pair of pants. They were turning into Lily's uniform. Still, mother had good days; Lily's boyfriend, Ken, was still dropping hints about their inevitable wedding; and she grew closer to God each day. Things were getting better. Becoming stable.

So why was she holding the letter opener in both hands? Lily ran the point of it across the envelope, tracing the letters in the return address: *The Next Design Diva*, Nia Network. Lily slipped the blade into the envelope's back flap, then pulled upward slightly, ripping the corner and—

"Are you sleeping in there?" A husky voice laced with laughter echoed in the hall before its speaker reached Lily's office.

Jean Guerra believed in giving people warnings of her impending arrival, even her friends. For everyone but Lily, the announcement was usually warranted, since people tended to find Jean a little intimidating. Lily saw through Jean's fast moves and loud talk . . . to her heart. She hoped her friend wouldn't see through her just as quickly today.

"Can't you ever stay in your office during the creative hour? We've got thirty more minutes. Take a nap, why don't you. Or color in a coloring book like that guy over in production." Lily's voice quivered despite her efforts to sound okay. She wasn't. The future, something she'd long locked away (except for her boyfriend) had come in the mail.

Though Lily chided her workaholic friend Jean for coming to visit when they were all supposed to be spending time alone to refuel their creativity, the interruption was a gift. For a moment she'd let herself consider something impossible. Something still caught on her letter opener.

Jean whisked into the office just as Lily swept the letter into her desk drawer, where it would accompany her secret copy of *Modern Bride* and a cigarette she'd found after quitting smoking and hadn't thrown away.

Lily squirmed under her friend's withering glance as Jean pushed Lily's huge fossil doorstop into place.

Jean shook her head. "Oh my. She's cramming things into that drawer again. Don't tell me. You were peeking at those silly ten-dollar wedding magazines. Or were you dreaming of that picket fence on Long Island with your doctor friend?"

Warmth rushed to Lily's face. "Neither. You need to stay out of my desk, you nosy thing."

Jean approached Lily like a lioness in a good suit. Laughter bubbled up from her throat. "Listen, honey, nobody needs to be nosy to know anything around here, especially when you stuff that drawer so full it can't shut. I can't tell you how many times I've had to come in here and pick up all that mess off the floor since you ran the custodian away."

"Here you go with that again. I told you. I did not run the custodian away. He can still clean in here . . . when I'm around."

"Uh-huh." Jean shook her head in pity.

"He was stealing my rocks!" Lily banged her fist on her desk, wanting to shove herself into the drawer too. She smiled, thinking of what might fly out if she tried.

"Listen to what you just said. Stealing rocks. Now, I admit you've got some of the best pebble collections I've ever seen, but you've got to let it go."

She reached around Lily and yanked out the drawer. A magazine unfurled as if she'd pulled the string on a parachute. Fabric swatches, neon note squares, and office supplies spilled over the sides and onto the floor.

Jean stuck her hand toward the back and came out with a pitiful excuse for a Virginia Slim. "You've got to let this go too. You haven't smoked in almost two years. What are you doing, planning a slow suicide sometime in the future?"

"I . . . I . . . just give me that, okay?" Lily reached for the cigarette, peeled back its skin, and emptied the tobacco guts into the trash while trying not to get too much of the smell on her fingers.

As she considered what she'd really saved up for later,

throwing away that letter instead of opening it, Lily became much less concerned with Jean and more concerned with her own heart. Sometimes it seemed like she'd come so far, but there were still those little secrets she tried to keep, parts of her life she tried to stuff in a drawer. And God kept having to come and pick up the pieces when they spilled over the side.

She grabbed a wet wipe from her purse and scrubbed her hands, only to realize what dangled from Jean's fingers.

The envelope.

The rumpled magazine had covered it, but as usual Jean had left no stone, or mangled bridal magazine, unturned. She looked as though she'd caught a tiger by the tail.

"They picked you! I knew they would. They had to. I told Raya I was going to call her father myself if they didn't."

Lily froze. She'd carried the envelope around in her purse for two days, wondering why the show had written her. She'd considered submitting sketches to *The Next Design Diva* several times, but each time something had happened with her mother's health to make her forget it. There was also the quiet that had come over her every time she'd prayed about it. She felt as though she was supposed to wait and see the salvation of the Lord, that what God had would come to her through another way. Now it seemed that her other way might have been from the office down the hall.

Lily blew out a breath. "What did you do?"

Beads from Jean's bracelets jangled as she shook her wrists. "Nothing much. I took a few sketches from your book and scanned them, and I sent that robe you designed for that stupid boyfriend of yours—"

Lily clenched her fists. "The kimono? That was Ken's Christmas present. I've been looking everywhere for it. How could you?"

Her friend smiled. "Easy. Now hush and open the letter. At least I don't try to match you up with men. Not that you couldn't use some help there too . . . Don't look at me like that. I care about you."

If this was caring, Lily didn't want to think of what being disliked might feel like. She pried the letter from Jean's fingers and placed it in the drawer, now empty except for a neon pink star-shaped paper clip and a pencil with no eraser. Lily's sketching pencil.

She stared up at the ceiling. "Why can't I have regular friends who don't care about me so much. Goodness, Jean, how could you? I mean, sure I'd love to have my own line of clothes, my own fashion show during fashion week, but I can't—"

"Here we go again. You really should have been a Catholic, you know. You're a natural at the guilt thing." Jean dropped into the chair a few inches away. "We've been over this a gazillion times. You can do this. None of your excuses hold water, especially your first one, that you're not good enough. You're good enough, and you have the sense to still question your talent. Good enough for me. As for your mother, she can go wherever you go."

Lily chuckled, though there was little humor in it. "Like the way your grandkids could go wherever you go, Jean?"

Her stoic friend grabbed the desk with a white-knuckled grip. "Okay, you got me. I still think you should open it. Just to know."

"No thanks," Lily said, taking the letter from the drawer and ripping it to shreds. "Some things are best left unknown. The things that count though, that people care about you and want the best for you, those are the prizes of life."

Jean's jaw tightened as Lily swept the torn bits of paper into the trash with her cupped hand. "Oh, please. You sound like a sappy commercial. This is it! Your shot. And you ripped it up. How could you?"

Lily covered her friend's hand with her own. "I don't know, but I did. If it's mine, God will bring it back . . . at a time when my hands are free enough to hold it."

1

Therefore . . . as you have always obeyed
. . . continue to work out your salvation with
fear and trembling, for it is God who works
in you.

Philippians 2:12–13

Six months later

Lily's pen scraped against the pages of her journal
like a scalpel, cutting away her thoughts and flinging them onto the page before someone entered her
office and reminded her how much work she had to
do. This time of day—the creative hour, as her boss,
Chenille, called it—wasn't about what work needed
to be done but about remembering why one wanted
to do it. Lily savored every minute.

It was in these times that the first germ of a sketch
or the image of an art project like the stone fountain she'd made last weekend brushed across
Lily's mind. Behind her, a thin stream of
water wept over the rock faces and into
the fountain's shallow bottom. The sound
reminded Lily of a nature CD but louder.

She must have missed something in the instructions. It was supposed to be quiet. This persistent sound would take some getting used to, especially during these times when she was used to quiet. With the rest of the day a blur of speakerphone conversations, computer clicks, and the cries of her co-worker Raya's baby, Ray, in the next office over, this hour of quiet gave Lily time to gather her scattered thoughts.

Sometimes the sounds of Raya's baby or her friend's soulful lullabies before nap time brought Lily to tears, though she wasn't sure why. Perhaps the fountain would muffle her tears and the baby's too. Lily hoped so. This year she'd bought a special journal to capture some of her prayers during the Lenten season.

This first entry, much more vulnerable and transparent than she'd expected, made emotion pool in the corners of her eyes. The prayer, a jumbled form of the words she'd held back before staining her best linen skirt and flying out the door late, had captured what remained of the thoughts. She'd given up on making her mother's favorite breakfast six months ago, but this morning the guilt had gotten to her again right before the prunes had.

Now, as Lily read the looping weariness of her own hand, she was glad that most of her thoughts had dissipated into the morning cold.

Lord, help me to obey you from a clean heart, to worship you with clean hands. My palms are stained with my own intentions, my fingers bloodied with a desire to do the right things for all the wrong reasons. Thank you for the opportunity to care for my mother. Forgive me for sometimes wishing I were somewhere else, doing something else. May my love for Mother be as your love for me—rain in summer, fire in winter. Shape me according to your pattern. Make me into a garment of praise.

That she'd mentioned her profession, pattern making, and the name of her employer, Garments of Praise Fashion Design, in the prayer surprised her. Her thoughts this morning had been about her mother, not her job. She silently added the requests she no longer wrote or spoke: for Ken to propose marriage and for her to someday get the opportunity to design her own line of clothes. Both things seemed less likely to happen with each passing day.

Lily began to hum, allowing the strains of a familiar Mahalia Jackson tune to well up inside her. She'd long since forgotten the words, but the prayer within the notes stuck with her. She closed her eyes, opening them only when Chanel No. 5 tickled her nostrils.

"Morning, Jean," she said, peeking through one eyelid. The fountain swished against the silence.

"Morning yourself. Mahalia, huh? You must be dreaming of that grotto of wedded bliss again. Is the picket fence still white?"

Lily sighed. She should have known that closing her journal wouldn't help. Jean saw through people like windowpanes. Everyone except herself, of course.

She straightened and stared at her friend. "It's a cottage, thank you. Stucco. And there's no fence, only a low stone wall."

Her lashes lingered as if wanting to close, to go back inside the stucco house, into the nursery where their baby slept, into the garden where her mother's orchids flourished, into the bedroom where her own love had bloomed. If only she'd stopped at that stone wall, dealing with Ken's ambivalence toward their relationship would be much easier. But she hadn't stopped there. She'd gone too far, seen too much. Worse, it occurred to her now that Ken was never actually in the house she imagined.

Jean's hands ruffled Lily's spiky hair. "I know you love him, Lil. Just love yourself too. That's all I'm saying."

"I hear you." Lily took a deep breath, wondering why the two of them always whispered at work, as though someone was listening. No one was—besides God, of course, and he'd already heard all the dish.

"Did you see the reruns of *The Next Design Diva*? Oh my goodness. Your stuff could have leveled the entire field. Do you ever wonder what was in that letter? You could probably get another one, you know—"

"Jean . . ."

"Okay, okay. I'll quit. This time. Don't think I can't wear you down now." Jean smoothed her cashmere turtleneck over her hips and adjusted the ochre belt circling her waist.

"You're wearing me down right now, silly, but not in the way you think. What are you doing in here, anyway? It's the creative hour, remember? I thought you were finally getting into it. I haven't seen you roaming during this time for weeks."

"I've been busy over there." She held out a bracelet of gold and olive beads. "It took me forever to finish it, but I guess I'm officially crafty like the rest of you. That project will do me for a while though. As for today, I have a hall pass," Jean said in a low voice. "I convinced Chenille that hanging out over here is about as freewheeling as I'm going to get. The new guy is finger painting in the cutting room. Can you believe it?"

Lily nodded. She could believe it. During the creative hour she'd seen (and heard) everything from batik fabric dyes to spoken word poetry. It was like an office-wide talent show for some people. A regular free-for-all. Not Lily though. She kept her creativity behind closed doors.

"I do believe it. I think Raya and Jay are rubber-stamping

Easter cards next door. If the baby will let them, that is. He was screaming a minute ago."

"I heard him. I don't know how you two can even think over here. You know how I am when the grandchildren have to come to work with me. I can't even concentrate for a minute. And here comes Chenille with a whole creative hour. That girl is so spaced out sometimes. If you all worked for me . . ." She paused.

Lily laughed. "Don't even joke about that. Sweatshops are illegal. If it'll help you loosen up any, I can teach you how to make one of those rock sculptures you like so much."

Jean rubbed her chin. "If you're serious about that, I may reconsider. I don't know if I can catch on to your rock thing, but I certainly like the results. I like the results of that haircut too. I'm so glad you did it. You needed a change."

"Thanks. I think." Lily ran a hand through the blades of the new haircut sticking out from her scalp like some new variety of grass.

The style had been Lily's Valentine's Day gift to herself. Her mother hated it, of course. Ken hated it too, when he got around to noticing.

"Give Chenille a break," Lily said. "She trusts us and she trusts God. After almost losing Lyle, she really gave a lot of thought to how we spend our time. I know it seems quirky, but I really need this hour. As for the rock sculpture, we can definitely do that. Just tell me when, and I'll bring in the supplies."

In truth, Lily probably had most of the things stashed away here in her office somewhere—all except a drill, and Raya kept a cute pink one next door to repair all the mannequins she managed to destroy. Raya always blamed the misshapen dress forms on her sons, but Lily knew that their

19

head designer tripped over most of them. That girl was the beauty and the geek wrapped into one.

Lily positioned a pattern adjustment on the drafting board on her desk.

Jean leaned over her shoulder, squinting to see the lines. Satisfied, she pulled back and put her hands on Lily's shoulders. "Hey, it's Fat Tuesday, isn't it?"

Lily nodded, then grabbed a handful of amber-colored pebbles from a glass on the corner of her desk. The jar had once been filled with Hershey's Kisses, then Jelly Bellies. "Your teeth will still rot, but at least they're fat free," Raya's husband, Flex, had said in a tone that only personal trainers and third-grade teachers can use.

One cavity later Lily had exchanged the jelly beans for some of her favorite rocks. Fiddling with the pebbles had proved as soothing as the candy. Well, almost.

"It's Fat Tuesday, all right. If I took off these pants, you'd be sure of it."

Even without the candy on her desk, her fast-paced life at work and Ken's choice of restaurants left her with a little extra flesh here and there, but it was nothing that couldn't be covered with the right clothes. At least not yet.

Lily watched as Jean walked over to the treadmill in the corner and folded the patterns dangling from the handlebar. She turned it on and started at a good clip.

"Do you want that thing?" Lily asked. "You can have it. I've finally accepted that walking on a rubber belt just doesn't thrill me. Rock-gathering walks are more my speed, but hard to get away for these days."

Jean's bracelet jingled as she picked up her pace on the treadmill. "If you don't mind, I'd love to have it. Speaking of giving things up, what are you giving up for Lent? Your fascination with that doctor of yours would be a good start.

You're too old to wait for him, you know. After thirty a girl doesn't have two years to give away. Either he's going to marry you or not."

It was the "or not" that scared Lily. She didn't want to have this conversation today of all days, before the start of her first Lent after years of Baptist-Pentecostal adventures. She was feeling insecure enough.

"The question is, Jean, what are you giving up? It was your babbling on and on about Epiphany and Advent memories that made me visit People's Episcopal again."

The treadmill buzzed as it inclined upward. Jean's breathing changed rhythm. "Lent? Me? Oh, I see. Ken is off limits with you like religion is off limits with me? Okay, I can play that game."

She wasn't supposed to work during creative time, but with Jean on the treadmill, Lily felt the need to do something. She picked up a pattern from her tray and penciled in a dart. Though Jean's retelling of childhood holy days had nudged Lily back to her Episcopal roots, Jean had no interest in discussing her own faith. She'd come to the Spanish language Eucharist with Lily a few times and cried from beginning to end, but they'd never said another word about it. Jean had once said church was for weak people, needy people. Lily couldn't agree more.

"Ash Wednesday was one of my favorites though," Jean offered between breaths. "I always kept my ashes on all day."

Lily smiled. Jean was a tall woman, solid but not fat exactly. Her workouts over the past few months had added muscle to her broad shoulders and leanness to her tall frame. Her new hair color, a sort of orangish red, would have seemed clownish on another woman, but Jean's inferno personality and dynamic style carried off the look easily. Her peach-colored lips seldom smiled. Jean smiled with her hands—cooking, cutting, and helping. A language Lily understood.

A mechanical bell sounded on the treadmill. Ten minutes had passed, and Jean hadn't even broken a sweat. The bell also coincided with the end of the creative hour. Lily would have to catch up on her journaling later as well as jot down a sketch that was forming in her mind, one she'd be sure to keep away from Jean lest she send it in to some other fashion reality show. Lily hadn't thought about the letter she'd received last year very often, but this week it seemed to meet her every morning at the edge of her mind.

Jean eased off the machine. "Thanks again about the treadmill and the craft lessons. Be good to yourself, okay?" She started for the door, then turned back. "And about that Fat Tuesday crack. You look fine. Just stop eating those Ding Dongs and get moving.

"Maybe you should give up those chocolate things for Lent. You already quit smoking and gave up your every-blue-moon beers. You've stopped buying new clothes. You won't take my advice and get rid of Ken. You really don't do anything else."

Lent. Lily sighed. For someone who didn't want to talk about her own relationship with God, Jean seemed fascinated with Lily's spiritual life. Much more fascinated than even Lily was, although this Lent thing seemed really important. She wanted to give something to God and expect nothing in return, to sacrifice the way Christ had for her. But what to give? She hadn't had a Ding Dong since her mother had caught her eating a whole box in one sitting two months ago. Of course, that happened to be one of her lucid days.

"In truth, Jean, I don't know what I'll give up. These years since Dad died all seem like an offering in a way. Sometimes

I feel like there's nothing left to give. Like I don't want anything enough to give it up."

Lily regretted the words as quickly as she'd spoken them. Lies. More lies. No desires? Yeah right. Did an hour pass when she didn't think about her bare ring finger or her dream of a Lily Chau tag fluttering on someone's neck? But there was that part of her that didn't care about any of it. That didn't care about anything. That numb part. That was the part of Lily that scared her.

Jean laughed. "Only you can make your complaints sound like poetry. Mine just sound like . . . complaints."

"Aren't you leaving? Just go already." Lily chuckled, then quieted, embarrassed that Jean might think her ungrateful. Sometimes it seemed like Jean was the Christian and she the unbeliever. She had to remember she was talking to people, not God. God could handle anything she had to say, even the hard stuff.

Jean checked her watch. "This creative thing is over, but I have a few more things to say, thank you. I think it's sad that a young, beautiful woman like you doesn't feel like she has anything precious enough to give up. If you'd listen to me and give Ken up for Lent and call that show, we could make this real simple."

Lily wadded a piece of pattern paper.

Jean ducked.

Lily shot it into the trash can instead. The dreams smoldering inside her under family commitments, a growing workload, and her own insecurities rose up all the time, groaning the same question in her ear: *What about* you, *Lily?*

Li Li, the good Christian, the faithful Chinese daughter in her, had an answer for Lily, her American, hip-hop, Hostess-snack-cake self.

What about *you?*

This was the part of Lily that gathered stones and whispered prayers.

Trust yourself to the One who can be trusted.

If only it were as easy to do as it was to say.

"Ken will give up Mars bars," Lily said, busying her fingers with making a slider to adjust an old pattern. The creative hour was over, and Lily felt herself craving silence, as much as she loved her friend. "He gives them up every year. He says I'm making too much of this, that I should just pick something, anything." Lily's home-manicured nails snagged the pattern as she reached for the scissors to cut out the form.

Jean touched Lily's sandstone lamp, one of her best projects. She ran a hand down the stack of rectangular slabs that made the lamp's base. "I hate to agree with Ken, but I think he's right. Pick something small, something you won't really miss."

The words of King David came to Lily's mind: "I will not sacrifice to the LORD my God burnt offerings that cost me nothing." As usual Lily empathized with the distressed and depressed king and felt the same sentiment building in her own heart.

"It'll come to me. I'll think of something before tomorrow. I'm just not sure what."

"You want to go big, huh? I'd say go for the rocks, then. They're a big deal to you." Jean admired the lamp again. "I still can't believe you made this. And that fountain is unbelievable. I couldn't envision it when you first described it to me, but it fits perfectly with the other pieces. I can't wait until you get your own line of clothes. You create stunning images."

"Thank you. Now get before our mild-mannered boss turns barracuda on both of us."

Still stuck on the thought of giving up her weekend rock

crafting, Lily considered who she might be, what she might do without her little projects to look forward to. She'd be waiting for a lot of calls from Ken that would never come, for starters.

That's how it had started, gathering pebbles while Ken was too busy to talk, too tired to go out. Her first big project had been the stone clock on her wall. Some of the numbers, hand chiseled and strung together like pearls on the underside, had taken many Saturday afternoons, but every minute had been worth it.

She looked around her small office at the things she'd made. The mosaic bench by the door, made of rocks from Israel and pieces of brown glass from her last case of beer. Flex was right. She hadn't missed the beer much, especially when Ken switched to red wine, which she hated. Spirals of copper wire climbed up from the lava rocks Ken had brought back from a medical conference in Hawaii. Quartz bookends held her work library—a sketchbook, her Bible, *The Book of Common Prayer*, *The Encyclopedia of Ethnic Clothing*, and her favorite copies of the first year of *Vibe* magazine—erect.

"I do love pebblesmithing. That would definitely be a sacrifice. As for fashion design, I don't hold out much hope for ever getting my own line."

Jean lowered her gaze at Lily. Though age had creased her face, Jean's fiery attitude and classic yet funky style often made Lily feel like the older of the two. "You're not holding out hope for a line? That makes me sad. We'll have to stone Ken if you keep talking like this."

Lily aimed a pebble at Jean. She missed wide on purpose, but her point was made. "If you keep up this Ken business, you'll end up at church with me tomorrow. And I'll wipe off your ashes so you don't enjoy it so much. Now get going."

Jean snorted. "On that note, see you later, hon." She exited quickly, her laughter clearing the hall ahead of her.

Lily watched her friend go, then turned back to her desk. A photo to her right, one of her and Ken smiling at their favorite dim sum restaurant, caught her attention. She blinked. Hadn't her mother been with them that night? She usually was, since Pinkie, as their neighbor Phyllis liked to be called, couldn't always sit with her. Jean came over when she could and did beadwork or knitting with Mother, but those occasions were rare. Lily scanned the photo again. A slender hand gripping Lily's arm at the edge of the photo cleared things up. Her mother had been there, as always quietly holding on.

If only Lily could do the same.

She took another look at Ken's smiling face. She could almost hear him saying, "Good morning, Miss Chau," just as he had on the day she'd met him, during her first breast cancer screening. He'd smiled just like that before explaining that the technician was out sick and slamming her already lacking chest totally flat. Lily had focused her eyes on the cross dangling from Ken's neck, praying that she wouldn't do either of the things she felt like doing—dying of embarrassment or kissing Ken senseless. She'd skipped both options, settling for a tender peck here and there a few weeks later on their first date.

Today, though, as always when talking with Jean, Lily had heard a grain of truth. She needed to give up her expectation that Ken would propose at the next dinner, that he was going to pull out a ring every time he knelt down to tie his shoes. Maybe if Lily's mother didn't check her finger every time she came home from a date with Ken, it wouldn't be so hard. Or if her boss, Chenille, skipped her "wedding status" email each week, perhaps it would be easier to accept that things might never lead to marriage.

Probably the only thing that would make it easier would be to accept the truth and decide what to do about it. That's what the old Lily, the person she had been before meeting Ken, would have done.

Lily wiped away a tear, knowing she might never be that woman again—a woman alone but not lonely.

A woman at peace.

It was all wrong.

Lily stared at the pictures she'd sketched onto the tagboard since last week's meeting with Raya. The Nia Network wasn't the only place Jean had shown Lily's designs last year. After seeing Lily's sketches, Raya had immediately talked to Chenille about having the two of them coordinate more closely on the Flexability line, a collection of sportswear based on Raya's husband, Flex. Now they met once a week, working through pieces at the idea stage, with Lily bringing up possible problems at the pattern and cutting stage.

Last week Raya had proposed two pieces with severe, straight lines. The look reminded Lily of Hart Nash, an eccentric and talented designer known throughout the garment district for taking risks and getting away with them. Nash had been absent from fashion week for the past two seasons, however, and Lily wondered where she had gone.

While Lily admired the woman's innovative artistry, she preferred sweeping pieces over the more constructed ones. She and Raya had agreed to come up with separate collection ideas. Now Lily looked at all of hers . . . and hated every one.

Creating for fun and creating to sell were two different things, and Lily wasn't sure if she could quite get the hang of considering anything beyond a great garment. The Flexability line had now established a brand and secured backing from Nike. Though Lily and Raya had to keep things fresh in the new designs, the look also needed to be familiar. Raya loved most of Lily's suggestions, calling them "fluid" or "a breath of fresh air," but sometimes she missed the mark as well.

The phone rang.

"Hello?"

Ken's voice, exactly the one she'd longed to hear, sounded in her ear. "What's shakin', Miss Bacon?"

Lily tried to laugh. Ken thought that little greeting was hilarious, but Lily always spent a few extra minutes checking her profile in the mirror whenever he said it.

"Not much. Struggling to get ready for the design meeting. I need to go over the fabric figures again and compare the measurements to the pieces in last year's collection."

Ken whistled. "Sounds mind-boggling, but don't worry, anything you come up with will be cute. It always is."

Lily stared at the receiver. Cute? It sounded like he was talking to a toddler who'd made a pretty picture. Sometimes his doctor brain couldn't fathom how difficult making clothes could be. After all, it was . . . making clothes to him, not brain surgery.

Lily didn't try to make him understand anymore on the condition that he stopped drawing gall bladder diagrams on their napkins at dinner to explain the wonders of laser surgery. It was a fair exchange, though sometimes it would be nice to be able to discuss more about her work. She laughed now, thinking of the robe she'd planned to give him last Christmas. It'd never been returned from the show, but she liked to think someone had appreciated it. Her work probably would have been lost on Ken.

Lily listened to Ken run down his day and tried to focus her thoughts on his words instead of on her upcoming design meeting. As was happening more and more lately, the fabric won. In fabric her creativity streamed and draped. When designing for her office and home, Lily's tastes favored stone. Sometimes she mixed the two together. A good friend as well as a great designer, Raya allowed Lily to search for her own style. During their meetings Raya gave her input and then released Lily to try to come back with something better. This week she just hadn't pulled it off.

The hum of Ken's voice, like background noise from a television set, buzzed against Lily's ear.

"Lily, you there?"

She blinked. "Sure."

"I was asking you about Ash Wednesday. The service. We're still going together, right?"

"Right." Lily smoothed a piece of periwinkle silk across the desk in front of her, then grabbed a handful of seed pearls from her desk drawer and dumped them into the center of the fabric. Minutes later a sloping splash of ivory emerged under her fingers. A beak? Maybe.

"Ms. Chau?"

"Hold on a second," Lily whispered into the phone before covering the receiver. She looked up from her desk at a woman wearing a linen sheath and a red silk jacket. It could have been a boxer's robe turned trendy, but it wasn't. The jacket the woman wore was a kimono.

Lily's kimono.

The phone slid past Lily's ear and clattered onto the desk, sending pearls raining to the floor. Lily tugged at the cord and brought the phone to her face. "I need to call you back."

"What—"

Click. Lily replaced the receiver in its cradle, shocked that she'd hung up on Ken for the first time but still too stunned by the sight of her work on someone's body to be worried

29

about his response. She'd explain later if she ever figured it out herself. This woman's face was familiar, especially her thick black brows and confident smile.

It can't be.

Unflinching, the woman held out her hand. "I'm honored to meet you. My name is Hart Nash, and I'm the new host of *The Next Design Diva.*"

2

And let the beauty of the L<small>ORD</small> our God be upon us: and establish thou the work of our hands upon us; yea, the work of our hands establish thou it.

Psalm 90:17 KJV

"I think you know why I'm here," Hart Nash said, taking the seat across from Lily and pausing to sweep the remaining pearls into her hand and fold the silk before putting it aside.

Lily managed a smile watching the acclaimed designer pause to tidy up a scrap of silk and a handful of pearls. A detail person who wasn't too high and mighty to do the little things. That earned Nash an extra point given her reputation as a diva extraordinaire.

"I have an idea why you're here. That robe you're wearing. I didn't submit that. One of my coworkers—"

"Jean Guerra? Yes, when we're finished here, you'll have to direct me to her. It was her name that kept your package from being thrown away when you didn't answer our invitation to come on the show. Little did I know that I'd find this—" She grabbed her lapels. "—inside the package. Someone left it in there, can you imagine?"

Lily swallowed, but her mouth felt like the desert. That Jean was something else. "I'm glad you like it. It was meant to be a gift for someone, actually, not a piece for your consideration. I've only recently started learning about commercial design."

Nash made a sour face. "Hopefully, we've caught you in time. Don't worry about that part right now. We'll give you a mentor on the show who'll help on that end. What I want is the passion I feel in this piece I'm wearing, the love I saw in those sketches." The woman slid onto the edge of her seat.

The whole thing sounded like a dream. Lily hadn't remembered mentors on any of the episodes she'd seen, but maybe they worked behind the scenes like the choreographers and voice coaches on all those "next big thing" shows that always seemed to be on. Not that she'd watched much lately. All reruns. But this time it seemed like it could be for real.

When had Lily last heard someone talk about design like this? Never.

"The show sounds amazing," she said. "You sound amazing. But the reason you never heard back from me the last time is because I can't do it. I can't move to California for weeks on end, not knowing when I'll get booted off and come home. I have a job here. My mother is older, and I take care of her . . ."

Nash shook her head. She tapped the desk with the point of her perfectly rounded nail. "You won't have to leave your mom. I had a few demands when I took over this show. One of them was that women wouldn't have to leave their children or families. If you're chosen for the final round, you'd have to fly out to LA, but we're going to shoot the individual stories in each contestant's location and piece the film together. There are no team exercises, so you really don't need to move."

"You'd come here? To Flushing, Queens, where I live? Or here where I work, or what?"

Nash smiled. "Both. Flushing is a visual area with so many types of people. We'll probably get most of the footage in this warehouse though. I like what your boss is trying to do here. I'd like to let a few more folks know about this place, especially with people like you and Jean working here. I checked out the Flexability catalog. Nice stuff. A little pedestrian for my tastes, but nice."

A fit of coughing overtook Lily at the woman's last sentence. What would Raya think to hear someone calling something she designed pedestrian? If only Nash knew. If Raya could, she'd be adding feathers and flowers to those workout outfits. The thought of Raya, let alone Chenille, knowing about Nash's offer made Lily's head spin.

"I don't know what my boss would think about this."

The woman reached into her kimono, into the secret pocket Lily had designed. She pulled out a small notebook, flipped a few pages, and read, "Garments of Praise is three years old. Ten percent of their proceeds go to clothing needy children from Queens to Queensland. Their current emphasis is sportswear backed by a large firm. Jean Guerra, of Yves Saint Laurent fame, heads up the cutting department. Lily Chau is the main pattern maker."

Eyes wide, Lily leaned forward across the desk. "Where'd you get that stuff? Some interview clips?"

When Raya's husband, Flex, won a modeling contest wearing one of the firm's designs, the media had swarmed for a few days, interviewing everyone on staff. Lily had never seen her quotes in print, but obviously, someone had printed something.

Jotting a few more lines in her notebook, Nash shook her head. "No, these are my own notes, from my research."

Whoa.

Lily rolled her shoulders backward, trying to ease the tension knotting her shoulders. Maybe she should keep her treadmill after all. "You did research on us? What are you writing now?"

The woman smiled. "I research everything. As for what I just wrote down, those are just some observation notes. Once you sign on to the show and we get down the road a ways, I may share them with you."

This was moving fast. Way too fast.

Lily squirmed in her chair. "Like I said, I need to talk to my boss."

"How do you think I got back here?" Nash shot her a knowing grin. "I called yesterday."

A large breath filled Lily's lungs. True enough, most people were cut off at the front desk before ever making it to her neck of the warehouse, but with a design legend sitting across from her wearing something Lily had made with her own hands, she couldn't quite think straight. She could hardly pull her eyes away from her work.

Nash nodded. "It looks good on me, doesn't it? A lot better than it might have on your boyfriend, husband, or whoever you were going to give it to. You've got about as good a chance as anybody to have your tag inside my clothes. That's saying a lot. But still, it's not saying everything. There are people with half your talent who want this twice as bad. I flew out here, but I won't beg."

A slow, easy smile arched across Lily's mouth. The flash of urgency in her visitor's voice helped Lily make the quick determination required of her. When in doubt, leave it out. Ken chided her rule as fear, but it'd served her well so far. Her mother might be up and around tomorrow or not recognize Lily at all. Senility gave no warnings and left no room for reality shows. True reality was interesting enough.

She extended a hand across the desk between them. "Thank you. You just helped make my decision easier. There are people who are more talented, more dedicated, and probably more suited for this than me. I'm flattered by the offer, but I'm going to have to decline."

Lily grasped the stranger's palm and quickly let go. She forced back the urge to reach into the jungle of her desk drawer for a napkin. The woman's hands were clammy, like Ken's when he worked too hard.

The visitor grabbed Lily's hand as quickly as she'd let go. "Okay, you want to play hard to get. I'll get right to the point. I need you on the show," she said, her angular nose and cheekbones jutting from her face as she spoke. "Whether you win or not, I'd like to have some hand in helping your talent develop. After looking over your package—thank God they didn't throw it out—it occurred to me who would be the perfect mentor for you. Until very recently having that person help you would have been impossible, but now there's a very good chance that it could happen."

Lily's mind reeled in confusion. They'd already gone out of their way to get a mentor for her without knowing if she'd come on the show? And evidently it was someone big, but who? In the first season, they'd already exhausted about every designer on the Fashion Walk of Fame who would do something like that. And it couldn't be Nash, since she was the host. That would have been Lily's guess if someone else had posed the question.

"You're wondering who, I can tell. I'll tell you what. You think this through. Sleep on it, mull it over—"

"More like pray about it," Lily said.

The woman paused as if wondering whether she'd made a mistake after all. "Yeah, praying. That too."

Glancing at the clock behind the woman's head, Lily got a head start on what would most likely be the most intense prayer session she'd had in a while. As the hands of the clock came into focus, Raya bumped the door open with her hip and came in dragging a playpen, a teapot, and her secret stash of white chocolate biscotti. The bead fringe on her salmon-colored dress made a clicking sound against with the cappuccino machine for their post-meeting laughter and latte.

From the look on Raya's face when she saw Nash, it was a good thing little Ray was now crawling and didn't have to be carried in his mother's arms. She left everything in the middle of the doorway for a second, then pulled it all inside.

"You're from the . . . so that means Lily's on the . . . oh, wait until I tell Jean!"

Nash smiled. "If news travels here anything like it did at the places I've worked, she'll know very soon. I'm heading to see her when I leave. Your father says hello, by the way, Raya. People at Nia have great things to say about you."

Raya's father had owned Nia Network before selling to Allied Media. After a flopped first year, they'd asked for Raya's input as a former production manager. Though Lily had liked the previous programming, she had to admit the shows were better now, though she didn't watch TV like she once had. Ken said it atrophied the brain. Why hours on a laptop seemed okay Lily wasn't sure.

Raya looked as though she was forming a response, when her baby, who'd been next door with his older brother, crawled into Lily's office. Baby Ray was just the thing to jar

Lily from this surreal conversation. Lily scooped him up and planted a kiss on his cheek.

Raya's older son, taking his morning break from his home-school studies, entered the office and dove toward the baby like an airplane. He waved slightly to their visitor.

Nash stood and started for the door as if she'd crashed a family dinner party. "This is a great place to work, I can tell. But I think they'll want what's best for you too. Pray over it, like you said, but know that I'd love to have you on the show."

Lily nodded but didn't speak. A year ago she might have taken her purse and followed Nash to whatever city she'd said was required. Today, though, with her friends and co-workers, Lily realized that maybe she was more content than she'd thought. She waved as Nash exited the office, wondering if she wasn't saying hello to a new phase of her life.

As the door swung shut on Nash, Raya's husband, Flex, wedged it open with his carry-on bag. He held a dozen pink roses in one hand and an arrangement of calla lilies in the other. He handed off one bunch of flowers to Lily before gathering Raya into his arms for a quick hug and kiss.

"Hey, everybody!" he said. "What's going on? I thought you two would be knee-deep in latte by now. And what was up with that pointy faced chick I passed coming in? She looked traumatized."

He released his wife and embraced his boys, taking the baby from his older son's arms. He kissed the baby's forehead.

Raya shook her head. "Flex, you are so silly. Traumatized. I'm the one who should look traumatized. Wait until Lily tells you who that was."

He turned to Lily. "Who was it, Lil? She looks sort of like that woman who used to make all those crazy designs on the fashion channel. The one with the big glasses."

Still shocked, Raya nodded. "That was her. Hart Nash. She's the new host of *The Next Design Diva*. It's on Nia. Dad says it's one of their highest rated slots."

Flex froze. He looked at his wife, then at Lily. "Do you know what this could do for you, Lil?"

His contest win on Nia Network had landed Flex's face on every magazine cover from *Essence* to *People*.

"Don't tell me, they want you on the show?"

Lily nodded, picking silently at her bouquet. Unless the wilted lei Ken had brought back from Hawaii counted, Ken had never bought her so much as a carnation. Still, he had his ways of letting her know he cared. She just couldn't think of any of them right now. Comparing him to Flex would be a bad idea at any rate. That guy was sickeningly thoughtful. In fact, sometimes he was just sickening. Like now. He looked like he was going to explode with joy.

She nodded. "They want me."

"Yes!" Flex said, pumping a fist. "You're going to do it, right? When do you leave?"

Lily shrugged. "I don't leave. I don't know if I'm going to do it, but if I do, they'll shoot me on location here," she said, wondering why she felt totally overwhelmed instead of happy. Why hadn't Nash taken her no and been done with it?

Raya lifted Lily's chin. "Don't look like that. God can make a way for this to happen, Lil. That's what you always tell me, right? Jesus died for this. All of it. Even the little stuff."

Lily fought back tears. "There you go, spouting my own stuff back at me when I least want to hear it."

Why was she crying? She hadn't even decided whether to go on the show. In fact, she was leaning toward declining again. It would just complicate her already busy life. And besides, nobody ever really had a chance on those things.

The prettiest people or the people best at hyping themselves always won.

"It's my honor to talk your stuff back to you, dear. Isn't that what friends are for?" Raya said, taking a bow. Her hair, a sea of braids and butterfly clips today, grazed the chair. "Now smile and go call that dry doctor boyfriend of yours and tell him your news. Flex and I would like to take you two out tonight. Jean has the grandkids this week, and Chenille is out of the office buying fabric, so you're stuck with us."

"Jean! I've got to tell her." Lily started for the speaker-phone.

Raya grabbed her hand. "Hart was going by Jean's on the way out, remember? Trust me, as soon as Hart Nash leaves, Jean will be down here, saying 'I told you so' in every way she can think of."

That got a smile out of Lily. It was all too true. Jean would get some real satisfaction out of this. "I hope Chenille doesn't think I'm going to just quit and run off. I'd never do that."

"We know that. Though if you had to leave, Chenille would probably be the first one telling you to do it. We'd probably be sending you patterns by courier, but she'd never want you to miss out on an opportunity."

Flower petals brushed Lily's lips as she pulled the bouquet closer to her face. She'd like to think Chenille would be excited for her, but she knew they were in a crucial period in their business, three years in. When Chenille had recruited them, they'd all agreed to stick it out for five years. The Nike account for Flex's line and the partial payment on the million-dollar wedding dress they'd designed had made a good start. The wedding had been postponed, and though Flex's line was selling well, the contract would be up soon. They needed something to move ahead, another big moment.

Like having an employee on *The Next Design Diva*.

Lily's hands tightened around her flowers. Chenille had stuck by her through all the ups and downs of the last eighteen months and her mother's varying needs for care, allowing her to work from home and giving her time each day to nurture the part of herself often consumed by her mother's care.

Could this show be a way of finally giving something back to Chenille and the group of co-workers she'd come to love as family? Or were the demands of her real family too much to consider taking on more? Her neighbor Pinkie was a godsend, but she was getting up in age herself. Lily didn't want to have to ask her to sit with her mother more than she already did. And the cost of a day nurse made that option out of the question.

A lump formed in Lily's throat. "I'm not sure there's anything to celebrate. I don't know if I'm going to go on the show. There's my mother to consider. And you guys too. But it might be good for GOP if I went on—provided I didn't bomb, of course."

"More like be the bomb," Raya's older son, Jay, said with a smile. He reached out and touched Lily's arm for reassurance the way she'd touched his many times when he was struggling with his schoolwork or trying to adjust to being Raya and Flex's son after losing both his parents to AIDS and his aunt to diabetes.

Having the two of them for parents had been Jay's dream since the time Raya and Flex had coached his basketball team, but having a family also meant having rules to obey and relationships to maintain. Sometimes things got overwhelming. Those were the days Lily would hear Jay's special double knock at her door.

"Thanks, Jay. I hope you're right. I'm still not sure if a celebration is in order."

Flex laughed. "Of course he's right. I haven't watched much of that show, but I'm pretty sure you can hang with the best of them. Rest assured that we'll do all we can to support you. As for tonight, we're just celebrating you, Lily. Let us do that, okay?"

Why was that so hard? To celebrate herself?

"Sure. Thanks." Lily blushed, heading next door to Raya's office to use the phone. Being this close to Raya and Flex when he came home was something she tried to avoid, especially when talking to Ken. It just made things harder.

"Great." Though Flex's words were aimed at her, his eyes were fixed on his wife. When they were like that, so happy without meaning to be, it was hard for Lily to look at them. And the kissing? Too much information. What was it about marriage that made people so uninhibited? Not that Raya and Flex had ever been restrained exactly, but still . . .

Everyone in the office—except Jean, who said marriage was overrated—assured Lily that soon she'd unfold the mysteries of matrimony and they'd all laugh about it. Even Ken. One day soon seemed so far off sometimes.

Almost on Lily's heels, Jay followed Lily with his baby brother, careful not to step on his mother's sketches as he entered the office. Next door in Lily's office, the door clicked shut.

Jay shrugged. "Sorry about them. You know how it is. Mom has on the welcome-home dress. They're pitiful."

Lily giggled, knowing Raya would faint if she heard her son talk that way. "You know too much, you know that?"

Jay tickled his brother's chin. "I don't know enough or I'd be back in school by now. I'm almost caught up though. By fall I should be in high school. What I do know is they'll be saying 'I love you' for the next ten minutes. At least."

Lily nodded, then dialed the phone. Ten minutes. It'd take her that long just to get Ken's answering service.

When Ken picked up himself, she fought to contain her surprise.

"Hey . . . guess what? You know that fashion designer reality show on TV? The host came in today and asked me to be a contestant. Can you believe it?"

"You? On TV? Seriously? That's great. Tell me all about it tonight. Dim sum. Seven o'clock. And can it be just us? Without your mother?"

Since Ken was the one who always insisted her mother come along, his question baffled her a little. Maybe he just said that because he knew she didn't have anybody to sit with her mother and would probably stay home if her mother didn't come along.

"Actually, Flex and Raya want to take us out, if that's okay."

"Okay. Whatever. Look, I need to go. Love you."

Click.

"Love you too," Lily said, though Ken was no longer on the line. Was this hang-up thing some new part of their relationship too?

She offered Jay a brave smile, half hoping she could get out of going out to dinner tonight and half wishing she wouldn't have to. She hated asking her neighbor to stay late, but she didn't know what else to do. And once she told Pinkie the news, she'd definitely insist on staying. Jean and Lily's mother got along well, but Jean's grandkids were a handful, and there was no way Jean could do both. Maybe she should call Ken back . . .

Look at me, I'm thinking about going on a TV show and I can't even go out to dinner.

Why was everything always so complicated?

Lily needed a rock.

Not a big one or even a perfect one with high polish, though both would be nice. She just needed a big hunk of stone, something to weigh heavy in her hand, something real. What had happened today certainly didn't seem real.

She couldn't have imagined this morning when she got off the train that she'd be heading for it tonight with the prospect of going on television. Or that seeing a stranger wearing her designs would both thrill and terrify her. She didn't know if her mother would be in a good mood tonight and let her go out for dinner and come home to an uneventful report or if tonight would be a bad night, the kind when she had to cancel and stay home.

There were a lot of things Lily didn't know as the wind whipped around her, blowing away the day's questions but leaving no answers. What she did know as she walked from the train to her apartment was that she wanted a rock. As she walked on, scents of curry and cabbage swirled around her, tumbling in the music of the evening reunions in the area's many dialects. On another day she might have stood still for a few seconds and allowed the languages and smells of her community to envelop her, but not today. Today she needed to get home, just as soon as she made one little trip, a detour to her rock spot.

Good rocks were hard to find, but there was a construction site by the Asian market where the workers left her rocks, sometimes hunks of asphalt, other times beautiful, unusual pebbles or stones. The construction crew thought Lily a little weird but knew the pieces meant something to her. Today Lily headed there with determination, hoping to find something different. Something special.

As she walked, she poured out the many questions ringing in her heart to the Rock of her salvation. Should she go on *The Next Design Diva*? It'd be more work and more stress, but it'd also bring Chenille some much-needed attention and give Lily a shot at her dream of having her own line of clothes. But at what cost? The two days a week she worked from home seemed to be the key to the arrangement she had taking care of her mother. Could she give up her rocks for Lent and become a contestant on a TV show just like that? She'd just gotten used to her church. How could she do all this?

With God, nothing is impossible.

Cold air vented her skirt as Lily passed the market. Atop a pile of concrete chunks, she spied a gift from her construction friends. A white stone veined with something shiny, gold looking. She'd have to get it home to be sure what it was, but it looked like a great catch.

Suddenly aware of the people milling around her, Lily weaved through the after-work crowd, pressing her body against the storefront. As she stepped toward the rock pile, a hand appeared and grabbed the stone.

Lily's eyes traveled up the arm of a worn jacket to a pair of piercing blue eyes, hidden at first by a shaggy crop of hair, a tousled mop of blondish brown highlighted with chunks of silver. Kindness creased the corners of the man's eyes. His lips were full and chapped. His skin was deeply tanned despite the cold air. A scar knifed down one cheek and into the collar of his shirt.

"Hey," Lily shouted, despite her plan to ask him for the rock calmly. "That's mine! Someone left that there for me." So much for being polite.

The rock thief extended his hand and formed his lips into something meant to be a smile. It would have been a magnificent one, actually, but his lips didn't seem to know what to do. He bit them instead. Lily made a note to never stop smiling, no matter how bad things got. Trying to remember wasn't pretty, especially in front of strangers.

Just as she was about to turn away and forget the whole thing, his lips remembered where to go. The effect was amazing. Give the guy some Chapstick and a haircut, and he'd be in business. Once he gave up that rock, of course.

"Here. You can have it." His voice sounded both irritated and amused, not to mention sexy.

Sexy? I'm definitely stressed.

Lily pushed her briefcase strap higher on her shoulder, realizing how crazy she probably sounded fighting someone over what was probably no more than a painted piece of New York street. Especially such a nice someone. She looked down at his feet and saw white socks stuffed into sandals. Her eyes traveled upward next, resting on the thing she'd been avoiding, that scar curving the outline of his jaw before trailing down his neck and into his shirt. Lily swallowed the sudden and irrational desire to kiss that line, to ask how it'd happened. She definitely needed to get home.

"You can have the rock. Sorry." Lily pivoted toward the crosswalk.

As she turned, the man touched her hand, placing the rock in the center of her palm and wrapping her fingers around it. "It's okay. I can find another rock. You keep this one. It's special."

Spices pricked the air as he came closer. She noticed the cloves first, so similar to the smell of Jean's studded Thanksgiving ham fresh from the oven. There was something else too though, something smoky and sweet. Something from a place far-off but just past the tips of her fingers. It wasn't cologne either. This scent was for anointing, for washing feet with hair. Something for weeping women to use when wrapping their Savior. Lily wanted to slump into his chest and fall asleep. Once she was done kissing that scar, of course.

What is getting into me?

Her briefcase strap slipped off her shoulder again as the man came within a breath of her and stopped, lingering there, looking at her as though he knew her. His confused lips looked as if they had definitely remembered how to smile . . . among other things.

Lily pulled her hand, and her mind, away. "What makes this rock so special?"

The man's eyes seemed to twinkle as he jammed his hands into his pockets. "It led me to you. God be with you, beautiful one."

With that, the handsome stranger disappeared into the market. Lily stared after him for a few seconds, then found her feet and followed. She stopped at the door of the market to peer inside.

He was gone, absorbed into the throng of customers shopping for dinner ingredients. The clock suspended above the cash register caught her attention, its hands mocking her with a truth more troubling than her chasing a stranger for a rock in Queens.

She was late. Again.

3

I will make your battlements of rubies, your
gates of sparkling jewels, and all your walls of
precious stones.

Isaiah 54:12

"You are late."

Lily nodded. She was running only a few minutes behind her usual time of arrival, but there was
no use arguing. Mother was obviously not herself.
Pinkie shook her head to confirm what Lily already
knew—it was going to be one of those nights. And
once again Lily would spend it without Ken.

There was no way she would make it to dinner
now. When Mother was like this, she couldn't be
left. If only Lily had passed by the rock spot. She
should have let the man take the rock and go.

Then you wouldn't have met him.

She was beginning to think that might have
been a good thing, not meeting that man.
What was she going to do when she went
to church? Tell everyone she was giving
up chasing guys in flip-flops for Lent? It

was more than a little embarrassing. Still, missing dinner was frustrating too. She plopped down on the couch and spilled out her news.

Pinkie rubbed her hands together, reluctant to leave. "Congratulations about the TV show. I've been telling you for years something like this was going to come to you."

"That you have," Lily said, slipping out of her shoes. "Did Mother eat okay today?"

"She did great. There are ribs in the oven for you. And some greens on the stove. She had some lo mein and a few vegetables. I'll pick up some of those spring rolls she likes and bring them tomorrow. We were talking like old times until—"

"Until I was late. I'm sorry. And thank you."

What else was there to be said? Pinkie was a grandmother herself, though her children seldom came around. How she and Lily's mother had come to be such good friends, no one remembered, not even the two of them. They never forgot their friendship though. Lily joked with Raya that she'd grown up with two mothers—one Chinese and one Trinidadian. Today as Pinkie looked at Lily with concern, she knew it was true.

No wonder I didn't have any boyfriends in high school.

"You are late!" Mother screamed at no one in particular, though she wasn't referring to either of them. Tonight was a scene Lily knew well, both from occasional rehearsals like this one and from the initial performance eighteen years before.

One weekend when she was twenty and home on break from Sarah Lawrence, her father hadn't returned from work. She'd worried all night and called the police while her mother had said nothing. On Saturday morning he'd appeared without explanation. Lily's quiet mother had lost it that day, screaming as she was now. Lily's father never explained.

Pinkie placed a hand on Lily's shoulder. "Are you sure you don't want me to stay? You've got a date and all . . ."

Lily shook her head. "No. You've done more than enough."

There were some things even Pinkie shouldn't see. Shouldn't know. Though perhaps Mother had told Pinkie. Lily doubted it. Lily had been there herself, and she still didn't know.

Pinkie gave her an understanding look. "Call me if you need me. And call the doctor if it gets too bad."

Already kneeling at her mother's side, Lily waved goodbye. She and Pinkie both knew Lily wouldn't call. As for the doctor, they'd already tested her mother twice. Old age. Slight dementia. Go home and do the best you can.

"Mother? It's Li Li. Let's get you into bed."

Usually they'd be heading to the tub, but Pinkie had braved the tub with Mother herself, despite her arthritis.

God bless that woman.

Lily stole a moment to try to catch Ken but ended up only leaving a message on his cell. She'd hoped to catch him before he made it to the restaurant. He wouldn't appreciate being stuck there alone with Flex and Raya. Though he and Flex got along pretty well, he and Raya just didn't click.

Mother clawed at her shoulder. "You are not Li Li. She is young. Pretty. You look old."

Lily hung her head. The most painful thing about dementia was her mother's brutal capacity for truth. Lily's fingers traced the lines teasing the corners of her own eyes. Although she faithfully slathered lotions and serums on her face daily, on nights like this, the lines on Lily's face, etched by other long, hard evenings, refused to lie flat or appear full. Her mother was right. She looked—and felt—old.

Despite Ken's belief that fifty was the new thirty, the

49

truth was, forty was staring Lily in the face. And she wasn't always sure she liked what she saw. "You're thirty-eight," Ken had written in a recent email. "We don't have to rush into marriage. Women are having children much later these days."

Was it really only last week that he'd said that? The conversation seemed a lifetime away. Lily's arms hooked under her mother's, bringing her upright. Though Mother didn't weigh much, she had a left hook that could drop a bull. Lily had learned that the hard way a few months before. She still wasn't sure where her mother had learned it. Her mother's eyes, now still and black, reminded Lily that there were some things she might not want to know.

It didn't stop Lily from desperately longing to have other things revealed. Treasures she could no longer open, like her father, long dead and still mysterious. He'd been a beautiful, intelligent, and often angry man. A puzzle of a man. And the woman with the pieces, the one whose bones pressed into Lily as they headed down the hall, held the key. Only, most days she couldn't remember where she'd put it.

Instead, Mother remembered the morning when Lily's father had opened the door and walked to the kitchen for tea as though he hadn't been out all night. The morning when Mother had made Lily promise never to leave her.

"Men mean well," Mother had whispered, not looking Lily in the eye. "But daughters do well. Good daughters, anyway. Promise me you'll be a good daughter."

"Always," Lily had answered. The promise had come easy then, when being a good daughter meant coming home every vacation and calling on holidays. Spending her summer vacations working in her father's laundry and trying to achieve his dream of her becoming a doctor had come harder. Giving up her father's dreams and finding her own had been even more difficult.

Though he'd been amused when Lily made paper dolls for the children in the neighborhood—dolls in every size, shape, and color—Lily's father had been furious about her decision to study fashion design. As she folded her mother into bed now, almost like a doll, Lily thought of those shapes she'd given the children. Little did she know then that cutting those edges so carefully would prepare her for a life in fashion.

Mother's hand brushed Lily's cheek as she tucked her into bed. For a moment the older woman's eyes cleared as if in recognition. A tear salted the corner of Lily's mouth.

"Li Li?" Her mother's voice sounded strangled, fearful.

She kissed her mother's hand. "I'm here."

She smiled, touched Lily's hair, which was much shorter than the last time they'd shared one of these moments. "What is this? You look like a little boy," she said in a throaty rasp.

The roses on the bedspread engulfed Mother's small body as though she'd gone to bed in a garden. Lily tucked her mother's long, white hair behind her ear before raking a hand through her own spiky tresses.

"It's just a haircut, Mother, remember? I'll grow it out again." She hadn't planned to grow it out just yet, but she would now.

"Good," Mother said, nearly in the arms of sleep. "My son-in-law does not want a chicken head for a wife. Where is the doctor, anyway?"

"Waiting for me at a restaurant," Lily whispered to the shadows.

A snore was her mother's response.

"New rock, huh?" Lily's boss pointed to the chunk of stone now perched on the corner of Lily's desk.

Lily turned to face Chenille and nodded, trying not to think about the latest addition to her rock collection or the man who left the stone behind and seemed to have walked off with a piece of Lily's heart.

"Yep. I got it in Flushing at the construction site . . ."

For some reason, Lily's words halted in her throat. Probably because if she talked about the rock, she'd have to talk about the man she'd spent the night thinking about while she couldn't sleep. He was best left in her dreams.

Chenille chuckled. "Did a cute construction guy dig it up for you or something? You've got man face."

Both hands to her cheeks, Lily nibbled at the inside of her mouth. Her face had a certain way of lighting up when talking about certain persons of the male persuasion. She'd spent months covering her face while she gushed about Ken when she'd first met him, to hear the folks around Garments of Praise tell it. Surely she wasn't getting goofy now over a total stranger.

Chenille took a seat in the empty chair and let her clipboard, full of notes about Hart Nash and the taping schedule for the show, slide onto the desk. "You totally have man face. You look like Raya when she comes back from lunch with Flex."

Lily cringed. "That bad?"

Chenille reached across the desk and peeled one of Lily's fingers away from her eyes. "Worse. So what's up? Is that rock Ken's twisted idea of a wedding ring? If it is, you can tell him I said—"

Didn't Lily wish Ken would be so romantic as to think

52

of such a thing? Ken wasn't answering his phone and he hadn't called. Strangely enough, Lily didn't feel bothered by it. The rock guy? Now he bothered her. "That's not it at all. Actually, a stranger is the reason for my man face. An older man. Sort of Bohemian looking but classy too, if that makes sense. Nothing like Ken. He had these eyes . . ."

Her friend's jaw dropped. "You've had it bad for Ken for so long that I didn't think I'd ever hear you talk like this about someone else. And a stranger, no less? How did you meet? Did he give you the rock?"

Oh boy. Now came the stuff that sounded strange.

"He stole the rock, but then he gave it back." She paused, trying to think of a way to explain but finding none. "I'll tell you the full story some other time, all right?"

Her boss cocked her head slightly. "Whatever. You know your rock stuff makes no sense to me, but I do understand that look on your face. Maybe you won't see the guy again, but it's good to know that your man face still works."

Lily rolled her eyes. Man face. Who had started that term, anyway? Raya, if she recalled correctly. As if that woman could talk. She had a framed magazine cover of Flex tacked onto the wall like a pin-up shot in a teenage girl's locker. The thought of that brought a smile to Lily's lips—for a second, anyway. One look at Hart Nash's name on Chenille's clipboard sobered her up. Despite all their girl talk, Chenille had come to her office this morning for a reason.

Chenille's eyes met Lily's. Silence echoed between them.

"I got a call from Hart Nash on my cell the other day asking permission to see you," Chenille said. "And Jean called last night. I guess I picked the wrong day to leave early, huh? It seems that some congratulations are in order."

"You could say that."

"I am saying it." Chenille crossed her legs. The pleats in her skirt resumed their positions.

Suddenly Lily wondered if coming in on her usual home day was a good idea after all. This conversation would have been better by phone or email. Chenille had a way of looking at people that could convince them of anything. Still, she'd come today because Pinkie had insisted and because she'd thought it'd be best to talk things through in person. Now it was time to do just that.

"Ready to discuss this?" Chenille asked with a cautious smile. "I wouldn't push, but there are some time-sensitive considerations here."

Lily reached for Beautiful One, her new favorite rock, and set it down right beside her. "Sure. We can get started. Do you mind if we pray first?"

"You know I don't mind," Chenille said. "I was going to ask if you didn't mind leading."

The women joined hands and dropped their heads, asking God's wisdom and love to guide them. After the amen, their grip lingered a few seconds more.

Chenille spoke first. "I've always known this day would come. Putting together the team I have here was something only God could have done. I'm thrilled and flattered that a national show wants to showcase one of my people. I think now is a great time for us to start considering expanding into a factory. And though you know I'd never push you, it'd be a great thing for the firm."

Lily opened her mouth, then closed it again.

Chenille gave her a few more seconds to respond. When Lily remained quiet, Chenille freed her papers from the clipboard and tapped the stack on the edge of Lily's desk.

"Though you wouldn't have to move to California or be taped with the other contestants, putting together an entire

54

collection from start to finish and being apprenticed by a mentor will take a lot of time. The question is, Lily, what do you want?"

"I'm not sure." Lily was surprised at her own words. "A year ago I'd have been jumping all over this office. But now the idea of leaving my flexible schedule and great friends, having less time with my mother . . . it doesn't sound so great anymore."

Chenille ran her tongue across her teeth. "What if you could do both?"

Lily felt her jaw slacken. "Keep my schedule here and do the show?"

Could it work? She couldn't see how exactly, but if Chenille thought it could work, it could.

"Not exactly. But we can try to keep it close. The stuff you're working on with Raya now is pretty critical for next spring's collection, so that will be your top priority as far as the firm is concerned. They can shoot around here as long as I know in advance and it doesn't become a distraction. On your off days, you could work on your designs at home and any other shooting they want to do. Oh, and your mentor. He or she could come here whenever necessary."

Lily's pulse raced.

"What's wrong?" Chenille lifted one eyebrow, Raya's trademark move. They'd all been around each other way too much.

"Do you really want to know?" Lily raked through her hair.

Chenille pushed the papers away and leaned forward on her elbow. "Do I want to know? Come on, you know the answer to that." She smiled and reached behind her and checked the cappuccino machine Lily had forgotten to return yesterday. "Almost done. Spill it."

Lily eased back in her chair. "Okay, here's the deal. I hadn't considered the possibility of my mentor being a man. I mean, duh, most of my favorite designers are men: Perry Ellis, Ralph Lauren, Joseph Abboud, Doug LaCroix—"

"Doug LaCroix? I forgot about him. Is he dead or what? He just disappeared after 9/11. Even *W* magazine didn't say a word. It's so hush-hush—"

"I don't know."

Lily pressed a fingertip to her scalp and rubbed in a circular motion. Doug LaCroix's work had made her consider menswear during design school, though his women's wear was his true claim to fame. She'd probably never meet him, but just the mention of his name reminded Lily just how high the stakes of this contest really were.

Chenille pulled a snack-size bag of cheese puffs out of her suit pocket. "Sorry I'm rambling. Don't worry. I've got listening food and everything. Proceed."

Pausing only to collect two steaming cups of cappuccino, Lily started again. "I know I didn't tell you the whole story, but that guy I saw yesterday? It was more than a casual meeting. I can't explain it exactly, but something happened."

Chenille's eyes narrowed. "Something happened? Whoa. Like what? Did he do something to you, because—"

"No, silly. Not that kind of something. The weird, time moving in slow motion, wanting to kiss a stranger for no good reason kind of something."

Chenille's cup stopped just short of her lips. "Are you serious? It was that intense?"

"So bad that I'm wondering if I shouldn't insist on a female mentor. I've been thinking I was in perimenopause for years. Maybe it's finally kicked in. I mean, Ken is a pain, but at least he's safe and predictable. This was something else. When I looked at that man, I felt . . ."

Chenille brought the cup to her lips. "I should be writing this down. It's classic."

Lily paused as the memory of a pair of piercing blue eyes and a shock of brownish-gray hair passed through her mind. "His eyes were so blue, they looked like those fake contacts at first. But then he came closer, and I knew they were real. And his skin. He was so tan. Not George Hamilton skin-cancer tan, but he had a sort of man-who-works-outdoors sort of thing going on. And that cologne . . . it smelled like the stuff they must have put on Jesus before they put him in the tomb. There was this smoky, woodsy smell."

"Vetiver?" Chenille shifted forward to the edge of her seat. "I used to have some in the diffuser on my desk."

Lily closed her eyes, imagining the smell. "Yes, that. Like a walk through tall grass. There were cloves too, maybe even myrrh. He smelled like a miracle like the Cana wedding where Jesus turned the water into wine."

Chenille picked up a few of the papers and started to fan herself. "Okay now, you just went there on me. I'm going to have to call my husband. I can't take it. Okay, yes I can. Tell me what he had on, and then we've got to get back to this TV show thing."

"That's just the thing. He was looking crazy, okay? Or at least I thought so at first. It was like nothing I ever would have put together. But on him, I don't know. He had on these rough-dried khakis and a V-neck sweater with a white button-down shirt underneath. And get this. Sports slides and socks. Who wears slides in New York before Easter?"

"Very hot old men who smell like Jesus, evidently."

Lily pinched her friend's arm. "Jesus smells good to me any way I can get him. Anyway, it was a trip. He was like a walking fashion show. Like he could become anything, but the essence of him would still be there. He wore that outfit like a prince playing at being a pauper."

"Though I hate to ask, and it probably isn't the godliest question I'll ever ask, I just have to know. The body?"

After taking a second's pause and closing her eyes for a moment, Lily answered. "Like a hungry tiger. Lithe. Lean. Sleek. Fluid." Lily halted before describing the muscles that had moved under that sweater as he'd disappeared into the store. And the scar and the way she'd wanted to kiss it. "His body affected me almost as much as what he called me."

"Okay, this is just too much. I think I'm going to have to scream." Chenille took a big sip from her cup. "Okay, go ahead. Hit me with it. What did he call you?"

The rock edges pressed against Lily's palm as she squeezed. "He called me . . . beautiful one."

"Okay, he's dangerous. Seriously."

"I know."

Lily had heard a lot of come-ons in her day, but for some reason she felt that that scarred, tanned, smiling man knew beauty when he saw it. She sensed that he'd known other things too. Painful things. He seemed like a man who knew how to be poured out like water or sit still like stone.

"And there was more, but I'd rather not get into it."

Chenille was fanning herself again. "Don't worry, Lil. I couldn't take any more anyway. It'll take me a while to recover from just listening to it, let alone experiencing it. Girl, you did good to make it to work today. No wonder you stood Raya up last night."

"That was about my mother, actually. I did call Raya, but I still feel bad. I hope she wasn't too upset. She seemed okay about it."

"No, it's fine. She knew something came up. Ken is probably the one you need to apologize to. Or was the one you needed to apologize to. After hearing that story, I'd say poor Ken is yesterday's news." She gathered her papers again.

Lily pushed the rock back to the corner of her desk. "It was just one of those things. I'll never see him again."

Chenille chuckled. "I wouldn't bet on that. There's dating, and then there's destiny. The latter is pretty hard to outrun. Look at Raya."

Lily had no answer for that one. Everyone in the office joked about the Cinderella story of how Raya and Flex got together. Or the Cinder-fella story, as Flex called it. Lily just never saw herself as the girl at the ball. She was too practical for fairy tales.

"I'm sorry I took us on a total tangent. What else did you want to tell me about the show?"

"That if you want to be a contestant, you'll have to decide today. And . . . you'll have to come up with a title for your line and at least two collection concepts."

"Today?" Lily's mind blanked as she tried to think of even one thing. Nothing came to mind. "Well, I guess that decides it, then. I've got nothing."

Giggles spilled from Chenille's lips, the deep-down kind of laughter that made a person's belly sore after. "Don't you see? That's it."

"What's it?" Lily looked around the room and back at her friend's face, glowing with more joy than she'd seen there in a long time.

"Your line. Beautiful One."

"But—"

Scribbling furiously with one hand, Chenille held up the

other. "That man. He is your line. His scent? Fresh. His body? Feral."

Lily's mouth hung open. Her stranger. Cloves, tigers . . . he was her destiny all right, but not in the way Chenille thought. Her fellow rock collector had just changed her mind. Lily was headed for the small screen.

"Okay. I'll do it."

4

You were in Eden, the garden of God; every
precious stone adorned you. . . . On the day
you were created they were prepared.

Ezekiel 28:13

"I'm sorry, Lily, but Dr. Lee is with a patient right
now. He's . . . he's booked up for the day." Ken's
secretary struggled to get the words out, as she always did when she was covering for him.

"No problem, Sara. Just tell him I called."

"He did mention something about Ash Wednesday services tonight though," the woman whispered
into the phone as though conveying a message vital
to national security. "I'd be there if I were you."

"Thanks," Lily said, before hanging up. If Ken's
secretary were shorter and Chinese, she could have
easily been Lily's mother.

Mother. No matter how excited Lily was
about agreeing to be on the TV show, she
couldn't help wondering how her mother
would take it. She wouldn't think it was
important, for one thing. ("TV? You have

61

no time for that. You'll be getting married soon.") How Lily's absences might affect her mother and whether Pinkie would be able to deal with the extra sitting the way she adamantly assured Lily she would was still left to be seen.

No matter how much Lily invested in her mother, she always seemed to fall short of the dutiful daughter her parents had wanted. Still, she refused to give up and put her mother in a home as some had suggested. Yet she knew that aging was the nature of things, the cycle of life. One day Lily too would grow old, look for a kind hand to guide her, for steady fingers to chop her prunes. Would Lily have a good daughter or a loving husband to do the job? Or would her needs be provided by whatever nursing home her feeble IRA could afford?

At the scent of Jean's rice heading down the hall, Lily smiled. How Jean always seemed to know just what she needed Lily could never figure, but she was always thankful after one of her friend's gift meals. And full.

"Busy?" Jean asked, peeking into Lily's office.

When Lily shook her head, Jean brought her whole body through the doorway, easing a casserole dish onto the desk. No oven mitts graced her hands, but the dish would be warm. It always was.

Lily's eyes brightened at the sight of her friend's kind, brown face and the sound of her speech, both as hearty as steel and as delicate as Spanish lace. In a way that Lily felt she never would, Jean knew who she was, and that was that. As the smell of perfectly seasoned rice enticed Lily's empty stomach, she was glad of her friend's sense of identity. Right now she felt like Alice in Wonderland.

I know who you are. You are mine.

"Hey, you." Lily was out of her chair to receive her friend.

Jean walked around the desk and gave Lily a big hug. She

didn't say anything about Hart Nash or the TV show. She didn't have to. The tears of joy soaking Lily's shoulder said it all. Jean's tears were almost a bigger event than the visit from the show's host.

Emotions overflowed Lily's eyes too, but she didn't speak either. After everything she'd told Chenille, she was almost talked out.

Finally Jean found her voice. "I wasn't going to come down here until I knew for sure that you were going to do it. I just couldn't. I might have hauled off and slapped you or something. Chenille told me about your line and the collections. Priceless. If you work hard, you could really win this thing."

"What?" Lily scrubbed her eyes with the back of her sleeve. "Are you kidding me? Now you think I could win? You didn't think I could win before?"

Jean laughed and kicked off her mules, orange silk with sequins. "Of course I didn't think you could win before. Everybody knows those things are rigged. I did think you'd get picked up by somebody and developed though, not to mention probably getting a great husband out of it."

Lily's mouth hung open. "You have got to be kidding me. A husband? You too?"

"Hey, I'm a mother, okay? You're like a daughter to me. I tried to tell you that you don't need a man, but the thing is, you want one. You can't help yourself. I get that. So I figure, let's widen the field a little."

What was going to happen next, an anvil falling through the ceiling? This was getting ridiculous.

"You are something else, but I love you. And I'm glad you sent my stuff in."

Jean dropped to the floor for some push-ups. "No problem," she said coming up from her second rep. "And thank you for taking this chance. I know you have reservations. Especially with your mom and everything."

Lily nodded. She was concerned about her mother and about herself. "I am concerned about Mother, but she's depending on me to take care of her, and this may be the way I end up doing it."

Rocking back on her knees, Jean agreed. "If you're waiting on Ken to sweep you off your feet, this is definitely a better shot. That fool might never propose. He's as much in love with himself as with anyone else." Jean stood and stretched her arms overhead.

Usually Lily would have defended Ken, but after the brutal pace of the past twenty-four hours, ignoring the comment was the best she could do.

"I was sitting here wondering who will end up taking care of me when you came in," she said.

"Me, of course. Why do you think I'm working out like a maniac? I realized way too late that I can't afford to die. You people don't listen to me, so I have to stick around and nag you. As for your future, it never hurts to think about those things. I didn't, and that was a mistake. Don't worry about it though. Focus on the opportunity in front of you. If you win this thing, you'll be able to pay somebody to take care of you. You'll have to invest wisely, of course, but I'll make sure you—"

"Will you cut it out? Everybody around here acts like I'm ten years old." Lily laughed a little and sat back in her chair, staring at the ceiling.

With Jean over fifty and walking around stronger than anybody, growing older took on a new meaning. Lily's graying angel man made her think twice about her possibilities too, but she still wondered whether she'd end up alone.

Lily stared at the photo of her and Ken, clipped to its rock frame on her desk. Sure, he was slow, but he'd propose. She was sure of it. It was foolish to think of things like growing old alone. She'd hear from Ken any minute. For all his pouting tendencies, he recovered quickly. She hoped this time would be no exception. Maybe hearing from him would clear up these feelings for the stranger. Maybe. They'd planned on attending Ash Wednesday service together, and Lily was going with him or without him. At the rate her life was changing, she needed God more now than ever.

"Taking your mom to church tonight?" Jean slid her feet back into her shoes and rotated her head from one side to the other.

Lily imitated the motion, then sighed. "Yes. Pinkie has her own service tonight. I'm hoping Mom won't scream hallelujah and throw the ashes or anything. She used to get pretty lively over at Pinkie's church. She's been good so far though, even recited some of the readings from memory. That almost made me cry."

Ken said sometimes dementia does that to people; they remember hymns from childhood but don't know what day it is. Pinkie, who'd cared for her sister with Alzheimer's for several years before she died, said Lily was lucky. "Your mother is just growing old, the way folks do," she continually reassured Lily. "Some do better than others."

"Did you decide what you're giving up?" Jean asked.

"The rocks, I guess. I can't even think straight enough to pick anything else . . ." Lily's voice cracked as she buried her head in her hands, finally feeling the weight of the past day and the many late nights that had come before.

Jean smoothed Lily's hair, the way Lily now did for her mother. "Another bad night?"

Lily nodded, thankful not to have to explain. She was glad to have friends at work, since it was the only place she went besides home. And church. She didn't really know anybody there yet.

Jean's brows knitted in concern. "Are you sleeping any better?"

Lily shook her head. "Not really."

Her friend sat on the corner of the desk. "All this talk about growing old alone, you need to focus on staying alive. You have to move your body, fuel your mind, and rest as often as you can."

Lily knew Jean was right. Sleepless nights were becoming more common to her than a good night's sleep. Last night she couldn't have slept more than a few hours between her mother's bad dreams and Scar Face marching through her mind. What scared her was that more than many hours later, she still wasn't sleepy. At some point she would crash, of course, but for now she was awake. Wide awake.

"You forgot the most important thing, Jean, feeding the soul. I know you're going to say no, but would you like to come to service tonight?"

Lily braced herself for one of Jean's signature moves, walking out and slamming the door, but she didn't. For a few seconds, she didn't move at all.

"Not tonight. Maybe next time. And don't ever think you know what I'm going to say. Sometimes I don't even know that," Jean said in a soft voice. "It was a good deflection, by the way, but it's not going to work. Have you slept all night in the past month? Can you even remember the last time?"

To Lily's horror, she couldn't remember. "I don't know. It's weird. I'm just up, you know. Sometimes I can't remember if I slept or not. Other times sleep overcomes me. I'm sort of numb. It must be something like the way people get when they're starving. They're not hungry anymore. A lot of times, I'm not sleepy."

Jean steepled her fingers under her chin. The tears of joy she'd had when she entered the room were replaced by tears of sorrow. "Those people aren't hungry anymore because they're dying, honey. Don't you see? This is a silent alarm. Your body has been crying out, and you've been ignoring it. Now your system has given up on convincing you that something's wrong, but something is wrong. I think you know that. I'm thrilled about this show, but it will count for nothing if you don't take care of yourself. Make an appointment."

"Okay."

Jean's words struck home. Inside Lily a bell was ringing. Something was wrong. The same something that had driven her to the offices of the HMO where she'd met Ken. She'd gone there for her first breast-cancer screening, a diagnosis regarding her insomnia and swinging moods, and perhaps a prescription. Chenille had taken Zoloft to get her through her depression during her husband's cancer recovery. Evened her right out, she said.

More a believer in miracles than in medicine, Lily had always been wishy-washy about people taking medication for depression. Didn't everybody have down times? King David would have needed a mega prescription the way some of those psalms sounded. The day she'd met Ken, though, Lily had been desperate enough to consider asking for a prescription of her own.

Until she saw Dr. Ken Lee.

Lily had sat there needing something, though she wasn't sure quite what. Whatever it was she might have wanted, after one look at Ken, she never asked for it. Having Ken skim a stethoscope across her flat chest had been humiliating enough. She wasn't about to tell him that her brain was less than normal too. How did she know it was depression, anyway? Doctors nowadays had a name for everything. Stress. That's all it was.

But what about now? What is this?

Lily shoved the question and its answer against a far wall in her mind. There were a lot of things she could be, but crazy wasn't one of them. Years before, when her father was still alive, he and Lily had lunched in Chinatown while her mother shopped with Pinkie.

He'd chosen his words carefully, as though they were his last. "This country now accepts Chinese. There are many opportunities available to you. You are like me, very smart. Almost too smart. Be careful. Sometimes intelligence brings other things. Crazy things. And America does not like crazy."

She'd thought the conversation itself a little crazy at the time. She didn't now. Now Lily saw the sadness of her father's eyes reflecting back at her in the mirror. Well versed in Chinese medicine when he came to America, her father had soon found that his knowledge was not accepted. He'd opened a laundry instead and offered health advice to the many Chinese who didn't speak English.

Pinkie's husband, Johannan, a Kenyan chemist, had experienced the same dilemma and ended up taking expensive classes he'd once taught to make himself employable. In the end he too gave up, opening Pinkie and Red's Caribbean Cuisine instead. Much of the food was African, and nothing in the place was red, but Pinkie said it sounded better.

Growing up, Lily had watched her father and her neighbor play chess and swap pipe-fogged stories of their pasts. At ten o'clock in the evening, both men would retire to their beds, never having spoken of the rib joint or the laundry, places that made them leaders in the community yet shadowed their American dreams. She hadn't understood the men's silent yet strong friendship then, but Lily saw the wisdom of it now.

Everyone needed friends, people who sought to accept more than to understand. Lily's friends didn't always understand her, but they did what they could. Chenille listened. Raya prayed. And Jean cooked. She said her paella was as close to heaven as she got. Lily was inclined to agree.

"I'm sorry. I was daydreaming. But don't worry, I hear you."

Jean smiled. "Daydreaming is good. And I hear you too, whether you believe it or not. Now eat up, Miss Design Diva, and go home and get some rest. It'll take more than working hard to win that show. You're going to have to start working smart." The door shut behind her.

Lily took a deep breath and a bite of the lunch Jean had brought. For the first time in days, hunger rose in her throat. She forked the food in as fast as she could without choking. How could she have been so hungry and not realized it? The same way she could be so sleepy and sitting here wide awake. Lily pressed Chenille's intercom button on her phone.

"Yes?"

"Since I'm really not supposed to be in today, I think I'm going to go home and take a nap if that's okay."

"Absolutely."

Though it wasn't her first time at People's Episcopal, tonight seemed different. Lily looked up into the high ceilings, stared at the organ, fighting the urge to reach up and touch the black smudge on her head. People who waved at Ken stared at Lily standing beside him, probably wondering if she was his wife or if her mother was his mother.

I am not.

She is not.

Ken's mother, Irene, was in Lebanon, Ohio, probably sitting in the St. Luke's Episcopal Church with a heavenly smile, her beautiful face no doubt framed by blond curls. After service she and her dashing Chinese husband would go to Friendly's for ice cream (which she would only pretend to eat). Later they'd fall asleep listening to *Masterpiece Theatre* and holding hands. Irene was seventy-eight, two years older than Mother, something Ken mentioned often.

Why Lily thought these things here, now, she wasn't sure. She was sure only of the ash print upon her forehead and the emptiness in her heart. People had talked before service about what they'd given up for Lent. Lily had said nothing, though her rock crafting would definitely be the thing to go.

How many weekends would that be with no projects? Five? Six? It wasn't like she'd have the time now anyway. Did that make her choice less reverent? She hoped not. She couldn't think of anything else. Even with the contest, she probably would have squeezed in the stone lantern she'd planned to work on next. Drawing close to God with no pretenses was more exciting than any hobby though. This was her first observance of Lent since childhood, and she was eager to see what God might do. Ken thought she was overthinking the whole thing. He gave up Mars bars again.

"It keeps things simple," he'd told her.

As one who knew nothing of simple, she'd only nodded in agreement, hoping he wouldn't see through her. Lily peeked at her mother as they read the next passage. The lips that had yelled at her last night easily recited the reading. Ken ignored both of them, allowing the prayer book to swallow his face.

Lily stiffened, realizing that perhaps she didn't like Ken so much. Did he always do this? Act this way? No, it was just her lack of sleep playing tricks. The nap this afternoon was a good start but not enough.

He squeezed her hand. "What's wrong?"

Everything.

"Nothing." Her afternoon nap definitely wasn't sufficient. Tiredness washed over Lily. Her fingers went prickly with sleep.

Another squeeze from Ken. "I think they're going to sing now. Could you, um, not sing along? I mean, I love that you want to do that and everything—"

"I understand." Lily's heart broke as the music began.

Ken had finally admitted it. He hated her singing too. Not that she was singing for him anyway. When Lily worshiped it brought her peace found nowhere else. Mother hated the sound of her voice, so there was no peace at home. At church and at work behind a locked door were the only places for her broken melodies. He'd tried to explain that the singing differed in this tradition, but to Lily worship was still worship.

She tried to make sense of the moment as the organ began to play. So he needed quiet. Isn't that what people came here for? Isn't that what she'd come here for? Unfortunately, she'd brought her booming voice along too.

Like Pinkie said, "Folks are what they are."

Lily reconciled all this while whispering the refrain of a hymn she loved very much and wanted to belt out with all her might. Even now she must have been too loud from the startled looks on some faces.

All the songs tonight had moved Lily, from the "Plainsong Psalm 103" to the "Gregorio Allegri" during the imposition of ashes. She watched the choirs—a mixed group of men, boys, women, and girls. At other services she'd seen them only separately. There was a lot to get used to, words to learn and such, but she savored every moment.

Just then a voice like a jackhammer broke through the quiet chorus, booming off the walls like a wayward ball. Ken made a face like he'd eaten sour candy. Lily couldn't help but smile.

When the song was over, she looked across the room to where the voice had come from, hoping to sneak a peek at the singer without being seen. No such luck.

The owner of the voice also owned a pair of piercing blue eyes creased with wrinkles. Pinkie had wrinkles like that. So did Jean. In truth, Lily was getting them too. That thought coupled with the man's mischievous smile almost made Lily laugh out loud. It was him. The guy with the rock.

The rock thief himself peered at her from the choir as though they shared a secret. His tanned skin looked even more stunning in the bright light of the sanctuary, but it was his eyes and their contented creases that held her attention. When Lily got home tonight, she would throw out every drop of age-defying liquid she owned.

That man sure knows how to wear a wrinkle.

Just then her stranger winked at Lily. She gasped as she read his lips, moving almost as though he were still singing the song.

Hello, beautiful one.

Lily made a mental note that religious holidays, sleep deprivation, and handsome men were not a good combination. The choir started again, with the man's voice knifing between the notes. His eyes, however, remained fixed on Lily. The others in the group stood still, but he moved his head and shoulders . . . and probably his hips, but Lily didn't dare look. She was probably committing some capital sin as it was. This was Ash Wednesday service, after all.

Lord, what are you doing to me? He isn't real. He can't be.

But those eyes stared back at her, and she knew he was all

too real. He was everything her collection would be: fresh, feral, and from the look of things, faithful. The thought of it all made Lily wish for just a second that she was back at her old church where she could shout. Instead, she laughed.

In the sanctuary.

With Ken.

God help us all.

Sandwiched between Lily and two small children, Mother tugged on a piece of Lily's "chicken hair" and nodded toward Ken, who was visibly horrified by Lily's less than reverent behavior. Her mother sat down so he'd have a clear channel to speak his mind.

"What were you laughing at?" he asked between clenched teeth as the music, and the service, ended.

Everything.

"Nothing."

Lily stole one last peek in the direction of the choir, where her handsome stranger had been a moment before. Like on the day she'd met him, he'd disappeared, reminding Lily that her heart was best focused on reality. Her gaze dropped to her lap.

5

Let the bridegroom leave his room and the bride her chamber.

Joel 2:16

"I think you're making a mistake here."

Doug LaCroix wanted to add what he really meant, that he'd made a mistake by coming back to America, by thinking he could blend into a congregation after over five years abroad on the mission field. Despite the varied cultures represented at People's Episcopal, Doug still felt like a foreigner in a city he'd once loved. Though the pace of his clinic had been brutal, the pace of New York overwhelmed him in a different way. Hearing God seemed impossible, especially with that woman bouncing around in his mind on top of the noise.

I am with you always, to the very end of the age.

The face of the priest, Patrick Kwan, only a bit more wrinkled than Doug's despite the fifteen years between them, gathered into a happy expression. "Stop pacing, friend. Sit."

Friend?

Doug's friends were back in Nigeria, struggling to keep the clinic open on limited funds, fighting back death in the face of a shifting state infrastructure with an ingenuity and tirelessness that made him feel guilty at the thought of sitting. *Friend.*

He'd once had friends like this kind priest. Many of them. Friends with soft wives, laughing children, and cute puppies. Friends who represented everything he'd given up. Some had died when the towers had crumbled. The other people he'd known could hardly be called friends, though he'd spent many years working with them. Without work to bloody his hands and the needs of people to bind his heart, would Doug be able to have a friend here?

Hoping so, he took a seat.

"The board chose right to have you come and drum up support for medical missions. You're passionate, honest, and hardworking." The older man placed a hand on Doug's shoulder. "You've changed a lot from the man I met two decades ago, but you still haven't learned one of the secrets of this Christian walk—pace. You've been running full speed for a long time. Will you now walk for the Lord? For this parish? We could use you."

The hand squeezed Doug's shoulder, but the words pressed his heart. Walk for the Lord? What good was that? There was work to be done, and here he was in New York City with a stomach full of plastic food, sitting. Were Ifyangi and the others at the clinic sitting? He hadn't sat much during his years in Nigeria, Uganda, or Haiti. At most he would lean on the counters before finally collapsing on a cot. Sitting here now seemed frivolous and lazy, like so many of the Christians he'd met since coming home.

Listen to me. I sound like Dad. Maybe I could use a little walk after all.

"I'm willing, though for the short time I'm here, I don't know how effective I can be."

The priest's laughing eyes grew solemn. He picked up a file from his desk. "About that. It seems you will be staying longer than anticipated."

Doug's hair, long and scruffy as ever, flopped forward as he buried his head in his hands. Before leaving his mission post in Africa, Doug had been required to do an exit interview to assess his mental state. He thought he'd come through with flying colors. Evidently not. Eighteen months earlier, in Uganda, he'd had a breakdown that required hospitalization for several days. Since then he'd been monitored closely, but many people broke down in the field. Doug felt it gave him more compassion, though now he wondered. He'd tried so hard to give the right answers to all their questions, but someone, most likely one of his co-workers at the hospital, had seen through his "all is well" responses. He wasn't in the danger zone he'd entered so many times before, but he was close. Perhaps too close if he hadn't realized it until now. Still . . .

Anger welled in his chest and up into his throat. He lifted his head.

"How long?"

The priest's smile returned. "One year."

One year. How many people he'd cared for would be dead when he returned? What about all the programs he was working on? The sickle cell treatment program? The diabetes screenings? The twin study? The much-needed dialysis clinic? His hands tightened around the armrests.

"No way. My team needs me." *And I need them.*

The priest opened a folder. Fashion sketches? What was that about? The older man thumbed through the pages.

76

"Someone else has already arrived to take your place," he said. "Things are going well, I hear. They'll be in touch soon. Until then I have a strange request. You've been asked to serve as a mentor for an up-and-coming fashion designer—"

"Fashion again?" Doug scrambled to his feet. "You've got to be kidding. I'm a doctor!"

The priest's calm voice climbed in volume, but his words came slow and clear. "You are a servant of Christ, Douglas. Don't forget that. If the Savior was willing to wash feet and build furniture, surely you can help someone create garments of praise."

Doug swallowed hard. Pride. So often it had caused him to fall, and his father before him. Though Reginald LaCroix, Doug's father, had started over a hundred churches in Thailand and China, no record of him graced the pages of missions history. No schoolchildren read his autobiography. When his father had taken his own life after yet another bout with depression, it was as if the good he'd done had been wiped away.

Though Doug had been against missions work after his father's death, he'd followed his parents' wishes and become a doctor, working his way through college in upscale men's shops and assisting tailors. His mother's love of fabric hadn't been lost on him. Everyone he worked for tried to woo Doug away from medicine. Uncle Sam succeeded, enlisting him as an army doctor in Vietnam. A year of stitching up soldiers under extreme conditions left Doug with no heart for medicine. He turned to the world people thought he was meant for—fashion. The attacks of September 11 had been last in a long line of troubling world events that had led Doug back to spending his days as his father had, saving lives . . . and souls.

Many times, though, Doug pushed himself too hard, both

in fashion years ago and now in medicine. Now looking at things through the lens of his faith instead of his swollen head, Doug saw that his overwork was more about thinking God's work could be done only through him than about simply trying to do his best. Doug sat, gripping the armrests again, this time in shame instead of anger. The idea that God needed him, and him alone, to do anything, to be anything . . .

"I'm sorry, Father Patrick. Of course I'll mentor or whatever they're asking me to do. I've been away so long though. I doubt I'll be up on what's going on in fashion now."

The priest nodded. "Good. It's availability, not ability, that our Lord requires." He handed over the folder full of sketches. "The background info on your apprentice is in this folder along with the sketches she submitted to the show—"

Doug struggled to get his breath. "Did you say show? As in TV show?"

The priest smiled. "Yes, that's who contacted us. *The Next Design Diva*. They somehow heard that you'd come back to the States and asked us if we could persuade you to be a part of their program. They're going to make a sizable donation to the medical missions fund and allow you to talk about the ministry and your experiences on the air. Knowing your passion for missions and your desire to help your clinic, we felt confident you'd agree.

"When they have a shooting schedule, the church secretary will give it to you. They have an initial meeting scheduled. The host, Hart Nash, is going to call you at the house."

Doug shook his head. "No calls. I'll contact her."

This was much worse than he thought. Nash had been off the scene a few years too according to the every-now-and-then correspondence he kept with a few people still in the business. This was going to be one of those shows with a bunch of has-beens trying to make a comeback. Not only was the thought of that revolting, it was also a little insulting. He'd chosen to leave fashion, but he could have kept at it for many more years. Obviously someone didn't think so.

That pride again, buddy. Let it go. This is about the clinic, not you.

Father Patrick gave him a consoling grin. "Just trust me on this one and go with it. And don't worry, we'll have some medical work for you soon. I'll get back to you on that once I know the details."

Doug nodded and took the folder, trying to ignore the churning in his middle. A reality show? When sending him off, the staff had held a prayer vigil and the kind of worship service he longed for now. No instrument had accompanied those broken strains of praise.

Though their prayer was that Doug would return soon with a dialysis and EKG machine, the needs were only a backdrop to the real need—for Jesus to have his way. Now it seemed those prayers had been answered, but not in the way he'd expected. He'd hoped to save lives, and now he'd be making clothes . . . and falling in love if he didn't watch himself. He'd had to run out of the choir once as it was.

How different this felt from the years he'd lived here as a rich idiot with a frozen heart, using women and being used by them. His last girlfriend had turned down his proposal and abandoned him when he'd divulged his plans to live out his restored faith by helping the world's poor at home and abroad. His heart had healed since then, but he had remained closed, despite seeing some of the most beautiful women in the world. He'd felt immune to the feminine power that had once held him captive—until that day in Flushing.

As happened most every hour now, a pair of kind eyes splintered his thoughts. Strands of raven slipped across his mind like silk. Though Doug felt alone since coming back to the States, his fellow rock collector somehow made him feel right at home. If he had to design clothes again, he'd use her for inspiration. Her laughter alone was enough to merit an entire season of clothes.

He opened the folder and scribbled something on the inside flap.

The Jade Collection.

The day had finally come.

And nothing, not even the ringing phone or the stack of work, both for Garments of Praise and *The Next Design Diva*, would mess up this day for Lily. The day Ken might propose.

He'd called today with no mention of the church fiasco. And his invitation sounded urgent.

"Can you make it to dinner tonight? I have something I need to talk to you about." Ken had paused. "It's important."

Lily had forced her hand to stop trembling and hold on to the phone. "What's the occasion?" she'd asked, trying to keep a smile in her voice the way Chenille advised them all to do when they wanted to scream during a phone call.

"I'd rather not say over the phone, okay? I love you, and I'm looking forward to seeing you. If you could wear your red silk, that'd be nice."

Lily had pinched her eyes shut. He loved her? Wear her red silk? Could this really be it? "Will do. See you tonight."

Now she found herself relaying the phone call to Chenille and trying not to sound too excited. Chenille looked excited enough for both of them.

"So let me get this straight. You're having dinner with Ken? A special dinner? Is he trying to come with it now with the fine stranger on the scene? I tell you, men can't deal with competition," Chenille said from the chair on the other side of Lily's desk.

She'd been sitting there when the phone rang and had heard the whole thing. She licked the nacho cheese from her fingers before reaching for one of Lily's tissues to wipe her hands.

"I don't think it has anything to do with competition."

Or did it? She and her handsome stranger had certainly been less than discreet during the Ash Wednesday service, something she wasn't proud of. How she'd ever go into that church again without being totally embarrassed Lily had no idea.

"It's all about the competition. Believe me. Though it's sad that's what it took to get him moving. But even a dead fish like Ken can read man face."

Lily grabbed one of the pebbles in her odds-and-ends jar and tossed it at her friend. "Will you cut it with the man face bit? So I met some guy and had some weird love jones going on. So I see him again in church and make a total fool of myself. It doesn't mean anything. It's like that stupid stuff you doodle on your notebooks in junior high. It isn't real."

Chenille put down her tissue and hooked her index finger in the corner of her mouth before grabbing a pencil and a piece of pattern paper.

"Oh . . . you saw him again! How dare you not tell. I'm writing it down this time. I tried to tell it to Lyle like you said it, but it wasn't half as juicy."

"Lyle! Tell me you did not tell your husband everything I said. Or everything you said for that matter. I don't think he'd appreciate us discussing some other man—"

"Oh, please. Stop trying to sound churchy, and spill the

beans. Lyle knows me, and he knows I love him. You'd be surprised what married people talk about."

"Don't put that off on all married people. You two are just interesting. As for the story, this one's simple. He was in the choir. He smiled at me, he mouthed some words, I laughed, Ken got mad, we went home."

Chenille grinned so wide Lily thought her lips would crack. The nut was actually writing all this down.

"Okay, okay, got it. Now go back to the words. What did he say?"

"That's not important—"

"I knew it! I know what it is now, you don't even have to say it. This is so romantic."

A sigh came from Lily's lips. "Will you let it go? It's not romantic. It's not anything. Lord willing, I'll be saying yes to a marriage proposal from Ken tonight and all this foolishness will be a bad memory."

Waving a yellowed finger in the air, Chenille shook her head. "Don't put the Lord in that, okay? You don't know what's going on here. But I know man face when I see it, and it's not happening when you talk about Ken. So for his sake, I hope he proposes tonight. 'Cause we've got a live one."

Lily gathered some of her hair into one hand, trying to make an updo. No go. Still too short. "I hate to say it, but somehow you were easier to deal with when you were all sad and quiet. Now that you're back on those cheese curls, you're giving me a headache."

It was a good sign, Chenille's yellowed fingers. Lily's boss hadn't eaten cheese curls, her favorite food, this much since she was pregnant with the baby she miscarried. After that Chenille hadn't been able to bear the sight of a cheese curl or a pregnant woman. When Raya had discovered she was pregnant several weeks after returning from her honeymoon, Raya had offered to take a leave of absence.

Somehow they'd all made it through, though not without a lot of Jean's cooking and several hundred Snickers bars (fun size, of course). With Lyle's cancer in remission and Raya's baby bouncing around the office, everyone's focus had drifted to Lily and her love—or loveless—life.

Chenille folded the piece of paper where she'd taken down the details of Lily's story and tucked it into her pocket, formerly full of snacks.

Lily took a sheet of paper too, thinking of the paper cranes her father had taught her to make. Perhaps those lessons of intricate folding had taught her to have the hope the cranes symbolized.

As she spoke she needed a huge dose of it. "I can't be sure if he's really going to propose, but Ken sounded serious on the phone. He said that tonight at dinner we needed to discuss something that would affect both of us. He said to wear my red silk." She took a breath. "It's his favorite."

"I hope you're right, but just know that I'm pulling for the old guy. Ken's great, and I love how you met him too, but this one is just too good. But for what it's worth, I hope all your dreams come true tonight."

Chenille grabbed Lily's neck, careful not to shower her with the remaining chalky cheese on her hands. All the GOP employees had mastered the fine art of eating around good fabric.

"Take off early. Get your hair done. Buy a disposable camera—"

Lily shook her head and held up both hands. Raya, Chenille, and Jean were great friends. Her best friends. But they all blew things out of proportion. They were still celebrating her spot on the TV show—even without her. She couldn't blame them. So many of the staff had dreams of their own, and Lily's chance was as real to each of them as if they'd been chosen. Same way with this wedding proposal, if that's even what it was.

"Let's not go that far, Chenille. I have lots of work to do, and so does Ken. If, and I say that strongly, Ken does propose, then those words will be all I need to make the moment special."

Her friend touched her hand. "You are such a gem. He's a fool for waiting so long. If he fumbles this, I hope the rock guy doesn't take as long."

The rock guy. It seemed he turned up in every conversation she had with Chenille. Why did Lily feel that there was a lot more to his story that had yet to unfold? It didn't make sense. She didn't even know his name. And by the time she did know it, she'd probably be engaged.

Lily shook her head. "Let the rock guy go. I'm going to do the same. It was just one of those crazy things that happens when you meet someone. Hopefully, after tonight I won't be so interested in rocks. Or strangers." She waved one hand. "And yes, you can go and tell the rest of them."

Chenille squealed and hugged Lily, this time not so careful with her Cheeto-coated fingers. "I can tell? Thanks!" She scampered out of the office, giggling.

At least someone was excited. Lily wasn't sure how she felt. She'd wanted Ken to make a commitment for so long, perhaps too long. At the same time, she'd grown accustomed to things as they were—dinner when they could catch it, a movie here and there. Ken was somebody to play phone tag with, receive messages from. It was nice to feel like someone cared. But marriage? Now she wasn't so sure. Ever since Ash Wednesday, when she'd seen those wonderful wrinkles around that man's eyes . . . something just wasn't right.

Maybe it was Lily who just wasn't right. She still wasn't sleeping or eating like she should. This thing with Ken was a no-brainer. The two of them were a perfect match. Her father would have been thrilled. And her mother? Well, Lily marrying Ken would make her fragmented life complete. A Chinese doctor for a son-in-law. And a Christian too.

Ken was a good man. The best man for her. So why had her heart thundered both times she'd seen that stranger? Did the enemy think her so foolish as to believe in love at first sight? Besides, Ken provided what she'd prayed for, a bond of respect and friendship with a good Christian man. Something safe. Something stable.

He hates your singing.

Lily took a deep breath. How would she get through life without singing? To most people it would seem a small thing, but those moments, times when she sang the hymns or psalms, were the times that got Lily through. Living with her mother required enough restraint. Giving up her rocks for a few weeks was proving to be a struggle. Could she hide another part of herself forever? Would life always be about trying not to disturb people? Or was it a small price for love, or something that resembled love so closely that even she couldn't distinguish between the two?

Pinkie needed to have time for her own life, which would probably fill with church events as soon as Lily's mother didn't require her care. A life with Ken would ensure a full-time caregiver for her mother and allow Lily to stay home with their children if she wanted to.

Children? She really was going a bit far. Some of Ken's comments lately made her wonder if he even wanted any kids. And after all, she was thirty-eight. She might not even be able to get pregnant. The doctor she'd had before Ken had reminded her of that somber fact when she'd turned thirty-five.

Kids or not, if God saw fit to give her a life with Ken, it would be more than enough. Exactly what she'd prayed for. She cleared her mind of blue-eyed daydreams and set to work brainstorming her sketches for *The Next Design Diva*. Though Chenille and Hart Nash were both supporting her, patterning and designing for a TV show and working for Garments of Praise was definitely a challenge, but a good challenge. Tonight brought a good challenge too, the dinner that might change her life.

The air sizzled with anticipation . . . and the scent of dim sum. Ken sat across the table from Lily, smiling and edging his egg roll around his saucer. Though Lily's appetite seemed to have vanished the past few days, tonight she felt ravenous.

Still, she restrained herself, chewing slowly and listening to the rundown of her boyfriend's day. Seven patients, three referrals, another run to the hospital after dinner. She nodded and sipped green tea, having long since learned the awkward dance that talking with Ken could sometimes be. Why had he sounded so urgent on the phone only to sound so casual now?

Everything about the evening said they'd come here for a special occasion. This was where they'd had their first date and a celebration dinner each year afterward. Everything was the same: dim sum; sizzling rice soup; a pupu platter of egg rolls, wontons, and Ken's favorite—chicken nuggets. It was all here, but something was wrong.

"The day was good on the whole. I accomplished a lot. I missed my Mars bars, of course. How was your day? Hear any more about the TV show?" he asked in a voice quieter than normal.

"Not yet. The host is going to email me tomorrow." Lily forced a smile.

How was her day? It was a blur of wondering about his invitation to dinner tonight and whether the ideas for her collection would be good enough to make it through the show's first round, let alone win. Things had been so much easier when her sketchbook was a secret, but Lily knew that hiding her talents wasn't going to help her reach her goals.

Though Hart Nash told her to forget what she knew about commercial design, she knew from watching previous episodes of the show that all those things were taken into consideration for the judging—market factors, whether the design had been done recently by another designer . . . On the train ride over, Lily had thought through her fusion of concepts, hoped they wouldn't be too different, but also wondered if they'd be commercial enough to appeal to a lot of people. She explained her thoughts to Ken.

"It's not done, right? You didn't make it yet. So if you think it's too out there, just start again. Give them what they want. That's the easiest way to win," Ken said with a shrug.

"I only wish it were that simple. It's easy to look at something and think you can make it. I do that all the time in my head with Raya's designs or something Chenille has made. But when it begins to belong to you, to make itself more than being made—"

Ken waved a hand as the waitress set down his plate. Orange beef. Something he'd never ordered. "That's the thing, see. You're all caught up in the artistry, the creating. These people have to sell the clothes. They know what their customers wear. Just make up something. Give it to them and get the money."

Lily's hunger fled as quickly as it had come, despite the steaming plate of rice and vegetables before her. It wasn't the first time Ken's mercenary streak had surfaced, but he'd always been sensitive to her feelings about her work. Even though he didn't understand exactly, he'd respected the notion that fashion design was more than just creating fodder for next season's discount rack. He'd acted as though her work had meant something. What had changed his mind?

She watched as he brought the beef to his mouth, waiting for surprise to register on his face. He'd mentioned a few times that the dish sounded good and that he'd have to try it sometime. Instead of surprise or wonder, Ken's eyes reflected a pleasant memory, the look of someone who'd seen an old friend. The way Chenille had looked earlier with those Cheetos.

He'd eaten orange beef before. Here, at this restaurant. And not with her. Lily's hands went limp. She pulled them into her lap under the table.

As if on cue, Ken avoided her eyes. "I invited you here tonight to apologize." He paused and cleared his throat. "I want to apologize for becoming so comfortable with you, for making you assume . . ." He paused again, his eyes searching Lily's.

She tipped her head forward, praying a tear wouldn't break free and betray her.

"I'm sorry for making you assume that we might get married one day." He said it in a rush.

Lily raised her head, smiled, and took a sip of tea. "I never thought that."

Liar.

His brows furrowed. "You didn't? I mean, we even talked about kids. And all this time we've been dating. I did think we'd marry, but when my parents asked me if I was willing to care for your mother, to have her live with us like you wanted—"

He'd gone too far. "It's fine. You don't have to explain."

Lily focused on a small dragon etched into her plate. She

ignored the sound of Ken's breathing as well as the lurch of her own uneven breaths. She also ignored the swollen pauses inviting her to ask the questions she refused to ask. ("So how long have you felt this way?" "When were you planning to tell me?") Ken would have to guide the knife so cruelly aimed at her heart himself. Though Lily hadn't been sure today if she was ready for marriage, she knew now that she wasn't ready for this rejection, for having her last hope of marriage and family drowned in her dinner plate.

This time a smile was more than Lily could manage. Her mother? His perfect, healthy parents had been discussing her mother and whether he was sure about caring for her? After all this time? She straightened her back against the booth, opened her purse, and sifted through her wallet. She threw a fifty-dollar bill on the table. It was more than she could afford, but what was the price of saving face when your last chance for a husband dumps you?

The prayer Lily had scrawled in her journal that morning came to mind:

Lord, protect me from all that makes me feel secure outside of you. Starve my self-sufficiency. In Christ's name, Amen.

Why did the words seem like skeletons now, phrases with the flesh torn from them? She tried to go back there, to recapture the moment when she'd written those words, but there was only here, only now.

Ken looked at her with pained eyes, as though she'd slapped him. "What is that money for?"

Lily stood and smoothed the red silk over her hips, hips that would never grow ripe with children. At least she'd be an old maid with style.

"That's for dinner. It's what friends do."

He rocked to his feet. "Friends? Wait, don't go so quickly. Just because we're not getting married doesn't mean we can't see each other, does it? Maybe we can still . . . Is it that guy from church?"

Ken too? Wouldn't anybody give that a rest? "No, I don't even know him. We met on my way home once. Just forget that."

He looked relieved. "Are you angry about what I said about your mother, then?"

Unwilling to dignify such a stupid question with an answer, Lily pushed her purse higher on her shoulder but didn't respond. Instead, she moved her mind in the sign of the cross, pushing across the evening prayer of compline, one of the fixed hours of ancient prayer she'd rediscovered since coming back to her Episcopalian roots. She'd forgone her prayer time to be here. To die here. Tonight before going to bed, she'd have a chance to say her prayers, to die all over again.

Ken took her hand again, touching his fingertips to hers. "It's just that after seeing patients all day, I wasn't sure I could live with one too. I know that sounds mean, but I'm just being honest. I guess I just don't understand why she can't go to a home. You keep acting like it's some Chinese thing, but my father is Chinese—"

"You're right, Ken. My taking care of my mother is not a Chinese thing. It's an honor thing, something you'd know little about."

"Look, Lily. I'm sorry. I do love you. And seeing you . . . in that dress. I'd planned to propose tonight. I know that's what you want. I'm sorry I can't give it to you. At least not now. Can't we just—"

"Good-bye, Ken."

Shaken and unable to say more without totally losing it and making a fool of herself, Lily left the restaurant, knowing that she'd never eat there again. Another table, the Lord's Table, also seemed violated before her, with the wine spilled and the bread scorched. She'd been fine living single and content. Why would God bring a man into her life, give her hope of having a family, only to wrench it away?

A pair of blue eyes assaulted her thoughts. She sniffed back a laugh. The singing stranger. Why did even she keep pulling him into things?

I know the plans I have for you . . . plans to prosper you and not to harm you, plans to give you hope and a future.

Lily waved for a cab, erasing the thought as she went. Though she had great friends, a cool new opportunity, and a mother who loved her, hope seemed laughable. And a future? For all her attempts to convince herself otherwise, Lily couldn't help but think she'd just left part of her future behind.

6

And Levi got up, left everything and followed him.

Luke 5:28

"What on earth are you making, Doug?"

Startled for a moment, Doug turned to face Father Patrick, the priest kind enough to offer both his friendship and his home. Making the paste for this chili took all Doug's concentration, and he hadn't heard his host enter.

"It's Thai chili, Father."

Father Patrick inhaled deeply, as if still considering what to think of the scent. "Patrick, Doug. Call me Patrick. Or should I take to calling you Douglas all the time?"

Doug winced as he poked at the garlic, curry, peppers, and beef tossing on waves of bubbling coconut oil. "We can't have that. Patrick it is, then."

He took a long whiff of the aroma that gave his priest such a doubtful look. For

Doug the smell contained memories of long walks along the beach in Ban Nam Kem, Thailand, where as a child he'd eaten gourmet meals cooked in gas-fired woks and served in open air. His only friends left there had been swept away by the tsunami, but Doug's memories of his father, legs folded and eyes ablaze, sharing about Jesu, as they called Christ, would always be with him.

He'd seen that same look in the dark-haired beauty who'd laughed like music on Ash Wednesday. Today, while Doug was singing one of the hymns from the service, Thai chili had come to mind. Though the recipe wasn't practical in preparation time or necessary ingredients, he had to have some of the spicy dish. If he was honest with himself, he had to admit that the chili was only a condolence until Sunday, when he would see the woman again. Hopefully, minus her male friend.

Father Patrick started to set the table for the two of them. "Thai chili, huh? I never knew you learned to cook there. You were so young, and then with everything that happened . . ."

Doug set the pot to simmer and joined Father Patrick, placing glasses for them both on the table. "It's all right. A lot happened in Thailand. Some bad things but some wonderful things too. This recipe is one of the wonderful things."

The thought of his mother with a mouthful of it was another one. Though her eyes teared up when she ate it and she had to chase each spoonful with water, Doug's mother couldn't get enough of the stuff. Until the day she'd died, it had been her favorite, along with the colors and fabrics of Asia.

"Mom loved it," he added.

Father Patrick nodded. "That settles it, then. I must have some." He stood. "Can I help out? I know nothing about

Thai cooking, but I can make a pretty mean pot of New York chili."

"I'll bet you can. I've already chopped the peanuts and the mint leaves, so there's nothing to do really," Doug said, laughing a little at his friend's troubled expression.

"Peanuts and mint leaves?" Father Patrick's face crumpled.

Doug smirked. "You must have some, remember?"

The priest sighed. "All right. I'm going to the study. Call me when it's ready. I'll make something cooler—and simpler—tomorrow night. Deal?"

"Deal."

Doug got up from the table and lifted the lid from the pot, stirring the recipe from his past with less enthusiasm than before. When Doug's mother had become ill and died, a veil of darkness had lowered over Doug's father, a dark shadow obvious to everyone but himself. Doug had no wife or children to reveal his extremes to him, but his co-workers had worked hard to fill the job.

He'd had several long relationships and many chances at marriage, but he saw now why none of them had worked out. With his heart finally in the right place, he'd tried to do things the right way, but when forced to choose love or service, he'd chosen service. Or perhaps it had chosen him. And he'd never regretted it, until now, wearing the apron of Father Patrick's late wife and stirring in her pots.

There would be no romantic dinners for Doug to remember, no legacy of children to teach about the world. His only measure of existence was lives saved or lost, and now he didn't even have that.

Doug punched the button on his CD player as Father Patrick reentered the room.

"Oh, and by the way, remember that medical position I mentioned?" Father Patrick asked. "We've had a doctor

94

coming in from Mount Sinai to do the adult day care, but he's taking a vacation soon. We'd like for you to fill in there until we find someone. We'd pay you, of course. And if it interferes with the TV show, we can probably get someone else by then."

"No need. I just hope I do a good job. Geriatrics can be challenging."

Strains of chanting filled the air, music that usually would have lifted Doug's spirits. Doug had come up with inexpensive treatments for many diseases in his work abroad, but something about the process of aging, of becoming a child again at the end of life, seemed too far beyond his control.

Then stop trying to control things.

"I'll definitely do it. You can give me a rundown of the duties after dinner. If you can talk after eating the chili, that is."

They met her at the door.

Lily took a deep breath and pushed past her friends, even Jean, whose concern strained the faint laugh lines around her mouth. Even so, Lily didn't want to talk. Not now. Last night's dinner with Ken and another long night with her mother didn't make for good morning conversation. Might as well nip it in the bud now.

"Seriously, I don't want to discuss it." She pulled her office door shut.

Raya, who wasn't even supposed to come in today, stuck her platform boot in the doorway. Lily took note of the shoe as the door shut against it. She'd have to borrow them for . . . well, something.

"You have to talk about this one," Raya said. "We all do."

Since when?

Lily held on to the edge of her desk for a moment before reaching into her drawer for the most recent issue of her now most hated periodical, *Modern Bride*. She flung it across the room at the trash can. She missed and hit her stone clock. The clock started coming apart before it hit the floor.

Tears streamed down Lily's face. "Okay, I'll make it easy for all of us. There'll be no wedding. There won't even be any more dates. Please don't say anything bad about Ken to make me feel better. It won't work. I love you guys, I do, but I just don't feel like talking right now." She watched in horror as Chenille and Jean came toward her. Raya closed the door firmly. "Really, guys. Later—" Lily wanted to scream, so she did.

Chenille looked at the others and then cleared her throat. "Lily, I'm really sorry to hear about you and Ken—"

"I'm not," Jean interjected.

Raya and Chenille shot Jean a look, which she ignored as usual. "Just calling it like I see it."

Lily's boss cleared her throat again. "Lily, we didn't come here about you and Ken. There's something else. A work situation."

Her eyes moving from Chenille to Raya, Lily tried to figure out what the problem could be. Had she forgotten to turn something in?

Raya's forced smile indicated something more, but she didn't say anything.

"We have a problem," Chenille said.

Uh-oh. This was not a girlfriend voice but an I'm-your-boss tone. And Jean, who never backed down from anything, looked as though she'd seen her own corpse. Raya was stroking the stapler like it was a cat. This was bad, like Ken part two.

Lily turned to Chenille. "So what is it? Am I fired? Did they call and say they hated my ideas for the show? What?"

Her mind reeled. She'd emailed her rough sketches only this morning before coming in. Had they looked at them and rejected them already? And if so, why contact Chenille instead of contacting Lily directly?

"It's Megan," Jean said and then paused. The name alone explained it all.

Before she knew it, Lily grabbed a piece of paper from her printer and began creasing and flipping it. A wing emerged between her fingers and then another. Soon she held a crane.

"She's back?" Lily asked.

Raya nodded.

More folding. "She wants her wedding dress?"

Raya nodded again.

Lily scrambled to remember Megan's dress, the bridal gown of doom. It had been a few seasons ago, after all. It was very traditional, she remembered, the kind of dress Lily would have wanted. To have someone like Megan wear it seemed almost like deception. The mother-in-law had liked it, though, and Raya had just wanted out of the project after making sketch after sketch (all while Megan was trying to win Flex).

Chenille put the folder on Lily's desk. "I'm sorry about you and Ken. We all are. But Megan, it seems, will be getting married after all. Since she's sticking with the design we prototyped, the next step is for you to adjust her pattern. She's gained about twenty pounds. I don't know if we'll end up with the full million when all is said and done, but the compensation should be enough for me to hire a replacement when you start designing full-time."

"Me, design full-time? I'm just going on a show, Chenille. That doesn't mean I'll win, and even if I do—"

"Oh, cut it and listen to the woman," Jean said.

For someone so happy that things hadn't worked out with Ken, she certainly seemed crabby. Wasn't Lily supposed to be the one upset?

"Lily, I'm planning for the best outcome for you and the worst outcome for us. No matter what happens, we're going to have to get some new blood in here and pull each of you up. You're all much more than the positions you hold now. So do you think you can deal with Megan? We're all here for you." Chenille sounded like a friend again.

"I guess. I'll put Jean on her if she gets too out of control."

Jean raised both hands. "I'm steering clear of that one as much as possible. Too moody."

Chenille rubbed her temples. "I know she's hard to work with, but we need to get through this."

Lily tried to breathe but felt her growing workload tightening around her chest. Hard to work with was one thing, but Megan could be impossible. Last time Megan had been a client, all four of them working around the clock couldn't please her. And there was still the TV show to deal with, her mother's worsening dementia, and the daunting task of convincing herself that Ken never existed. She grasped mentally for the prayer she'd mumbled through this morning while brushing her teeth.

Lord, may I not yield to a mind-set of power, but rather one of peace. Amen.

The echo of the words in her head quieted her soul but troubled her mind. How could she get a new mind-set when she didn't even have time to think?

"I'll go through the file and get an initial report to everyone by close of business. Have Megan call me so we can set up a measurement schedule."

Chenille pointed over to the blinking line on the phone. "I hoped you'd say that. She's holding on three."

"Sorry about this morning. We were sort of like a firing squad, huh? It's just that we had so much drama with Megan last time that we just want to get it over with."

Jean's upper body curled up from the body ball she was sitting on, exposed from where it was usually hidden under her desk. Like her face, Jean's body hinted at her age, but mostly it was the coarse wisdom in her voice and the stab of her eyes that told of battles fought and lessons learned.

Lily would have joined her friend, moving through a quick circuit of push-ups, crunches, and squats, an office workout program Flex had designed, but today all she could do was watch.

"I understand, Jean. It was just bad timing. I'm praying Megan's project will move forward, not sideways. I really don't know if I'll be gracious with her this time if she starts with the hourly phone check-ins. This is just a pattern alteration. I hope she gets that."

Jean pulsed upward, working her lower stomach, so flat these days that it put the younger crowd to shame. "She won't understand, you know that. But enough about her. I don't want to push, but this thing with Ken really seems to have rattled you. I'm sorry Chenille got your hopes up before you went. You can't give men that kind of power—"

"Let's not go there, okay?"

Jean had been Lily's tutor in How to Protect Yourself 101 since the day they'd started working together. "They come when you least expect them," Jean had said. "And in your moments of weakness, they steal your heart." Now, feeling like her chest was filled with the Jelly Bellies she'd once loved, Lily wondered if she shouldn't have listened to Jean more closely.

Still, Lily knew there were good men around. Her father had been one, along with Pinkie's husband, Johannan. The priest at People's Episcopal seemed nice too. When she'd gone to apologize about her behavior during service, he'd been very forgiving. If she didn't know better, she thought she might even have heard him chuckling as she walked away.

She'd received an email this morning from People's Episcopal with some information about medical missions throughout the world. The stories of the murdered child soldiers in Uganda and the wounds from political unrest in Haiti and Nigeria broke Lily's heart. Whoever had written the piece had used a soft hand but had given enough detail to make her care about the people and the ministry to them. The email said one of the mission's doctors would be visiting their church to collect funds for medical equipment in Nigeria. She hoped she'd be able to attend. It was great to see doctors doing stuff like that. Ken would never be able to squeeze in even a short-term missions trip between work, downloading B movies, online stock trading, and the few church services he struggled to attend.

Didn't you tell your friends not to tear Ken down? Let it go.

"It'd be great to listen to you bash Ken, but I just can't. Ken was as good to me as he could be. I accept that. I just need to be better to myself."

Jean rolled off her ball. Her knit skirt fell right into place. The wonders of good fabric. "You've got that right. I still want to know what his excuse was. I think I have a right to know, as much food as I cooked for that bum."

Lily laughed, despite how much this conversation pained her. The reason Ken called things off? Could she really say it?

"It was Mother. I thought he was okay with my plans for her to live with us, but evidently not. Seems he thought we could continue dating though, just not get married. Don't blame him. It's my fault."

Jean sipped the water that was on her desk. "Your fault? Oh, please. Don't give me one of your sin of Eve speeches. How is wanting to care for your mother your fault?"

Lily shrugged. "Not that. Other things. For one, I placed all my hope in Ken. And he knew it. Before he came along, singleness was all I knew, all I wanted. Then somehow I made marriage the measure of my value. To put all my hope in one thing, in one man, was foolish."

Jean's cheeks brightened, sort of like man face but worse. "You didn't put your faith in Ken. You put your faith in God. Still maybe not the smartest thing in my opinion, but watching how you trust God has been making me rethink my position. You were trying to do the right thing. Don't blame yourself for that."

The tear that had threatened at the restaurant last night rushed down Lily's nose and onto her lips. She licked it away. "Me? Faith? I can only hope that maybe there's some truth to what you're saying, but sometimes I don't know. Do you know what I was doing an hour ago in my office?"

Jean didn't try to guess.

"I was looking through the yellow pages for nursing homes, that's what. I even used you as an excuse. 'Jean did say I was taking on too much. Maybe it is too much.' For my own happiness, I really considered it."

When Lily finished, her palms were sweating and Jean looked troubled. This was usually Jean's role, the ranting doubter, with Lily to comfort and reassure.

Jean placed a hand on Lily's. "Again, you've got to stop this. You're human. These are hard choices. I wouldn't mind if my kids put me somewhere clean as long as they came to visit. Thing is, they probably wouldn't. They'd just let me rot in the back room. Don't wreck your faith on one stupid guy, even if he is a cute doctor."

Lily laughed. "He was hot, wasn't he?"

"Like five-alarm chili. On the outside, anyway. But he's too old for that to carry him. What is he, forty? He'll turn into Silly Putty in ten years."

"Jean!" Lily tried not to laugh, but she totally lost it. Her friends said the funniest things and always when she least expected it.

"I'm serious. And ten years after that, he'll need a bra like the rest of us. Gravity gets the guys too, you know. Dr. Ken has been treating us poor slugs so long he's forgetting it's going to happen to him too. Have you ever considered that instead of punishment, this might be a blessing? That maybe you would have ended up married to a person who wasn't for you? Maybe God has somebody for you who's hot inside and out."

"So let me get this straight," she said. "Now you're a theologian?"

"Not exactly—it's complicated. Look, this isn't about me. With you everything is about God, so I'm just trying to help make sense of things."

"For me or for you?" Lily put her lunch in Jean's refrigerator. It might taste better after a good zapping by the microwave later.

Her friend lowered her voice. "Maybe the answers are for both of us. It's complicated."

Lily walked into the hall, wondering if Jean didn't already know some of the answers.

It's complicated.

That was the best answer yet. How could she feel totally committed to caring for her mother on one hand and then find herself wondering what it would be like to have a full night's sleep in the arms of a man who loved her on the other?

Lily shuddered, remembering her mother's trusting eyes before she'd left that morning. In those eyes she wasn't Lily Chau, up-and-coming designer, but Li Li, the only daughter of a woman who'd worked her entire life to send her daughter to college. Though their relationship hadn't been the best in the past few years, Lily's mother deserved the honor her daughter had pledged to her—and to God. Wherever Christ's hand was in all of this, Lily would have to trust him for the strength to fulfill that promise. At this point anything other than the numbness she felt would be welcome.

Though still not totally used to New York City, Doug took solace in the smells of Flushing, Queens: wisps of curry; spicy clouds of kimchi, the Korean pickled cabbage he loved; the sound of soy sauce and scallions simmering a duet in a hot wok; the sharp staccato of long-handled spatulas dicing shrimp. Each made Doug's mouth water as he ran for the subway station. Perhaps he'd cook tonight, even though it was Father Patrick's turn, he thought, entering the train and taking a seat.

He considered possible menus as the train shot through the underground tube, taking him to another part of the city. It was the easiest way to travel here, but next time he'd probably borrow a car from the church. Or maybe take the bus. At any rate, he'd save his dinner thoughts for later. The Thai chili had brought Father Patrick to tears (and cleared his sinuses). It'd be best to let him try something else, perhaps some Nigerian spinach soup.

For now Doug had to go and meet his apprentice for that silly show before he started thinking about filling in as the doctor in the adult day care. Though he'd been concerned about taking the position, the patients he'd met on his visit to the center this morning were endearing. He was still smiling from the kind faces and intriguing stories of escaping dangerous countries and overcoming overwhelming odds.

And who knew, maybe someone else would take over the fashion thing while he devoted his energies to the adult day care instead of wasting his time on something he hadn't thought about in five years.

I waste nothing.

He sighed at the truth of those words. How many things had he learned to do over the years that had nothing to do with medicine—construction, plumbing, carpentry, cooking? Yet all of it had been in the Lord's service.

Perhaps what was really bothering Doug was how he'd reacted when he'd seen that woman in church. He'd probably looked like a patient himself, smiling and mouthing words like that. This morning he'd almost asked the secretary for the woman's name, when he realized he'd pretty much made his affections known by staring at her like a lost puppy. As the request for the phone number had come to his lips, Doug had decided against it. He had work to do. The train stopped, and Doug made quick work of the blocks leading to his destination.

He stopped on the street, reading the sign in front of the squat warehouse. "Garments of Praise Fashion Design," same as the paper in his pocket. The title and the Scripture it came from, Isaiah 61, cheered Doug. How often had the Lord given him something new to wear over his despair?

Even this sabbatical, a rest he'd fought against, seemed to be clothing the gray feelings that sometimes overcame him. At his first assignment in Uganda, he'd become so overcome with concern with the children taken from their homes and forced to murder their families and friends that he'd stopped eating, sleeping, or anything but praying and working.

Three months and thirty pounds later, he'd had to be reassigned. He still prayed for those children every day, but he knew he didn't have the detachment necessary to work in that environment. He longed to clothe people with praise instead of despair, though he knew how strong the sadness could be. The resiliency of the people he'd met during his travels still astounded him, as did the bravery of the men and women of the armed forces, where he'd also served and seen his share of horrors. All of it made thinking about clothes seem rather silly. At least this firm was small. It wasn't as if he'd be working there or anything. It didn't take too much to see potential. Either you had it or you didn't.

As he opened the door to the building, Doug knew no darkness could exist in such a bright place.

"I'm here to see . . . L. Chau," Doug said, reading from the page in front of him.

He took in the room, a melting pot of pink and tangerine, turquoise and jade. While he never would have put those colors together anywhere except in a carton of sherbet, Doug had to admit the combined effect was captivating.

A bronze Amazon in a pink skirt and matching lipstick gave him a warm smile. "You must be from the show. We thought you were coming later."

Time. He had to really focus on that again. In Africa you just sort of showed up. It wasn't as if anybody was going to turn you away.

"I'm probably a little early. Sorry." Doug nodded, noticing the way the woman's kinky hair hung in gold corkscrews around her ears. Though the woman was a bit taller than him in her stacked shoes, Doug kept stride with her easily.

"I'm Raya, by the way," his guide said, looking more like a

woman from Port-au-Prince than a New Yorker. She stopped abruptly in front of a set of double doors. She turned the knob, but it remained stiff in her hand. "If you'll wait a moment, I'll go and get the key. It's usually open."

"No problem," Doug said, remembering to smile as Father Patrick was constantly reminding him. ("You look angry. Smile sometimes.")

Though the woman seemed as no nonsense as Doug was, the memories she'd provoked of his mother's scent and the kind women of Haiti had earned her a smile.

While she disappeared behind a partition, Doug rested against the locked door, debating what to do about this mentorship. Though he'd seen a few guys wandering around the sherbet-colored foyer, L. Chau was most likely a woman. If so, he'd be professional. Detached—

"It is well with my soul . . ." A sorrowful yet full voice sounded from behind the door. Some of the notes poured out powerfully and others lower, in a more reluctant tone, which made it sound even more beautiful.

Looking through the Plexiglas panel on the door, Doug stiffened. It was a woman all right. *The* woman. Though he'd watched blood pour out of people without so much as a twitch, the thought of facing that woman right now made him want to run and hide. At the same time, he wanted to be closer to her. He sighed as his mind wrapped around the truth. His beautiful one was definitely Asian. Could she be the L. Chau he'd been sent here to mentor? If so, then either both his heart and his priest had played a trick on him or God was doing something Doug wasn't sure he wanted to be a part of.

As the song ended, Doug whispered a chorus of his own, the song of his troubled thoughts. "Bless the Lord, O my soul, and all that is within me bless his holy name." Even as he spoke the words, Doug wondered what was really in him. Though he'd balked at being part of the show, right now he knew that he'd agree to make all the clothes in the world if the sweet blossom beyond that wall would give him a chance to know her better.

What on earth is happening to me?

Before he could sort it out, the lady in pink returned with the key. She held it up with a smile and put it into the lock, but before she could turn it, the knob turned in her hand and the door opened, revealing the woman Doug had envisioned so many times lately. This close, he could see better the sadness in her almond eyes. A beautiful sadness so different from the store-bought prettiness on so many women in this city. There was despair in those eyes, but hope too. She was a woman who could endure hard things without forgetting how to laugh.

"Lily, you were locked in there? Girl, this man is here from *The Next Design Diva* to meet with you. I had to go all over the building to get the key."

The woman now identified as Lily looked at her co-worker, then at Doug. She froze at the sight of him. Did she remember him too? Or was his lack of a haircut as scary as Father Patrick had indicated?

"I'm . . . I'm sorry," she said, opening the door wide. "Do come in. And sorry to you also, Raya."

Raya shook her head. "It's okay, Lil. We just have to treat the people right if you're going to win. Isn't that right, Mr . . ."

Here we go. You might as well get it over with.

"LaCroix. Doug LaCroix."

Lily's friend wobbled on her beautiful heels. "LaCroix? Are you related to the designer by that name?"

He laughed a little, tugging at his jeans. Calvins. He'd forgotten how comfortably they fit him. "You could say that. I am him."

107

His new apprentice rocked forward on her toes and looked a little queasy at the revelation of his identity. He steadied her, watching the sadness in her eyes turn to humiliation.

Lily gave her friend a narrow glance. "Could you bring my cell, please? I'm going to have to call the show. I can't do this. I just can't."

Her friend paused, as if wondering whether to carry out the request. At Doug's almost imperceptible shake of his head, she said, "How about I just leave you two alone for now and we talk about that later, okay? You can do this. You've been doing it. Mr. LaCroix is just going to help you do it better."

If the war whoop Raya let out after shutting the door was any indication, Doug was going to help Lily do whatever she'd been doing a whole lot better. Lily was close enough for him to smell her now. Almond shampoo and Dove soap. He'd never known the two could smell so good. She licked her lips but didn't say anything.

He swallowed back what he wanted to say, things that weren't supposed to be in a missionary's vocabulary. Were they going to be alone like this every time they met? No matter. He could do this. He looked at the stack of papers on the table. A proposal sheet for her line for the show.

"I see you've brought your ideas. Good."

Her eyes widened. She snatched the page and put it behind her back. "That? No. I'm going to have to come up with something else. I—"

Doug silenced Lily's protests . . . with a kiss. It was his first in a long time, and despite the man she'd come to church with, Lily's response made Doug think it was her first good kiss in a long time too. He stopped himself from running his fingers through her hair, daring only to touch the ends of it with his fingertips.

All at once she pulled away. "What did that have to do with fashion design?"

Doug snatched the paper she'd been holding, folded it, and tucked it into his jeans. "That had everything to do with fashion design. One, we'd both be thinking about it for this entire meeting and not remember a single thing either of us said. Now it's over and we'll be thinking about doing it again, but we may actually get some work done. Two, I couldn't think of another way to get that paper from you. It'd be a little awkward for someone to show up with a camera and find us chasing each other around the conference room."

Lily wiped the corners of her mouth, still breathing hard from the kiss. He was too.

"Don't you think it'd be just as awkward for them to come in and see us kissing?"

Doug smiled. "Probably, but I don't think you'd let me get too carried away."

"You are unbelievable. This is never going to work." She started for the door.

He blocked her path. "It is going to work. It has to. Your boss needs to get on TV to take this place to the next level, and I need to do what I came here to do, raise money to save lives."

Lily snorted. "Raise money? Why don't you just give the money yourself?"

Doug chuckled, knowing she'd asked what many people wondered. He almost gave in and told her everything. "That's none of your business."

He reached into his pocket and unfolded the paper, holding it high over his head as he read it. When he'd finished, it took all his restraint to keep from kissing her again. Her collection was him.

"I should have met you sooner. I could have saved a lot

of money in therapy. You pegged me clean without even knowing my name."

She avoided his eyes. "That line isn't about you. It's about who I thought you were."

"So now I'm just some insensitive jerk?"

"Pretty much." Lily's hands balled into fists.

He stepped away from the door. "Good. I'm not supposed to be your friend. I look forward to seeing your sketches and any photographs you have at our next meeting."

She ran out of the room, but not before looking back at him with a wounded expression. When the door banged shut, Doug rested against it, holding a hand over his heart. He willed it to stay under his ribs where it belonged instead of following Lily down the hall. Though his own life beat in his ears, his emotions rushed after Lily, defying all his efforts to call his feelings back. Though he'd thought he would never have feelings for a woman again, Doug couldn't deny it—he had a thing for Lily Chau, and he had it bad.

To give her any chance of winning the show, and to save his own heart, he'd have to keep pushing her away like he'd done today. There was no way that a sweet, soft-spoken woman like that could ever love an old foghorn like him.

7

So is my word that goes out from my mouth:
It will not return to me empty, but will ac-
complish what I desire.

Isaiah 55:11

"So you're telling me that the cute old guy is Doug LaCroix? And he's your mentor for the show? How can that be?"

Lily had been asking herself the same thing all morning, but when the question came from Chenille's mouth, it took on another dimension. She'd known word would spread quickly with Raya on the scene, though Lily couldn't blame her. If Ralph Lauren showed up to talk to one of them, she'd be screaming down the hall too.

Her boss twirled a finger in her auburn curls, so often restrained into a bun or French twist over the last year. The sea of red hair cascading down her shoulders meant that not only had Chenille's husband been cancer-free for six months, but he was definitely alive and well. Playing in Chenille's hair was one of Lyle's pastimes.

"So what happened?" Chenille asked. "I hate to ask because you look so upset, but the suspense is eating me up. This is just too good."

Lily swallowed, measuring her words like ingredients in a favorite recipe. Not unlike in a court of law, everything said around this place could be used against you. "I really wish Raya could keep her mouth shut sometimes. I know you guys don't think I have a life, but there are some things I'd like to keep to myself!"

Before Chenille could respond, Lily stormed out of her office and slammed the door, as stunned by the crashing sound as Chenille probably was.

She ran down the west hall, stopping to catch her breath only when she reached her own office door. Was that as over-the-top as she thought? If not, Chenille's heels would hit the cement floor any second, clicking down the hall as she scrambled to apologize.

The hall was silent.

Not even Jean, who occupied the office next to Chenille's and could hear a mouse on the other side of town, had emerged from her door. Raya's door, however, clicked shut quietly on Lily's arrival, probably to receive the news of the outburst by intercom. Lily retreated into her office, thankful that profits from the Flexability line had afforded them actual rooms with doors instead of the makeshift cubicles they'd once had.

She eased her door shut so no one would think she'd slammed it, then dropped into her chair and cried. She'd been stretched out and overextended for the past few years, but today every carefully stacked piece of Lily tumbled to her feet. All her hard-won peace fell down as well. To have her mentor turn out to be the man she'd been daydreaming about for days was bad enough, but to have him turn out to be Doug LaCroix? That was just cruel. Maybe if he hadn't been such a recluse and world traveler, she might have recognized him and known to steer clear.

How could this be happening to her? For two years she'd shared dim sum and dreams with Ken, only for him to dump her without a second thought. (He'd left a few friendly yet remorseful voice mails, but those didn't count.) How could someone she barely knew have such an effect on her? Rather than talk about Doug kissing her, she'd jumped on her friend and stormed out of her office. How could she be upset? When Raya and Flex were dating, hadn't Lily, Jean, and Chenille had daily powwows to share whatever juicy tidbits they'd gathered? Hadn't she herself prodded Raya for updates at every turn?

She lifted her head, then stood, preparing to apologize, to somehow communicate better how desperate she felt, how her life seemed to be spiraling out of control. As she reached the door, her three friends came in.

Raya led the procession with her baby perched on one hip. "I'm really sorry, Lily. I didn't mean to invade your privacy or gossip or anything. I guess that's just sort of what we do around here, but that doesn't make it right. I'm really sorry. It's just that when I saw who it was, I knew you were going to win. We love you so much—"

Lily's hug cut off Raya's sentence. She rubbed the baby's back. Somehow Lily found her voice. "I love you guys too. I don't know what I would have done without you. Any of you. Chenille, forgive me for that outburst back there. I'm not . . . doing well."

Jean stroked Lily's hair. "You'll be fine, sweetheart. Nothing a good meal and a week of rest won't cure. Did you sing today?"

She nodded. Did everyone know about her singing excursions in the conference room too? "I did. Right before the cute old guy thing."

Raya took a step back. "He's the cute old guy? Doug LaCroix? Oh my goodness, Lily! No wonder you're freaking out."

Lily rolled her eyes at Chenille. They were all blabbermouths.

Jean looked like she was the one headed for a breakdown. "So it really is him?" she asked in a hoarse whisper. "He was here? Today?"

Lily laughed through her tears. "Oh, he was here, all right. Why, do you know him?"

Jean felt her way to one of Lily's chairs. "Know him? I almost married the man. We were friends for years. We lost touch though, and the next thing I knew, he was gone. Some said he joined a cult. Others said he joined the Peace Corps. Quite a few people are convinced that he's dead."

The room might as well have been a mannequin closet. Not one of the other women moved. Lily was losing feeling in her fingers and toes. Maybe all her blood had just rushed to her head. She shook herself to stop the effect.

Chenille shook herself too, but probably more to make sure she wasn't dreaming. "This story just gets better and better. So you've got the hots for him too, Jean?"

Jean made a face that she saved for special shows of stupidity, pursing her lips tightly together. "First of all, the only hots I've got are hot flashes. What would I want with a man now? Even a man as sweet as Doug. No, he's not for me." She turned to Lily. "But for you . . ."

"You can forget it. He's not what I thought he was at all. He's an arrogant jerk. Do you know how he started our meeting?"

Raya leaned so far forward that Lily thought the baby would fall. He didn't. He hung on for dear life.

"He kissed me, that's what. Just like that. No warning. Nothing. Said we'd both be thinking about it the whole time, so it was best to get it over with. Can you believe that?"

"That's my Doug! He must not have gone soft like everybody says. He's still the real deal." Jean clapped her palms together.

Chenille took two pieces of pattern paper from Lily's shelf. She handed the second one to Raya. They proceeded to fan themselves like two Southern belles in August.

Lily threw up her hands. "And here I was thinking I'm losing it. You're the ones coming unglued. I don't know what I'm going to do."

"I know what I'd do," Jean said. "Of course, I'd have to be substantially younger, thinner, and dumber than I am now, but I'd do it all the same."

The other three women stared Jean down.

"What? I'm just telling the truth. I go along with all your little prayer meetings and sing-ins, so leave me alone. I just say what you're all thinking."

Lily took another piece of paper from the pile, covered her face with it, and took a deep breath. That Jean was something else. She peeled the page down from her face.

"I'm going to have to call Hart Nash and tell her to get somebody else. There's no way this is going to work."

All her friends exchanged glances, but Chenille took the chance. "You're kidding, right? There's no way you can quit now. This is priceless. People will be buying DVDs of this for years after you two get married. They'll all swear they saw it coming."

That was the last straw. Lily opened the door and waved them all out. "Go. Every last one of you except the baby have lost your minds. Don't come back until you find them."

Raya went first, waving good-bye with a goofy smile. Chenille was next, pausing to say something, but Lily gave her a little push into the hall that made her think twice.

Jean ambled her way to the door and leveled a stern warning. "If you quit that show, I will never talk to you again. I mean it."

Lily laughed in her face. "Do you promise? Can I get that in writing?"

Jean stomped off down the hall, mumbling about how nobody listened to her.

Lily dropped into the chair Jean had been sitting in and leaned forward on the warm seat. How on earth had she gotten herself into such a mess? Hart Nash was already developing a schedule for shooting Lily's segments. Doug wanted to see her sketches the next time they met, as if there'd be a next time. Though she needed the $100,000 cash prize and contract for her own clothing line more than ever now that she was an old maid again, if winning the show meant being with Doug, she'd have to pass. Wasting two years like she had with Ken was an experience Lily wouldn't let herself go through again. No matter how good Doug LaCroix kissed, it was better not to create any more loose threads.

Lily heard the scraping long before she reached the door. The sound, accompanied by the smell of soy sauce and onions, stopped Lily a few feet short of the door. It opened anyway, and her neighbor emerged.

"She's been cooking all day. I can't stop her," Pinkie said with a smile.

In disbelief, Lily trudged into the apartment. She'd fixed her mind on the task of forcing another bowl of tapioca down her mother's throat, waiting, and watching for her to swallow. Instead, she was met by a fiery stranger with a spatula in her hand and quick words on her lips.

"Come in! Shut the door," her mother said, making another swipe through the wok as the plump, gray shrimp turned pink before her eyes.

Pinkie shut the door before Lily processed the command. There had been many days like this before, days when her mother was thumbtacked in the present, lucid and aware. Lately, though, those times had been confined to dark moments in the night that came and passed like a breath of wind. Not knowing whether or not the moment would stay, Lily didn't speak but watched instead as her mother's wrists flipped the spatula so casually. Her father's spatula.

Though her mother didn't turn and look at her, Lily knew that her appearance had been inventoried in that first glance. She looked down at her platform boots and zippered dress and ran a hand through her growing-out-but-still-spiky hair. Her mother's silence now said as much as her words would later.

"After you left this morning, she just got out of bed, went to the dresser, picked out her clothes, and got in the shower. We've been going ever since. Been to Chinatown and everything. If you need to go out with your young man, just call me. She'll be good company tonight," Pinkie whispered before sliding out the door.

Tonight. Her young man. She'd have to update Pinkie on that situation, though knowing her neighbor, she'd already figured things out. The only young man on Lily's mind wasn't so young. She'd recounted her meeting with him today a hundred times, it seemed, each time coming up with another reason why she couldn't meet with him again tonight like

117

he'd suggested by email. Their initial meeting might have been a bad start, he'd said in his note.

You think?

Actually, it was too good of a start if that kiss was his rule of thumb. After that there was nowhere else to go but down. Although if Jean had thought about marrying him at one point, the guy couldn't be all bad.

Still, Lily had cited excuse after excuse for why she couldn't meet him tonight. Her mother, first of all. When he'd offered to come to her apartment, she'd wiggled out of that, saying she needed to work on Megan's pattern, which though true, was still lame. The wedding wasn't for months, and Megan wasn't even in town.

The whole thing had ended with Lily going home a few minutes early, only to find her mother chow cooking the way her father used to, releasing the scents that had some-times shamed Lily in childhood, smells that had clung to her clothes, seeped through her lunch pail. Smells Lily now loved.

"Why are you standing there gawking like that? Come, get the plates. You don't want him to think that we are lazy, do you?"

Lily ignored her mother's frown as well as her own as she walked into the kitchen. It was nice to have Mother back to herself, but not if she was cooking for imaginary guests.

"Who, Mother? There's no one here but you and me. Pinkie has gone home—"

A sigh of exasperation escaped her mother's lips as she pushed past Lily for the blue and white patterned dishes, her mother's first real purchase after arriving in America. Even with the move from San Francisco when Lily was young, most of this set of dishes had survived. Her mother held three plates in her hand.

"The doctor, Li Li. Don't you know anything? And take off those ridiculous boots. Put on your red silk."

The doctor? Lily froze. Ken? Had her mother called him, not knowing about their breakup? They hadn't been exactly close, but her mother had been fond of him. Once when a breakup had threatened, Lily's mother had come to her in tears. "How can you do this? Don't you love me?" Back then Lily had reassured her mother—and Ken—that she loved them both. Today she would have to make another declaration of love—for herself.

"Mother, Ken and I aren't together anymore. He would have no reason to come here. So if you invited him, I'll call—"

A knock sounded at the door.

"He's here!" Lily's mother shot her a disdainful look and started for the door.

Suddenly uprooted from her spot, Lily ran to the door and flung herself in front of it. She'd played it cool with Ken that night at the restaurant, but she couldn't let him see her now. Would he actually explain his reasons in front of her mother? No, for all Ken's funky little ways, he wouldn't say anything in front of Mother.

Don't put anything past him.

True enough, Ken's twisted little reality made perfect sense in his mind. Lily couldn't risk letting him humiliate her or her family any more.

"Don't open it, Mother. I mean it. I know you can't accept it, but Ken and I will never be married. Never."

Lily's mother darted around her like an NBA guard and turned the doorknob. "Not that doctor. He's an idiot. And his mind is not Chinese. Pinkie told me about it. This doctor is better."

Pinkie knew? "What—"

119

The door opened, and there Doug LaCroix stood with that same mysterious look and those piercing eyes. Lily squeezed the back of the couch beside her.

He stepped inside. "I'm sorry. When I couldn't get you at the office, I called here. I mentioned that I'd spent some of my childhood in China, and your mother and I had quite a time catching up. She insisted that I come for dinner."

Unable to think of what to say, Lily extended her hand. "Do come in, then." Doctor? Her mother really was losing it.

Her mother nodded, waving him straight to the pot. "Chow food," she said. "Like you said on the phone."

Doug nodded and looked down at the pot as though he wanted to cry. "Yes. That's exactly it. It smells so good." He turned to Lily, who was now shoving plates around the table. "But I won't stay. I think we have become fast friends, but I don't want to intrude on Lily—"

Before Lily could answer, her mother waved her hand. "Intrude? What does she have to do? Go to work and make paper dolls? She needs a husband. You need dinner. Sit down."

So Doug sat, but not before his lips curled into a sympathetic smile. Lily placed a fork beside his plate, wishing she could melt through the floor. As if to keep her from doing just that, Doug placed his cool, steady hand on hers.

"Sorry about tonight," Doug said to Lily as they drove Father Patrick's car home from the church, where they'd tried to have another, more focused meeting. Doug had picked the place thinking it would cool things off between them.

It made things worse.

He didn't know about Lily, but he'd spent the whole time praying and trying to figure out what he was supposed to do next. Despite his efforts not to, every time he was with Lily, a little more of him left with her. Whether it was love or hate he wasn't sure, but he obviously had an effect on her too. She hadn't sketched more than a few lines.

And Doug couldn't blame her. Dinner, although charming and delicious, had proved too much for both of them. Their encounter this afternoon had been more than overwhelming, and then he had to go and add to it by making her create on demand? Unfortunately, the show's schedule demanded that they come out of the day with something. They'd succeeded in that, only it wasn't anything they could use on the show.

"I really didn't mean to intrude. With dinner, I mean," he said, both glad to be so close to Lily and wishing the traffic would move so that he could get her home.

Her hair was sticking up after she'd raked her hands through it while sketching, and her lipstick, a beautiful neutral shade he couldn't name at the moment, was smudged across her mouth. It was all he could do to keep from kissing her again, and that scared him.

Lily surprised him with a smile. "It's okay. Thank you for coming. Mother hasn't seemed that excited about anything in a long time. I'm just tired, and well, you have to admit, it's been an eventful day."

Doug appreciated her words but still felt angry with himself. Even if God did have plans for the two of them (which he seriously doubted), why would he show his eagerness like a grammar school boy?

The traffic, which most New Yorkers avoided by taking the subway, gave Doug and Lily time to talk. They discussed places they'd been—her to Israel with her mother and Pinkie, him all over the world. Red lights lent themselves to world history, wine, politics, even a commentary on the state of the church. By the time they'd touched on Rwanda and rap music, something Doug had been fond of during its inception, he knew he was in trouble.

Lily was as smart as she was beautiful, and he'd probably scared her away. Or if he hadn't, he would now.

"So why aren't you married?" he asked. "I don't mean to be rude, but I don't get it. I guess when I was here, it made sense, everybody dating until they're forty. In Africa a good woman marries young—"

Lily's head turned toward the window.

"I mean quickly . . . I don't know what I mean . . . forget it."

She faced forward again. "In America, if you recall, good men marry slowly, if at all. I think a better question would be, why are you still single? Jean Guerra told me today that she almost married you once. I'm sure she's not the only one. As for me, perhaps I'm not as wonderful as you think."

Fear jolted through Doug at the mention of Jean's name. He'd even gone as far as to buy Jean a ring. She'd pawned it, bought a red convertible, and married one of his army buddies. He hadn't seen her in years. What would she be like now? Probably the same.

"Jean? How is she? Where is she?"

Lily snorted. "Funny. She asked the same questions about you. She's one of my best friends. She's probably the same as she was when you knew her. Just a little older and wiser, to hear her tell it. She works at Garments of Praise, the place where you were today."

Doug didn't try to hide his shock. "You're kidding."

"I'm not."

"Do you know who she is? What she can do?"

"Sure," Lily said. "She's head of the cutting department. She's amazing."

Doug felt like leaving Father Patrick's car here and walking home at the thought of Jean Guerra cutting out pieces in that little warehouse. "Are you guys crazy? Jean's not a cutter, she's a designer. The best menswear designer I ever knew. We all tried to steal her from Yves Saint Laurent. We used to joke that one of Jean's suits could get a guy married well, hired on, or buried handsomely."

Lily looked shocked. An awkward pause poked through what had been a volley of conversation.

Finally she spoke. "So that's where you know Jean from, then? Menswear?"

Doug turned the wheel quickly to move into the next lane. "No. I knew Jean long before that. Long before either of us had much of anything. We met in Vietnam. I was an army doctor, and she was one of the nurses. A very good one, at that. She stayed on her feet through things that knocked me on my back. Once she held me up while I cut a bullet out of a guy. I do remember her patching up everyone's uniforms, but I didn't know what she could do until we met again in the city years later."

"So you are a doctor?" Lily whispered.

"Of course. Did you think I lied to your mother? I hadn't practiced for years until lately, but I kept up all my certifications. It just wasn't something I talked about."

"So you were in the Peace Corps like everyone said?"

He shook his head. The Peace Corps thing again. He'd done that too, but thirty years ago. "I've been in the Peace Corps but not recently. For the past few years, I've been part of the medical mission."

She covered her mouth. "A missionary? I read about that ministry in an email from the church."

So they had run the piece he wrote. "Good. It took me

a while to write that. I hope it gave the congregation some sense of what we do."

Lily looked amazed, as if he'd stepped into the driver's seat from outer space. "The piece was excellent. In fact, I was planning to make a donation on Sunday."

"Thank you. And thank you for having me in your home tonight. Your hospitality made me feel at home. Thank your mother for me too."

The blare of car horns made Doug think of Africa and the annoying buzz of insects that he'd learned to ignore.

The driver in the car behind Doug honked for him to inch forward, littering the air with a string of curses. Doug noted the frustration and humiliation under the words. Beneath the bright lights of this or any city, there were forgotten people, poor and angry people. People who sometimes needed to hear the thunder of their own voices in their ears, even when speaking to a stranger.

Lily shook her head. "Sorry about that. We can be pretty expressive, us New Yorkers."

"It's okay."

Doug understood. Right now he wanted to scream too, at the futility of his presence in a place where he had nothing to offer but clothes because he'd failed to act happy enough for someone's satisfaction during his exit interview. And on top of everything, he'd somehow let himself be deluded into thinking he could fall in love. Maybe Lily was right and they should give up on the idea of working together and he should go somewhere, anywhere but here. He would send Lily a note of apology when he was long gone, adding in something special for Su, her dear mother.

Doug took a deep breath as they approached the intersection. Confused for a second, Doug let the car inch toward the middle line, then guided it back.

Lily laughed, not knowing how glorious it sounded in Doug's ears. "Staying on the right side of the road must be pretty hard now, huh?"

"Not unless I'm distracted. Like now." He braked for another light, wishing he'd had a similar mechanism for his mouth. What was this woman doing to him?

He was already mentally writing his letter of regret to Father Patrick, explaining why he'd be unable to stay. The last thing Lily needed was some missionary doctor trying to hit on her. If he were home, it would be different. The women, the wives and daughters of his friends, would carry messages to Lily for him, tell him what to do. Here it was all about dating, something he'd never been good at, even after doing so much of it. Perhaps he couldn't return to Nigeria, but that didn't mean he had to stay here—

A squeal of tires sounded in Doug's ears. His body, uncoiled in resolution a moment earlier, knotted now in preparation for impact. Something—a car out of control from the sound of it—was coming, and there wasn't anything he could do about it. He threw a hand across Lily. "Hold on!"

Jesus, help us.

Metal hit metal in front of them as an old Buick smashed the side of a blue minivan in the next lane. Lily sat next to him, silent. Her eyes were closed.

"Lily? Are you okay?" Doug said, fumbling for his seat belt, then hers.

He was unbuckling her belt when Lily opened her eyes. "I'm fine. I was praying. Don't worry about me. Go on. Check on them."

Doug looked between the seats for the cell phone Father Patrick insisted he carry. Once he found it, he punched 911. His eyes darted between Lily and the scene as he explained to the operator what had happened.

"I do want to check on those people, but I don't want to leave you here."

In truth, Doug had already visually assessed the situation—the passenger of the minivan, a black woman, leaned against the window of the smashed door. She looked unconscious. The driver of the Buick was trapped also but looked alert from Doug's view.

Lily pressed Doug's shoulder and grabbed his phone. "Go on. I'm fine."

Nodding, Doug left the car and stepped onto the street. Seeing no way to get to the passenger from behind, he walked to the driver's side of the minivan. Though the man looked unhurt, he was upset, yelling and swinging his arms.

"Help her," the driver screamed in Ibo, the Nigerian language of Doug's last mission station. "She is pregnant!"

The words penetrated Doug's mind. The man either could not or would not speak English. Many people defaulted to their native language during trauma. Either way without Doug to translate, the woman and her baby may not survive. Doug reached into his jacket for the small Bible and pen always tucked there. On the inside cover, he scribbled all he had seen, then in Ibo asked the man for the woman's medical history, which the medical personnel would ask for when they arrived. Matthew was the man's name.

Sirens whined nearby. Unable to breech all the cars, the paramedics cut across the traffic on foot with stretchers and tools. Doug was talking to the woman in Ibo, trying to keep her conscious, when the paramedics reached hem.

"Step back, sir," a paramedic cautioned him.

Doug obeyed but not without offering his assistance. "I can help."

126

A weary ambulance driver waved him away. "Give your statement to the police. That will help."

Doug stared back at Lily, still in the car but making motions with her hands, pointing to the police officer nearby. "Tell them you're a doctor," she mouthed.

Hadn't he said that already? He hadn't, but when the driver became animated about his wife, Doug marched back to the paramedic.

"I'm a doctor," he said, flipping open his wallet for the American Medical Association card he seldom used.

By this time the paramedic didn't seem to care what Doug was, because the driver of the minivan was screaming for Doug, "the African." The rest of his words were in a dialect the medical team couldn't understand.

Doug spoke quickly. "The wife's name is Chioma. She's thirty-seven weeks pregnant with their first child. No medicines or conditions. He doesn't know the blood type." He added soothing words in Ibo for Matthew.

A hand touched his back. Lily's hand. When had she gotten out of the car?

"Make sure they help her," she whispered as sweat poured down Doug's face. "I'll get the car home to Father Patrick and tell him what happened."

Matthew reached out for Lily's hand, since she was closer to him than Doug was. "God bless your husband," he said. "For helping my wife. My baby."

Lily nodded but didn't correct the man's assumption. "God will help them." She paused to give Doug an encouraging look, then walked back to the car without saying more.

Doug piled into the ambulance and prayed for all of them, Matthew and Chioma and their baby and Father Patrick, who would be surprised to see Lily instead of him. Lily, the woman who'd made Doug feel certain there was no place for him in Flushing a few minutes ago. Lily, the woman who made him feel certain God had a plan for him a few minutes later.

Lily.

The woman he'd waited his whole life for.

8

Rise up and help us; redeem us because of your unfailing love.

Psalm 44:26

After rummaging through the glove compartment to find the priest's home address, Lily had finally gotten the car to Father Patrick's home. The priest, though concerned, had remained calm, thanked her for bringing the car, and brought her home.

"Douglas has a way of finding people who need help. I'm sure he'll be fine."

She hoped Father Patrick was right.

Many minutes had passed since her priest had delivered her in front of her apartment. She gathered the strength to go inside, to tear her mind away from Doug, from that accident scene. "God bless your husband," the African man had said, his only words she could understand. The only words she wished she hadn't comprehended.

She could still feel Doug's arm restraining her when the cars collided in front of them. Like a man protecting his wife. Like a mother protecting her child. Like a daughter protecting her mother. The seconds had passed in slow motion as Doug had called the authorities and helped the African couple. She recalled what had happened when she was with Ken once and a man passed out in the grocery store. She'd urged Ken to help him, since he was a doctor, but he'd refused, citing help on the way. "Malpractice insurance isn't what it used to be," Ken had said.

Doug had no malpractice insurance, she was sure of that. His concern was for protecting others, not himself. Not that she could compare Ken's work in a health maintenance organization with Doug's service in missionary medicine. Both men were needed, although right now she needed Doug a lot more. While her mind turned over these things, she keyed into her dark, silent apartment.

She put down her keys and slipped out of her shoes just inside the door without flipping on the light.

A groan rose up from the floor.

She swiped at the wall, flooding the room with brightness as she flipped the switch. Pinkie lay on the floor clutching her chest.

Though Lily hadn't screamed when those cars crashed, she screamed now. A stone mosaic fell to the floor as she reached for the phone and dialed 911, never leaving Pinkie's side.

"What is it? Chest pain?"

Pinkie's head moved only a fraction of an inch, but it was enough for Lily to know that was a yes. Sweat poured off her neighbor's forehead. Lily's mother wandered in from the hall.

"Pinkeeeee!" she screeched, wadding her nightgown in her hands.

Lily shooed her away. "Go back to bed, Mom. The ambulance is coming." She couldn't deal with both of them right now.

Her mother ignored her. "Aspirin! Get aspirin!"

Yes, aspirin. Hadn't they given that to Lily's father in the ambulance when he'd had his heart attack? It hadn't saved him, but it was something. Lily nodded, reaching for her purse and dumping it on the ground. Jean insisted that Lily take two baby aspirin a day along with her vitamins. She'd been slack with the regimen lately but still carried the pills. She pushed two small tablets into Pinkie's mouth.

"Swallow these, Auntie," Lily said, surprised to hear herself using her childhood name for her neighbor.

Her mother grabbed a towel from the kitchen and mopped Pinkie's brow, reciting Psalm 91 as she went. "He who dwells in the shelter of the Most High will rest in the shadow of the Almighty."

"Yes," Pinkie whispered. "Yes, Lord."

Her mother held her friend's hand.

Lily froze, listening to the clarity with which her mother spoke the Scriptures, amazed at how a mind usually so clouded with confusion could be so clear at a time like this. She didn't understand it, but she was thankful.

"Ambulance!" someone called outside the door.

Lily struggled to get up and let in the same paramedics she'd seen at the accident earlier this evening. They moved right past her, showing no recognition. Good. She had neither the time nor the energy to explain.

"She's seventy-two," she told them. "I'll call her daughter and get her things from next door."

The men already had Pinkie on a stretcher and half out the door. "Follow us to the ER or come along. We've got to get her in."

Lily grabbed her purse before realizing she couldn't leave her mother alone. "I can't—"

A bony hand tapped her in the back. Lily turned to find

her mother wearing her best housecoat and a pair of Lily's father's penny loafers. "We come in ambulance." She patted her purse. "I have information."

They'd had a good run, Pinkie and Lily. A run that was over. They both knew it.

"My heart's too big, I guess," Pinkie said during that long night at the hospital. The cardiologist in attendance agreed.

Pinkie's daughter, Barbara, wanted to lay some blame too. "I think all of this could have been avoided had you not used my mother as your babysitter."

Barbara never had liked Lily much while they were growing up. She'd thought it strange that Lily's Asian family was so close with her Afro-Caribbean one. "Aren't you supposed to only eat rice?" she'd asked Lily on a summer day, her eyes questioning Lily's plate full of jerked chicken and fried plantain.

"Aren't you only supposed to eat watermelon?" Lily had countered, pointing to the spring rolls and Chinese vegetables gracing Barbara's Chinet dish. They hadn't shared many words since, except to exchange the salary Pinkie refused to accept. Just as adamant to compensate her mother's friend, Lily slipped the money to Barbara instead. It was a strange arrangement, but as long as Pinkie's rent was paid and her refrigerator was full, what did it matter?

Barbara and Lily were adults now, and their relationship, or lack of one, didn't make a difference. Pinkie did. Lily motioned for Barbara to step into the hall and shut the door softly.

"Barbara, maybe you're right. Your mother was willing to sit with my mom, and I needed the help. I didn't know anybody to ask, and I'm not sure if I would have trusted them anyway. Pinkie is family to me, and if her helping me hurt her, then I am truly sorry."

Barbara's forehead furrowed. "I didn't expect you to say that." She paused. "Yes, I did. You're a good woman, Lily. Maybe a little too good. Anyway, thanks for understanding. I'm going to bring Mama home and see if we can't get her better. I guess I'm sort of in your boat now."

Lily only smiled. No one was in her boat but Jesus, and even he seemed to be asleep. Not only was there no one else to sit with her mother, but it seemed that losing Pinkie's company had taken any remaining clarity in her mother's mind.

In the days following Pinkie's heart attack, Lily's mother had slid in and out of sleep, moving from past to present.

Lily had spent her day off making arrangements for her mother's care at the People's Episcopal Adult Day Care Center. Though it seemed to be a wonderful place, its title gave her chills. Still, she had to work, and now the time had come for her to turn her mother over to strangers. Her heartbeat slowed as she fingered the clothes she'd laid out for her mother the night before.

The morning sifted through Lily's fingers as she spooned oatmeal into her mother's mouth and took turns buttoning her mothers clothes and her own. Instead of the morning metro girl she'd once been, dashing for the train with her briefcase, Lily was now part of a wobbly and wonderful unit of two. With each careful step, Lily focused on a phrase from Amy Carmichael that had brought her much serenity over the years.

In acceptance lieth peace.

It was a hard sentence, simple yet painful on the lips, especially in a world that taught people to accept nothing but the best, to follow their dreams no matter the cost. The phrase flew in the face of teachings that said Lily should never feel the darkness so often edging at her soul, that she should always be happy, prosperous, healthy. And yet today, with every step she took, pressing her mother's wiry body forward while supporting it at the same time, Lily wanted to accept where she was in her life, to open her hands and hold it, to stop struggling to be perfect. As they climbed the steps together, Lily let go of her end of the rope holding her soul taut and erect and allowed the darkness, the winter of her heart, to blow in.

She paused on the top landing, gripping her mother's trembling hand. A cold blackness stung her mind and she had an overwhelming urge to cry, but in the midst of the pain, she realized that the numbness she'd hated had fled. In its absence peace had come in.

Whatever happens, Lord, I'm yours.

Lily and her mother stopped in front of the door Lily had heard so much about. The blue block letters spelling out "Adult Day Care" had been the topic of discussion when they passed it before. Her mother had said they were embarrassing, like a babysitter for old people.

"I don't need to go there," she'd said. "I have a good daughter. Li Li."

Yesterday the thought of her failure might have torn Lily apart. Today she chose to accept her limitations and pray that God would make up the difference. Her mother looked at the letters but this time said nothing.

Lily pressed the buzzer and checked her watch. By the time she got her mother checked in and made it to work, she'd have lost half the morning. Lily smiled, accepting that too.

The door opened electronically, and Lily's heart opened automatically. Doug stood on the other side of the door.

"Good morning," he said tenderly, taking her mother's hand. He greeted Lily too, with a soft kiss on her cheek, one that left his scent lingering behind. She finally recognized the components of his smell, vetiver, cloves, frankincense, and myrrh. The combination was fitting. This morning he was nothing if not a gift.

Lily pressed her feet into the floor to keep from jumping into his arms. She had no idea why Doug was here in place of the stern doctor she'd talked to on the phone, but she was grateful.

"Li Li, who is this man?" her mother asked in an agitated voice before pulling away from Doug.

She'd been easy enough all morning, but a storm was brewing in her now. Lily didn't try to get out of the way.

Doug gave Lily a comforting look, one that brought her feet a little off the floor. He took her mother by the elbow and bowed toward her.

"Good morning, Su. I'm Doug, a friend of Li Li's." He reminded her of their previous meeting in her own language.

Lily hung back, listening, remembering feeling left out when Doug and her mother had spoken Chinese at dinner a few nights before. It had reminded her of when her father was alive and her parents talked across her at the dinner table. While her mother had been adamant that Lily learn Mandarin, Lily's father would not allow it. "They may never see us as Americans, but they will know she is American."

His words could not have been truer. The one time Lily had visited China as a teen, her Chinese cousins had laughed at her accent and funny clothes. She'd accepted then that though she hated hyphenated perceptions, Chinese-American

135

pretty much summed her up. Still, if that were true, what exactly was Doug?

Cute-American.

When it seemed her mother and the good doctor would never stop talking long enough for Lily to say good-bye, Lily turned to buzz herself out of the center. She silently prayed that the center wouldn't have to call her back before the end of the day and that she'd restrain herself from calling every hour. She pressed the button, and the door swung open.

"What's wrong with you?" her mother called behind her. "Aren't you going to say good-bye to this man? He's a doctor!"

Lily grabbed her cheeks. Man face for sure. "Good-bye, Mother," she said softly. "And good-bye, Doctor."

Doug gave her a smile that made her toes curl.

"Good-bye, beautiful one," he said. "Have a good day. We need to meet again soon."

Lily nodded before ducking into the hall and walking at a steady clip but slowly enough to wipe her tears. Once the street began to blur in front of her, she blinked back her fears and ran . . . for the train . . . for everything.

"So what do you have for Fluid?"

Lily tucked a wisp of hair behind her ear, tuning out her mother's cooking sounds in the background. She rested on a pillow on her living room floor while Doug rested his back on the couch.

"Not much," she said, handing Doug a sketch.

He stared at it, then took a deep breath. "What do you think of this?"

"Good, not great. More structure than movement."

Doug smiled. "Exactly. Flint. Start a pile for that. What

do you think of when you think of the word *fluid*? What comes to mind?"

She closed her eyes. What came to mind when she thought of most any word these days was Doug, but she tried to concentrate and come up with a more suitable answer.

"Fluid, huh? Let's see. I have this fountain in my office. The water washes over the rocks and into the bottom pool, then it's pumped back to the top again. The sound is steady but soft. When I watch it, it reminds me of crying."

Doug nodded, making notes. "Good. More."

Lily rubbed her neck with one hand. "I think of molten lava flowing down the side of a volcano, glowing red-hot. Long legs. Pencil drawings that can be erased. Flow. Outpouring. Flexability."

Doug's hair hung in his eyes as he scribbled on his tablet, making sweeping arcs and circles with his hands. When he turned the tablet around, he'd made circles and adjoining lines. Mind mapping. Hadn't she taken a class on that in college?

He tapped one circle with a pencil. "You spoke of fire and water. Both can flow. Move. Flexability in your mind is both an ability to bend and a sportswear line. The fountain cries. The fire burns. This collection is alive, hungry, but moving." He sat on the couch beside her.

She sat up and pushed the pillow aside, crossing her legs in front of her. She covered her mouth for a second, then took the paper from Doug.

"Oh my goodness. It's like me and Jean. She's the fire and I'm the water. Classic cuts that move with the body. Clean pieces that flow." Lily reached for a pen and began scratching notes in the margins of an old *Vogue*.

When her pen finally stopped, Doug put an arm around her shoulder. He kissed her temple, then the top of her ear.

"Actually, I was thinking that it was you and me, with you being the fire, but go with that. It's good."

Lily turned, bringing her lips to his, celebrating making some progress, celebrating being alive. This kiss, much like the first, left both of them lost in each other. Lost and found too.

Doug was first to pull away this time, though his chest heaved beneath his shirt. "Now, that was good. But your mother's in the kitchen. I wouldn't want—"

Lily jerked him down by his collar and kissed him again quickly, holding his face in her hands. "Thank you for caring about my mother's feelings. And mine. Let's go check on her."

He took her hand and pulled her up, pulled her close. "Yes. Let's."

"You don't look well, Doug. Lovesick?"

"Basically," Doug said, picking through the spinach soup in front of him and rolling a ball of dough between his fingers to sop up the juice. Not only had the Oyobos, the couple he'd traveled with to the hospital after their car accident, survived the crash, but the baby, taken by C-section that night, was healthy.

When Doug had visited them at the hospital, the couple had insisted he join them for dinner. Doug hadn't gone out much since coming to the city except for a few visits with old friends. But this invitation had drawn him out of hiding. The thought of having some Nigerian food hadn't hurt either.

"I feel like a silly boy, Matthew," Doug said. His new friend seemed as capable of reading his emotions as his old friends had been.

"It is the beautiful Chinese girl? The seamstress I thought

was your wife? Your eyes go soft when you speak of her." Matthew laughed and hit Doug on the back.

"Yes, she's the one. I forgot what it was like to be in love. I don't know if my heart can take it. I'm too old for this."

His host shook his head. "Too old? There is no such thing. I married Chioma at forty-nine. How old are you?"

"Older than that," Doug said in a gust of breath.

"Ah, this is nothing. Your blood is still hot. Look at me, fifty-two and the father of a son."

Doug smiled but said nothing. Such things were more than his mind could grasp. As much as he felt for Lily, that their lives were very different was undeniable. She had her mother to take care of and a great talent to develop. He would never ask her to give up her dreams or her family and trudge off across the world to follow him. He couldn't imagine leaving New York without her either.

In the other room, the soft voices of the women from Matthew's church who'd come to care for Chioma and the baby rose to Doug's ears. How he missed that sound, the clacking of tongues and high cooing notes of mothers and friends. No matter the culture, baby talk was pretty much the same.

Today he'd heard the workers use some of the same sounds in the adult day care with great success, especially with the clients who either didn't speak English or no longer spoke at all. He'd enjoyed talking with Lily's mother and many of the center's other characters, like the eighty-five-year-old Pakistani gentlemen who had beat him handily at chess.

One of the women from Matthew's church pushed another plate under Doug's nose, a stew of chicken, fish, and beef, a stew he'd eaten often in Nigeria. The rice, measured carefully from a twenty-five-pound bag and cooked to perfection, lined the plate beneath the stew.

"Thank you," he said, but the woman was gone, leaving only Matthew again, with his piercing eyes and hard questions.

Matthew chewed slowly, then swallowed. "Listen," he said, speaking in the English that had eluded him on the night he and Doug met, "when it comes to women, sometimes it's best not to think too hard or talk too much. You saved our family, and we are thankful. We are praying for you every day. Do God's will and be at peace. He is a good God, even in matters of the heart."

Do God's will. Be at peace. His new friend made it all sound so simple. It used to be that simple. Save lives. Go where needed. Pick up your cross and walk. In places where survival was the driving force, Doug's choices had been easy. Here things were more complicated. Here there was abundance and need. Wealth and poverty of spirit. It was easy to mistake the rich for the poor and vice versa.

"I'm filling in at the center for the elderly at the church. Lily's mother came. She's a delight."

Matthew nodded. "The mothers of good women. They miss nothing. Be careful. What did you discuss?"

"I'm not too worried," Doug said with a chuckle. "We spent most of the day in 1967."

Matthew, a biology professor and a quick study, gave Doug a probing look. "Hmm. A turbulent year around the world. My father was in the Biafran War then, I believe. Is her mother all right? Is it Alzheimer's, do you think?"

Doug took another bite of the steaming stew. "I wonder. I'm no specialist in that area, but there's a difference between dementia and something more. I may talk to Lily about it."

"Tread softly when you talk to her, and remember what I said about the mothers of good women. There are tests, not definitive, but close enough. She should know what's ahead, if possible," Matthew said, taking another bite of the hearty stew. "It's best."

Best? It was, of course, best for Lily's mother to be diagnosed and for her to know what she was up against, but being a doctor in Vietnam had taught Doug that for some people, not knowing was what got them through. Unaware of which camp Lily fell into, he'd have to just give her his opinion and hope she'd act on further testing and treatment.

The baby cried in the next room. The sound tugged Doug's heart back to Nigeria, to the baby he'd delivered before leaving. The mission had been right to worry about him. Doug was worried about himself. His arrangement with the show had already allowed him to send some needed funds to the clinic. To get the rest, he'd need to be Lily's mentor and a final round judge. He knew already that his feelings for her would make partiality difficult. He'd wondered when he left Nigeria how he'd get back with what was needed. Now he wondered how he'd ever be able to leave New York . . . and Lily Chau.

9

This is the one I esteem: he who is humble
and contrite in spirit, and trembles at my
word.

Isaiah 66:2

Lily looked up from her desk in surprise. Her boss's
husband, Lyle, smiled down at her, his thin face
more drawn than the last time she'd seen him but
just as radiant.

She reached out for him. "Hey! What are you
doing here?"

Though it'd been months since Chenille's husband had been declared cancer free, Lily was still
startled sometimes at the sight of him, especially
around the office. Today, though, his kind eyes
were just what she needed.

He took a seat. "I just wanted to stop by and chat.
I haven't really been keeping up with everyone. How's your mother? Better? Worse?"

That was the thing Lily liked about Lyle.
He didn't sugarcoat things, not even when
it came to his own illness. If he had noth-

ing good to tell, he just didn't tell anything. Lily both feared and respected that about him.

"She's worse. They've said on several occasions that it's just old age. Senility—"

"But you think it's more." His words lined up evenly like shoes at the edge of a closet. Lily had often thought his voice would have been perfect for singing lullabies if Chenille's baby had lived.

"It's happening all at once. I don't know much of Mother's family history. Pinkie used to fill in what I couldn't remember from stories Mother told her. Most times I think she's just getting older. But lately I wonder—"

"If something is wrong." Lyle finished Lily's sentence, then shifted her paperweight, a medium-size rock she'd brought back from the Edom Valley, from hand to hand. Beautiful One, the rock Doug had given her, was carefully wedged in her desk drawer.

Something was wrong. That summed it up perfectly. Both for Lily and her mother. Lily needed to make an appointment for herself.

"Yes. Something is wrong. I'm trying to accept that. I hope I can face whatever it is . . . alone."

Lyle touched Lily's shoulder. "You're never alone, Lil. Never. And I don't just mean Chenille and me or Raya and Jean. Jesus is here, hands outstretched. I've seen death close up these past two years enough times to be sure of that. He just doesn't always come in the ways we expect."

Lily pulled away, her eyes filled with tears. She had many friends, most of whom were Christians. People she could laugh with, show a few layers of herself to. Lyle was someone she didn't speak to often, but when she did his calm truths sliced her to the bone. Death? She couldn't even think in those terms, for her mother or herself. Yet if she truly trusted

God, was death the end of everything or just another beginning? She wasn't sure. Lily only knew that today she was in the land of the living, along with her mother, and both of them were struggling.

Lyle smiled, cutting into her despair. "And from what I hear, being alone is not a problem you need to be concerned with. Cute Old Missionary Guy is legendary around my parts. My wife has even taken to dressing me in clothes he designed." He touched his slacks before burying a hand in his pocket.

Doug LaCroix trousers. How had Lily missed them? Getting to know Doug now in person, she could see his handprints all over them. The generous pockets, easy-to-wash fabric, draping hem at the bottom that skimmed the tops of Lyle's shoes . . .

Fluid.

Water.

And right now Lily could use a long, lean drink of it.

Lyle stayed a few more minutes, prayed with her, and shared a short song he'd written. Lily didn't catch all the words, but the chords stuck with her. It was the sound of acceptance, the bluster of winter that rushed in despite the birth of spring. A song of darkness pierced by light.

After Lyle left, Lily dashed off an email to Doug regarding the first scheduled taping and the changes he'd recommended to her first set of sketches. She felt her entire body relax as she tapped the keys.

I accept all changes.
Thanks,
Your flame

"So when is my friend coming back here again?" Jean asked, rushing into Lily's office like a ball of light. "I've been on the lookout for him."

Lily scoured her desk for her daybook. "Let's see, we've been meeting at my apartment to keep Mother comfortable, but the show will be coming to do some taping here next week. He'll be here."

Jean clucked her tongue. "Working at the apartment, huh? Sounds like you may just get more out of this than a design contract after all. Is that going to work okay for the show though? Do they have rules about stuff like that?"

"Um, I don't know. I really didn't think about it. I guess I'll have to talk to Doug about it."

Jean looked over the top of her glasses. "You do that. At any rate, I wouldn't be too personal on camera. For starters, it'd probably be good if you called him Mr. LaCroix instead of Doug."

That sounded reasonable. She probably shouldn't send any more emails signed "your flame" out into cyberspace either. Why hadn't any of this crossed her mind before? Probably because until the past few days, she hadn't thought she had any chance of making the first cut in the contest. Doug's confidence had bolstered her belief in herself. If she could just get a couple of full nights of sleep back-to-back, she might really feel good about things.

"You're just blooming right in front of my eyes. It's beautiful to see. How's Pinkie?" Jean asked.

Lily's face sobered. "Better. I'm going home to get Mother and take her by there now."

"Okay, tell Doug I said hello. Tell him I expect to see him before I get a wedding invitation or I'll be very unhappy."

Jean was out the door before Lily could say anything. Wedding invitation? Though such things had been her daily concern for the past two years, Lily had lost her taste for *Modern Bride* magazine. *Architectural Digest, Birds and Blooms, National Geographic,* and other periodicals with inspiring pictures covered her desk now. Lily eased her desk drawer open. The only thing shoved in it now was Doug's rock and her prayer journal, which she really needed to pull out.

The phone rang. It was Barbara, Pinkie's daughter. "Mom's sleeping now, but she's been asking all day if you and your mother are coming by tonight. You are coming, aren't you?"

Lily pushed the drawer shut and grabbed her purse. "Yes, I'm coming. I'm going to get Mom right now."

Forty-five minutes later Doug greeted her at the adult day care center, his eyes darting around the empty day room.

"Good to see you," he said, twining his fingers in hers. "I've had a hard time concentrating since I read that email."

Lily'd had a hard time concentrating since she met him. "About that. Jean pointed out today that our little . . ." She pointed at Doug and then back at herself. ". . . whatever this is might be a problem with the show. I guess I didn't think I had a chance, so I didn't think about it."

Doug opened the palm of her hand and kissed it. "I did think about it. When I wasn't thinking about you. I may have to opt out of the judging phase. I'm thoroughly biased."

Lily bit the inside of her cheek, happy that Chenille and the others weren't there to see her. Man face was in full effect.

"Stop it, okay, before you get us both in trouble."

She grabbed his collar with both hands, then smoothed her hands down over his sweater, the same V-neck he'd worn when she'd met him. She could see now that it was one of his own designs. It fit him accordingly.

He blew out a breath and shook his head. "My flame indeed. Where are you headed now? Home? I've seen all the

146

patients and planned to head out myself. Maybe we can take a look at Flint. We need to try to keep on schedule, since we waste so much time making goo-goo eyes at each other." His eyes creased with laughter.

Man, he's beautiful.

"No, I'm going to the hospital to see Pinkie, Mom's friend who used to sit with her. She's recovering from a heart attack."

Doug threw back his head. "The infamous Pinkie! I must come along to meet her. From your mother's funny stories, I feel like I know her. Is it true that she owned a barbeque joint that sold African food?"

"Absolutely true. And no one ever asked about it either. You're welcome to come along. Just be ready to be quizzed and prayed for. Pinkie is my other mother."

Doug kissed Lily's right thumb and then her four fingers. "Your first mother is pretty tough, so I'll have to pray that I'm prepared. Let me get her. Have you eaten?"

Lily paused. Had she eaten? She'd taken a few Cheetos from Chenille and picked through some old paella from Jean in the fridge at work . . .

"Not really."

Something flashed in Doug's eyes. Was it amusement or concern? "Okay, we'll fix that too."

Lily hated hospitals. Every time she visited one, she remembered the long hours following her father's emergency surgery, the downcast eyes of the surgeon, announcing her father's death before saying a word. But Pinkie, as much Lily's family as her father had been, was here, so Lily and her mother were here again, this time with Doug tagging along.

Pinkie was smiling and sitting upright in the bed when they arrived, despite being crowded by an overgrowth of bouquets heralding well wishes from well-known ministers from all over New York and across the country. Pinkie held up a hand, crisscrossed with tape to hold down her IV tubing.

"Ah, look at this. Friends come to see me," she said, fluttering her eyelids shaded with her signature cocoa shadow.

Doug stepped forward and offered his hand. "Doug LaCroix. Pleased to meet you. I had to come and meet the woman who has meant so much to my two new friends." Pinkie craned her neck to the right. "New friends, huh? By the way you're holding Li Li's hand, y'all are a lot more than friends. What do you think of him, Su?"

Lily's mother nodded several times. "Good doctor. Better than the other one. Eats good. Prays hard. He even knows Chinese. I don't like his eyes, but maybe the babies won't get them."

"Mom!" Lily shaded her face with one hand. Between her mother and Jean she didn't know what they might say next.

Doug cracked up laughing. "See what I mean? I had to come and be a part of this. I feel very much at home."

Pinkie folded down the sheet covering her chest. "Home? That's a good word. Where is your home, Mr. LaCroix? That name sounds familiar."

Lily's mother hooked a finger in Doug's pocket and shook it up and down.

"Pants. Johannan's pants," Lily said.

Pinkie's eyes opened wide. "LaCroix! Oh my, how my husband loved those pants! And how I loved them on him." She wiped a tear away from her eye. "How is it that you come here without a haircut when you made clothes like that?"

A whistling sound came from Lily's mouth as she dropped into the chair at the end of Pinkie's bed. How could she have been so foolish as to let Doug come along? And Mother, who'd been so quiet lately, certainly had a lot to say.

"Pinkie, please. Don't."

Doug patted Lily's shoulder. "It's fine. I guess you're right, Miss Pinkie. I've been living abroad for a few years and haven't had a need for the finesse I once had."

"Just get a haircut." Pinkie pulled the sheet up around her chin and patted the bed for Lily's mother to sit down.

She didn't. Her feelings about hospitals mirrored Lily's.

Lily's mother motioned for Doug to bend down. She ran a hand through his hair. "Yes, it is too big. Like a dog. But still handsome. Only the eyes are ugly."

"The eyes are fine, Su," Pinkie said. "Nice even. He's old though."

"So is she!"

Pinkie chuckled. "She is not. She has an old soul though. Always did. They'll be fine."

By now Lily was near tears, and Doug's tanned face was red from laughing.

He walked to Pinkie's bed and took her hand. "Thank you, dear lady, for your honest appraisal. You remind me of my mother."

She nodded. "I imagine so. She'd turn in her grave if she saw you looking like this. And what happened to your face there. You've got plenty of money, I know. Can't they fix that scar?"

At that Doug fell silent.

Lily shot to her feet. "Auntie, I'm going to let you visit

with Mom. I'm glad Doug came along, but I think you two have gone a little too far—"

"It's okay." Doug leaned over the rail of Pinkie's bed.

The old woman traced the edge of the scar, stopping her hand at his chin.

"It hurt, didn't it?" she said.

"Very much," he whispered.

"I'm sorry." Pinkie didn't wipe her tears this time. She let them flow.

Doug smiled. "Me too."

"Don't fix it. Just leave it. It's supposed to be there," she said through her tears.

"I know," Doug said, reaching for Lily, who was now at his side.

She turned his face and pulled it toward her, until the scar tracing his cheek was in full view. As she'd wanted to on the day she met him, Lily cradled Doug's head in her hands and kissed his scar. She stopped short of his collar.

"Li Li!"

First her mother, then Pinkie shouted Lily's name, jolting her back into reality. Had she really kissed him like that in front of them? From the grin on his face, she definitely had.

When Lily turned back to the two older women, her mother was sitting on Pinkie's bed and the frowns she'd been expecting had turned to smiles.

Her mother spoke first. "So when is the wedding?"

How he talked himself into these things Doug wasn't sure, but this time it was worth it. Father Patrick had been a little surprised to receive visitors ("You have a cell phone, Doug.

Use it."), but he'd adjusted quickly, talking to Lily and her mother while Doug rifled through the refrigerator.

Most of the spices and special ingredients he'd bought on his last trip to the market were gone, and only standard ingredients remained.

"It looks like the menu is American tonight. Shepherd's pie."

The casserole of meat, potatoes, cheese, and corn had been his favorite as a child visiting church potlucks when home on furlough. The conversation came from a simple recipe as well—family, friends, and faith.

Father Patrick took the lead, telling stories about church dinners past. Lily and her mother listened in earnest as he concluded his tribute with a prayer for them both. Finally, he turned to Lily and inquired about Pinkie.

"I'm sorry to hear about your neighbor. Is that why your mother had to come to the center? Because of . . . what was her name?"

"Pinkie," Lily's mother answered with a smile the likes of which Lily hadn't seen in a long time.

Was her mother flirting? True enough, she and Father Patrick were probably close in age. To both Doug's and Lily's shock, the priest seemed to be smiling right back.

I can't believe this, Doug thought. He tried and failed not to laugh. For all his concern, Lily's mother seemed quite aware today.

"Yes, Pinkie," he said. "You'll have to meet her too, Father. She gave me some makeover suggestions much in line with your own advice."

Lily groaned. "She sure did. She's really something. She's like a preacher, a police officer, and a gourmet chef rolled into one. Everybody on the block misses her."

Doug paused in his potato mashing and leaned over

Lily's ear. "I miss you. Meet me in the other room after dinner."

Even as he said it, Doug knew how crazy it sounded. How could you miss someone you saw every day? He had no clue, but it didn't make it any less true.

The priest shook his head. "Whispering is rude, Doug," he said in mock anger before turning to Lily's mother. "I'll bet you miss your friend, although you seem very interesting too, Mrs. Chau. I am grateful to have you in our congregation again."

Lily turned up her sleeves and lined the baking pan with ground beef. She pulled the pan closer to her face before dumping the meat back into the strainer again and washing it with hot water.

"So you miss me, huh?" she asked Doug, now stirring the corn.

Doug wiped his hands on a towel. "Every second. By the way, the Oyobos send their greetings. The family from the accident, remember?"

She nodded. "Oh yes. I got the picture you emailed of their baby. How are they? Chioma and Matthew, right? Remember how he thought you were my husband?" Lily laughed.

Doug didn't laugh. "I do remember."

With Lily's help, he assembled the casserole and put it in the oven.

"The food should be done in about thirty minutes," he said to Father Patrick and Lily's mother. Both of them waved him off.

"Thanks," the priest said, not bothering to turn his head.

Doug took Lily by the hand, marveling at the unlikely places love chose to bloom. Though he'd taken her hand first, it was she who led him into the sitting room. Doug closed the door behind them and pulled Lily to his chest.

"You didn't tell me your mother was such a flirt. You Chau women don't give us guys a chance."

Lily punched his chest. "It's not funny. I can't believe it. I mean, half the time Mother doesn't even know what day it is. How on earth can she be in the kitchen batting her eyelashes like that? And at her age? It's reprehensible."

Doug moved in to kiss her but fell back against the door with laughter. "Reprehensible? This from a woman who kissed my face at her neighbor's sickbed? You've got a lot of nerve."

Lily squeezed her eyes shut. "I didn't mean to do that . . ."

He took her face in his hands and returned the favor, speaking between kisses. "Oh . . . yes . . . you . . . did." She'd meant every kiss.

And so did he, though he stopped at her throat. What he'd wondered about at sixteen he knew for sure now. There was no need for exploring fire out of curiosity. He already knew it burned.

She closed her eyes and held a hand to her throat, tracing the kisses with her finger. "Okay, so I guess I can't say anything about Mom. That was pretty crazy kissing you like that at the hospital. It's just that . . . I've wanted to do that since the first time I met you. I guess I've been thinking about it ever since. I was a little jealous when Pinkie touched it first."

Doug loosened his grip on Lily's waist, wanted to turn away from her. His scar hugged the curves of his face so well that many people missed it. The ones who didn't miss it either did a bad job of ignoring it or stared at it all the time. Lily had never once mentioned it or touched it, until today. To know that her first thought had been to kiss it made him want to pick her up and take her home, to their home. Only they didn't have one. They didn't have anything. And Doug didn't know how they could have anything. But he'd have to figure it out. And soon.

"So what do you think about Matthew's mistaking me for your husband? Who knows? Maybe Matthew is a prophet."

"I hope so," Lily said, running her fingers through the fluff of hair that shielded Doug's eyes.

Warmth traveled up his spine and down again, right into his shoes. He wanted to kiss her again but stopped himself, knowing that the way he felt right now, he wouldn't be able to stop. Could this really be happening after all the failed relationships of his life? Could this love be God's gift to him after all this time?

As if sensing that they'd crossed over into a new place, Lily stepped back from him and offered her hand. They walked back to the kitchen in silence and passed the rest of their dinner with eager looks instead of words.

Lily wasn't hungry in the weeks since her dinner with Doug; she'd lost her taste for just about everything . . . but him. As wonderful as that seemed, Lily knew it was dangerous too. She needed to get back to the rock, and not the one wedged in her desk. More than anything, her hands craved something to make, something to pile and shape, something to create a shelter against her mother's future, the deadlines for the show, Megan's dress, and finally, her growing feelings for Doug. Though she wanted to make something, anything, with her rocks, it was God she needed now, to still her, guide her. To keep her . . . fluid.

She'd sent off two pieces for her Fluid collection to Doug a few minutes before: an A-lined Tibetan coat and an Indian sari. The pieces were unstructured, made with minimal cuts, created to drape the body in elegant folds.

Though she needed two more pieces for that collection, the clothes coming to her mind now were like structures built on bricks of layered fabric. Fashionable stones for the Flint collection.

In a flurry of creativity, she'd sketched out her ideas in pencil right after sending the other sketches through. She looked at the new designs now, collars protruding out of ringed blouses and cobbled pants. The pieces were very different from the first set but just as beautiful. As she drew them, her heart leapt with a joy she thought had left her. A joy she felt most often in Doug's presence. Now she hoped to get back to the place where she felt that kind of joy in the presence of God.

She still read her Bible and wrote out her prayers, though not as much as before. These days, though, she felt nothing when she did it. Blah. Some mornings it was a fight just to get out of bed. If she hadn't needed to keep working on her line for the show and Megan's pattern, she might have stayed in bed on more days than she could count. If the teacup-sized hollows forming below her collarbones were any indication, Lily's appetite could use a jump start too.

The intercom buzzed. "Megan's here."

Lily calmed herself, determined to get the right measurements. The forms and pattern from her first appointment had been off by a few eighths of an inch.

"You're going to get it right this time, aren't you? I can't keep coming down here." Megan swept into the room in a celery-colored pantsuit and matching shoes. Her lips were greenish gold.

Lily swallowed. There wasn't enough left of her to try to counter Megan today.

"I'll try."

Megan's voice gentled, but her words didn't. "See that you do that."

The prayer scratched in Lily's journal whispered to her heart.

Lord, free me from fear and occupation with self. Help me to love first and evaluate later. Bless me to love each person I meet with intense, personal care, even those who don't deserve it. Amen.

Why was she always so spiritual at the start of days like this, times when she sank her lowest? It was a tall order, that prayer, but a good one.

"So how are things, Megan? Is your mother doing any better? What about the wedding? I know you said it's not until next year, but are your plans coming together?" Lily spoke around a mouthful of pins and held Megan still with a firm hand. She wasn't going to use just measuring tape this time. She'd mark off her fabric with tailor's chalk too, just to be safe.

Megan seemed taken aback by Lily's concern. "I'm doing well with the wedding plans, but thanks for asking. Maybe I could bring in some things for you to look at, the flowers and the cake. That kind of stuff."

Lily motioned for Megan to lift both hands and took several measurements of her bust and arms. "That'd be fine. I'd love to see them."

"Really?" Megan's voice faltered. "Thanks. And thanks for asking about my mom. She doesn't have full-blown AIDS, they say, and she's able to do quite a bit with her meds. When she does get sick, though, it scares me."

"I know what you mean," Lily said, writing down the new numbers. "My mother is growing older, more forgetful. I don't know how much longer I can care for her myself. Or how much longer I'll even have her around. It's scary."

Megan sniffed. "Yeah. *Scary* is the right word. I'm glad

Raya's mom turned out to be negative after her HIV scare. I wouldn't wish it on anybody. But some days it seems okay. Like nothing is wrong. Like before."

Lily nodded. Those days were fewer and farther between for her now, but she took them when she could get them. She moved quickly but precisely with the tape and fabric, this time leaving nothing to chance.

"All done," she said finally, standing.

"So what about you?" Megan asked. "Are you seeing anyone? You look all melancholy since you broke up with your boyfriend."

Had she told Megan about Ken? Oh well. It was such a big deal around the office that Megan had probably overheard. She was good at that.

"Actually, I am seeing someone. Sort of." She knew better than to give Megan too much information about anything. She borrowed a phrase from Jean. "It's complicated."

Megan nodded. "I hear you on that one. Even though I'm getting married soon, it's still complicated. Good luck with it, or blessings or whatever."

Lily smiled. "I don't know how it will turn out. It's not like I don't have enough on my mind."

The phone rang before Megan responded.

"I'll go so you can take that," Megan said.

"Thanks," Lily said, picking up the phone.

"Lily, this is Doug."

Her grip tightened around the phone. "Is Mom all right?"

"She's fine. I'm the problem. I can't get you off of my mind. Can we talk when you come to pick up your mother tonight? I'd like to talk more about Matthew's prophecy of me being your husband."

She paused as both fear and joy tightened around her mind. Unfortunately, only the fear remained as the dread she'd fought through to leave the apartment this morning settled over her.

"I don't think I'll have time to talk about that tonight, Doug. But I'd love to hear what you think of those sketches I sent you."

10

Which of you, if his son asks for bread, will give him a stone?

Matthew 7:9

She could hardly look at Doug, but she couldn't turn away either. The hours since his call and Megan's fitting had passed all too quickly, leaving Lily to face the object of both her affection and her fears. Though she'd wanted a husband more than anything just a few weeks ago, now she wasn't sure if she should make any promises to someone else when she couldn't keep her promises to herself.

When Doug met her at the door as he always did, his eyes were filled with both understanding and disappointment.

Lily's gaze alternated between her feet and his eyes and then moved to the center employees waiting to go home. She was the last pickup of the day. Heeding Jean's warnings, she'd decided to create some distance between her and Doug, in the minds of others at least.

"Well, thanks again, Mr. LaCroix, everyone. Sorry to hold you all up. Come on, Mother."

Her mother lingered, muttering something to Doug in Chinese, then pointing at Lily and laughing. Doug kept a straight face.

Lily tugged at her mother's elbow, no longer interested in trying to figure out what her mother had to say. "Come on, Mother. Now."

Doug followed behind them, holding open the door. "She said that you need some of my potato pie. That your paper dolls are eating all your dinner."

Hooking arms with her mother, Lily paused to pull her coat closed. Did she look that thin? Was everyone thinking the same thing about her but only her mother had the nerve to say it?

In spite of the other people present in the room, Doug grazed Lily's collarbone with his calloused fingers. "I think Li Li looks beautiful, Su, but I will bring some potato pie for you if you'd like some."

Deflated, Lily's mother shook her head. "No potato for me. Only for her."

His fingers skimmed down Lily's arm and meshed with her fingers. His eyes looked straight into her heart, easily speaking the message he'd planned to share with her in the space of a few movements. She wanted to lift her hands and touch his muscled shoulder or tuck some of that wayward hair behind his ear, but the emptiness, gnawing at her once again, wouldn't allow it. The long walk to the train and then home would take everything she had. She offered what she could—a smile.

Doug smiled back, his eyes overflowing with compassion. As the employees buzzed out the door, he held the back of Lily's hand to his face and kissed it.

"Take care of yourself, okay? The sketches look good. Let's take a break for a few days so you can rest. I don't want you fainting on TV next week."

She didn't notice the note in her pocket until she hung up her coat at home.

Lily passed her mother's bead basket across the table, tuning out the buzz of the TV. She took out the note Doug had slipped in her pocket, wishing she'd noticed on the train when she'd had a pole to support her. As it was, she chose her father's old recliner while her mother sat on the couch, stringing beads.

Lily,

Sorry to slip you this message. I would have liked talking better, but I understand you're not up to it. I have a few things to share. The first is something that came to me when praying for you this morning. Overlook it if it doesn't make sense. I'm rather gifted at nonsense, it seems. I'll start with what I wrote down this morning. Here it is, word for word:

Take comfort, Abram's daughter, your nation will be established, hammered out from stone and clothed in silk. Your eyes will see the promise, your mouth speak a new name.

Hope that meant something to you. I felt compelled to share it, almost as much as the second thing, something difficult but necessary for me to say.

I love you.

I feel silly saying that in a note, but it's true. I spend most of my days trying to figure out how we can not only be together but stay together. I just wanted you to know that my intentions are noble and this is not something casual between us.

Enough with mush and on to harder things. I can't be sure, but I think your mother may be in an early stage of Alzheimer's disease. Please get her to a neurologist as soon as possible.

Sincerely,
The Rock Thief

"Li Li. You crying. What's wrong?" Her mother's busy hands kept threading, but her eyes were fixed on her daughter.

Hugging her knees, Lily let out a breath, releasing all her fears, all her plans. The one thing she'd consoled herself with, the fact that her mother didn't have Alzheimer's, that things could be worse than they were, inched out of Lily's reach. As for the other things, love, being together forever . . . they just seemed too good to be true. Fairy tales were for Raya and Flex, not Lily. Had she loved Doug more because she'd known he'd be leaving? Because she wouldn't have to commit?

"I'm okay, Mother. I just have some things on my mind. I need to think it through."

Her mother put down her project and cradled her daughter's hands. "Yes. Do. Think is good."

Lily let her head relax, not bothering to contest her mother's words. Thinking might be good for some, but the thinking she would have to do now seemed anything but good. Doug had opened something she might never be able to close—both in her heart and in her home.

⟢

"I understand your concern, Douglas," Father Patrick said, using Doug's full name, since Doug couldn't bring himself to call the priest Patrick anymore.

Doug didn't like being called by his full name, since only his mother had called him that, but he couldn't bring himself to drop the "Father" either. It probably hadn't helped that he had startled Father Patrick from behind. The priest had almost spilled his cereal.

"Lily needs help. I can see it. All the signs are there. She's losing weight, she's withdrawn—"

The priest's eyes narrowed. "With all due respect, Douglas, you've known her only a short time. If my memory serves me, which it often doesn't, she was always a quiet girl. As for the weight, I haven't scrutinized her appearance as closely as you have."

He ladled a spoonful of cereal into his mouth. "It's obvious that you have feelings for this woman; just remember, pace yourself. If you're that troubled about her, get on your knees every time she comes to mind. Either God will move or you'll need some knee pads. Whatever you do, don't pounce on her like you pounced on me just now. You'll scare her away."

Doug bit into his apple, all the breakfast he wanted today.

Scare her away. He'd done that before and didn't want to do it again. Still, Lily had stayed on his mind.

"Okay, I'll see you over at the church."

The priest frowned. "But it's only 5:30. Where are you going?"

Bending slightly, Doug touched his knees, then pressed his palms together as though praying. "I'm going to take you up on your advice," he said, heading upstairs.

After singing a few hymns and studying the day's Lenten readings, Doug knelt next to his bed and began to pray—for his new parish, his friends and patients in Nigeria, the choir, the Oyobos' baby, the clients at the adult day care center. Friends from all the places he'd ever been seemed to come to mind as Doug prayed for everyone and everything.

With sweat trickling down his forehead, he brought Lily's mother before the throne, asking forgiveness if he'd made a mistake giving his opinion and asking for the grace of a good neurologist and a swift diagnosis. For Lily his prayers were more halted. He stopped often, realizing that many of his prayers started out being for her and ended up being for himself.

"Lord, let my love for her be without deceit. Help me to do good, seek justice, correct oppression, defend the fatherless, plead for the widow. Help me to stay in the safety of your hand, the cover of your hiding place," he whispered, once again crucifying his need to be the source of someone's information and protection.

Lily wasn't his wife. He had to be careful not to overstep, no matter how great his concern.

At work later that morning, Doug found himself turning every time the door opened, wondering which Lily would arrive, the frazzled one who was going to be late for work or the solemn, quiet one who'd passed her mother's things to Doug without saying a word the day before. If it had been anyone else, he'd have thought she was angry with him for some reason, but something in her eyes, glimmering slightly, like a firefly trapped in a jar, called out to Doug as if asking to be freed from the blues that had hold of her.

Blues he knew all too well.

Doug rinsed his hands and went back to the day room where many of his client-friends were enjoying breakfast. Today was clinic day, so he'd need to get all the charts in order and make calls in the afternoon to any of the clients' private doctors if he found any problems. Doug retreated to his office and, against his better judgment, put in a call to Lily's mother's private physician, the man who'd escorted Lily to church on Ash Wednesday. Never one to play it safe, Doug punched the numbers and talked to the receptionist and waited for Ken to come to the line.

"Ken Lee."

"Hi, this is Doug LaCroix from over at the adult day care at People's Episcopal. I'm calling about Su Chau."

Ken grunted into the phone. "Yes, what about her?"

"Well, I suggested to Lily that she might want to have her mother tested for Alzheimer's, and since you're the primary care doctor and they'll need your referral, I thought maybe you could sign off on that and get things going."

Obviously, he'd thought wrong, and Ken didn't hesitate to tell him so. "Miss Chau hasn't mentioned anything to me about further testing for her mother. Once she does I'll discuss the next step with her. Since this isn't your area, you should probably stay out of it. In fact, what are you even doing over there? I thought Dr. Stahl was in charge of that center."

"He is. I'm filling in for him. I only called because I thought we both had a personal interest in the case. I was wrong."

Ken was silent for a moment. "I'll look into it. Until then please don't play doctor with the cases over there. I don't think the doctor who runs that facility would appreciate it.

Perhaps you should go into the city and see if there are any fashion shows going on."

Doug couldn't help but laugh. The poor guy. He obviously wasn't taking this change of command very well. Doug thought he'd caught Ken giving him a funny look when he'd walked Lily to her car on Sunday. He'd been right.

"You know what, Dr. Lee? I think that's some great advice. I'm going to see what's going on in the district. Perhaps Lily and I can catch a show. Good day."

Though he'd thrown in his last statement to ruffle the good doctor's feathers, some of it was true. It was time to stop hiding in Father Patrick's apartment and look up some of his friends in the fashion industry. Though he'd lost a sense of himself the past few years, it seemed that he would always be Doug LaCroix no matter what.

Maybe it was time he accepted that and flowed with it instead of against it. His first call would be to his former stylist at Man-O-Cure in Manhattan. A few hours there and he'd be a new man. A little too new, he feared, but it was time all the same.

As worried as he was about Lily's hollow look, a good long look in the mirror revealed a man trying to hide behind a mop of hair and a pair of sports slides. Were missionaries allowed to wear three-piece suits? Doug wasn't sure, but he also knew that God was bigger than any rules he could make up for himself. He'd left fashion because he didn't believe he could serve God there, but now he wasn't so sure that was true either. Things in his life were changing by the minute. He had a choice: stay fluid and make the transitions or become flint and be shattered to pieces. Having done both, he preferred the former.

He realized that before he could love Lily, he had to be whole and able to see his own blind spots, lest the same

166

depression that had clipped at his heels over the years, and that had eventually swallowed his father whole, dog him too. The blues definitely seemed to have Lily's graceful neck with both hands. Each day it seemed the once subtle sadness that had drawn him to her grew closer to the surface, giving Doug a glimpse of how he had probably looked to the exit interviewer for the mission board. Though his practiced answers said the right things, the person across the table had seen his tired eyes and heard the impatience in his voice. And now Doug was glad of it.

In the bathroom this morning, he'd taken the time to stare at his face after shaving instead of turning away. What he saw there had surprised him and comforted him too. There were pinched and drawn places under his cheekbones, scooped out from too much work and not enough play. What comforted him was that they were filling in nicely and that his eyes still showed the joy that remained in him.

In the wake of so much loss the past few years, Doug had often passed off fun as frivolous, unnecessary. It was work that was redemptive, he'd thought. Now Doug saw that such a life was just another form of pride—a way of drawing people to himself instead of drawing them to Christ, making the clinic programs dependent on him instead of dependent on God.

Doug knew now that this furlough had been a gift, and aside from meeting Lily, perhaps the best one he'd ever been given. For once he would have to do the thing he'd told his patients so many times—stand and see the salvation of the Lord. As for Lily's state of mind, Father Patrick's advice had already earned Doug a few scuffs on his khakis. Knee pads might be in order by the end of the week. Still, as much as he didn't want to scare her away, he couldn't help his concern. He had another call in mind, one that he'd probably regret much more than the first.

"Garments of Praise."

"Chenille Rizzo, please." Doug hoped his subtle accent didn't give him away. In person it wasn't as noticeable, but on the phone it made him very easy to identify.

"Chenille, how can I help you?"

Doug gripped the phone harder. "I'm not sure that you can help me, but I hope so. This is Doug LaCroix, Chenille, how are you?"

A fit of giggling ensued that almost made Doug laugh too. Finally Chenille pulled herself together, though Doug could have sworn he'd heard the phrase "cute old missionary guy" whispered in the background.

"Mr. LaCroix. Yes, what do you need? Is this about the taping of the show?"

He cleared his throat. "In a way. Let me just get to it. I don't know Lily as well as you do, so I can't be sure, but it seems that maybe she's been a little sad the past few days. Overworked maybe? I'm wondering if all these different demands aren't pushing her too hard. The show's schedule is a little grueling, plus there's her work at Garments of Praise and caring for her mother, and of course, there's me wasting inordinate amounts of her time."

"No, you're not. We're very glad to have you helping Lily. I, too, have wondered if all this is wearing on her. And don't feel bad for bringing it up. She and I have discussed this before you, the show, or any of these new developments. Are you saying you think she should drop out?"

What was he saying? "No, I don't think so at all. I guess I just figured that since you two were friends, you could tell me if I was off base. I suppose I hoped I was off base."

Chenille sighed. "Unfortunately, I think you're dead-on. You do what you can do from your end, and I'll do what I can from mine. I got a similar call from a customer about the same situation, so it sounds like the Lord is trying to tell me something. I'll keep an eye out and talk to Lily soon."

Doug took a deep breath. Maybe this call wasn't such a bad idea after all. "Thanks, Chenille. I'm glad Lily has friends like you. I look forward to coming over there in the next few days."

More giggles. "We're glad that you're Lily's, uh, friend too. Very glad."

He was smiling himself. "Right. Okay, well, I'd better let you go."

Doug hung up and emerged from the office of the doctor he was filling in for. As he stepped into the corridor, one of the center employees brushed past him. He stopped her.

"Hey, are you busy tonight?"

The woman, a college student, looked confused.

For a moment so did Doug. "Oh, no, I'm not asking you out or anything. I was just wondering if you could stick around this evening and look after Mrs. Chau so that her daughter and I can discuss a project we're working on. I'd pay you, of course."

She let out a breath. "Sure. I'd love to. Mrs. Chau is really funny. She makes nice jewelry too. You don't have to pay me."

"I insist," Doug said, hoping he'd brought enough Thai chili to share with Lily if she wanted some. Not exactly the right dish to tempt the appetite with, but it was all he had. He thanked the attendant and checked the clock. Was it Lily's day off today? She changed up often, and sometimes he got confused. Maybe he was trying too hard, doing too much. Again.

The buzzer sounded at the front. With a salute to the Caribbean grandmother who loved to tell him sugarcane stories, Doug headed for the door and opened it eagerly, like he was opening a Christmas gift.

"Sorry I'm late," Lily said, fumbling with her mother's things as the attendant came and took her mother away. "She didn't sleep well last night, but she ate well this morning. I was going to stay home, but we—she wanted to come, to see you."

Doug fought the urge to chuckle at her blunder. He didn't want to push her too hard. "I'm glad. I enjoy seeing you—her too."

Though the comment would have made Lily laugh a few days ago, today she froze like a deer facing a hunter. No doubt she had read his note.

He'd done it again. Or had he? The look that had concerned Doug so much, the way Lily's eyes seemed to drift off and fade away, passed from her face. What replaced it was not an absent gaze but a look of acceptance. Her shoulders relaxed and her breathing seemed to slow, giving him time to recognize what he saw. Peace. Had he been without it so long that he'd mistaken it for nothingness?

"I enjoy seeing you too, Doug. Probably a little too much," Lily said, scribbling her name on the roster next to her mother's name. "Have you heard from your prophet friend lately, by the way?"

Doug tried to hold it in, but he couldn't. Laughter spilled from his mouth, filling the space between them. "Matthew and his family are fine. They ask about you whenever I call. It's good to see you smiling, Lily. You have a beautiful smile."

She shrugged. "I guess, if you go for toothy grins. You're not too bad yourself, handsome. That mission field has been good to you," she added.

It was Doug's turn to freeze. Had he read Lily totally wrong? And was she trying to be funny calling him handsome? He'd been called a lot of things in his life: suave, debonair, sophisticated, daring. Handsome wasn't usually in the lineup. He cleared his throat, suddenly painfully aware of his long hair and rough-dried khakis. If she thought he was handsome now . . .

"Keep talking like that and I might have to clean up and surprise you. I can't keep up with you, of course," Doug said, reaching for her hand in spite of his thoughts to the contrary.

Today Lily wore what was fast becoming his favorite outfit, a pair of flared black pants, some ballet-slipper sort of shoes, and a white blouse that wrapped around and tied at her waist. Though her jacket was pulled around her, he was certain what was underneath—she always paired those pants with the white wrap shirt. He'd thought Lily to be in some deep funk. He wondered now if he hadn't totally missed the mark. It wouldn't be the first time. Calling Lily's boss now seemed to be a very bad idea. Doug made a mental note to call Chenille back and explain that maybe he'd overreacted.

He cleared his throat once more, diving in for the kill. He'd planned to ask for a meeting anyway, but since she seemed okay, he was going to go for it. "Do you think we can meet tonight? About the collection, of course—"

She shook her head, pointing to the clock. "Probably not. I don't know. I've got to go in to work today and catch up on some things, and then there's Mom—"

He held up a hand before she could protest any more. "I made arrangements for the woman who just took your mother back to stay behind and care for her while we work. Just show up with your thinking cap on. I'll even have dinner waiting. After we sing I'll take both of you home."

Lily stared at him for a minute, then gave in. "Okay. You didn't need to go to so much trouble, but since you did, we'll talk about it when I get off. I've got to run."

171

Doug watched as she did just that, escaping the day care like a princess, her pants flapping as she went. Doug turned quickly to rejoin the group in the day room before starting his exams.

Lily's mother's table was his first stop.

Chenille awaited Lily in her office. Her hands held no clipboard. She looked as though she'd come as a friend and not an employer, or maybe as a little of both.

"Maybe you should see someone," Chenille said softly, wasting no time in getting to the point. Her husband's charms seemed to be wearing off on her.

Lily looked at her boss in shock, trying to make sense of the words she'd just heard. Sure, there had been that outburst a while back, and she'd been late a few times, but her work had been good. She hadn't been chatting up the place or anything in the past few days, but was something wrong with keeping to herself?

She sat in her office chair, flicked on her computer, and turned her back to Chenille. "See someone? I don't know what you mean."

Chenille came closer, leaning over Lily's shoulder. "Sweetie, something's wrong. You're skin and bones. We talk to you about it, but you don't hear us. We've all noticed it, discussed it. This week two people outside the company expressed concern."

Lily's heart pounded. She looked down at her waist. She'd had to wrap her blouse around an extra time to tie it shut, but there was plenty of meat left on her. There always would be. Her mother had been quick to tell her that all her life. ("It must be the American food. Fat and big feet. Perhaps someone will still marry you.") But customers expressing concern? That couldn't be true.

"Who? What people?"

Chenille paused, winding one of her red curls around her finger. "Megan, for one. She asked if you were . . . on drugs or something. She said you seemed depressed and looked like one of those Calvin Klein models. The old, scary ones, remember?"

See what happens when you try to be nice to people?

Lily shrugged. What could she say? Megan was nuts, everybody knew that. Still, something rang true. This week she just didn't want to talk to anyone, not even Pinkie, who called every evening from the hospital explaining new developments in her illness, like bypass surgery and other tests. It was as though Lily was just all tapped out. After work at night, she crawled into bed, sometimes ignoring her mother's midnight noises instead of running to her side as she once had.

She'd developed an ability to be present but absent at the same time. A memory stabbed her mind—an image of her father, sitting at dinner, staring through her into some far-off place. Was this how he had survived? Half alive?

"I wouldn't put too much stock in anything Megan says, Chenille, but I'll admit I'm not myself. Who is? Life changes all the time. Sometimes it takes time to adjust."

Chenille touched Lily's elbow softly, as though she were made of porcelain. "Sometimes it takes help to adjust. And that's okay. If I hadn't gotten help during Lyle's illness, I might not be around to enjoy his health now. Thank God I had friends who loved me enough to tell me that something was really wrong. You lost a dream when Ken broke things off, and you've had new job responsibilities piled on, all while your mother is getting worse. Not to mention a whole new relationship that could really turn into something. I applaud you for getting some help for your mother, but now it's time to get some help for you."

Tears streamed down Lily's face, though she fought to keep them back. Some help for her? The only help she needed was God.

"I can do everything through him who gives me strength," she whispered through a veil of tears.

Lily clutched her friend. It had taken months for Chenille to emerge from the strain of Lyle's illness and care. That someone as strong as Chenille had needed to take drugs to overcome her depression seemed a blow to Lily's faith. Was God enough or wasn't he?

You're asking the wrong questions.

Chenille let her go. "Just talk to your doctor, okay? God's grace is sufficient even when it comes out of a pill bottle. I had one prescription. Eight weeks. It made all the difference."

Lily didn't know what to say. It was hard enough to process the fact that her co-workers and customers thought she was some kind of mental patient.

"I'll think about it."

Her boss nodded. "That's all I can ask. At any rate, your work has been phenomenal. I just want you to know that work isn't the only thing we care about around here."

That made them both smile. Chenille's caring heart had been one of the things that had drawn Lily to this job. She could have easily gone to another firm, worked with big name designers, but Garments of Praise lived up to its name. She could still remember when Raya's oldest son's photo was passed around at their staff meeting. A child from one of their Monday meetings had become Raya's family. Lily still enjoyed those meetings, though they were less frequent now.

Though she wasn't sure if she agreed with Chenille about the drugs, she knew her boss had her best interests at heart. Lily stopped her friend before she left.

"Chenille, one last thing. You said Megan was the first customer worried about me. Who was the other one?"

Chenille sighed. "I'd rather not say. I wouldn't want—"

Lily smoothed her forehead. "Who?" she asked, though she already knew the answer.

"I guess he's not a customer exactly. Your mentor. Doug LaCroix."

11

Blessed is the man who trusts in the LORD, whose confidence is in him. He will be like a tree planted by the water that sends out its roots by the stream. It does not fear when heat comes; its leaves are always green. It has no worries in a year of drought and never fails to bear fruit.

Jeremiah 17:7–8

Lily came through like a hurricane. All hair and pants. She shoved her mother's water bottle and other personal items into the bag marked "Chau."

"Wait, what about our meeting?" Doug said, following after the walking ball of fury. And here he'd worried about her frozen emotions.

"What about the meeting? You do the designs. You win the contest. I'm tired, I'm crazy, and I'm going home."

He swallowed, trying not to get upset himself. "Look, you need to calm down. There are still people here."

That really set her off. "People, huh? We wouldn't want to make you look bad on your job that isn't even your job. We wouldn't want anyone calling the priest to say that you're nuts, would we? Call just to say they're worried about you? Because that's what people who supposedly love me do."

Oops. "About that. I think I overreacted. I was going to call Chenille back in the morning. I was just worried—"

"And I guess talking to me was just too much. If you'd waited another day, you could have at least written me another note. The first one was great, by the way, only now I think I'm going to go home and burn it!"

She walked into the day room in giant strides. Doug was foolish enough to follow, praying that no one else came to pick up their family members in the midst of this.

"Lily, I am so sorry. Please, don't be like this. I wouldn't have done that on a whim. I really am worried about you."

"Worried, Doug? You don't even know me. What do you need to be worried about? Perhaps you should be more concerned about yourself. Fashion designer? Doctor? Missionary? Who are you? Maybe I should make some calls of concern too."

Doug paused and rested against the wall, blinking a few times and taking a few deep breaths. Had he really thought this woman was some calm, quiet soul when he first met her? She was definitely fire. What he wasn't sure of was if she was still his flame. It certainly didn't sound like it. He could play her game and start yelling and making a scene right with her. He'd been great at that. It was the mess that came after, the apologies and embarrassment, that he'd rather not deal with.

Lord, help me out here.

When Lily squished a hat on her mother's head in the day room and Mrs. Chau made a funny face, Doug went to the microwave and got the dinner he'd had waiting for them.

He hoped that seeing her mother with that sideways hat and funny expression would break down Lily's anger.

He was wrong.

"Here, have some dinner," he said, extending the plastic bowl like an olive branch.

When it zipped past his ear like a Frisbee and splattered against the wall behind the day room sink, all the employees who'd been straining to watch from around the corner scurried away like insects. Doug stared at Lily in disbelief.

She looked shocked too, looking down at her hands as though they weren't part of her body. Fighting back tears, she pulled her mother along toward the door. She turned back as she reached it.

"I'm sorry. Please tell everyone I'm sorry."

Doug walked toward her. "Lily . . ."

The door slammed in his face.

Doug spent the next fifteen minutes cleaning chili off the wall and evading questions from the other employees. As embarrassed as he was to have had a fight with Lily in public, what hurt most about the whole thing were memories of all the times he'd exploded on co-workers in the past, saying thoughtless things and brushing it off because it got the results he needed. Acting as though God's rules didn't apply in certain situations. Being on this side of a flying bowl gave him a fresh perspective, one he hoped would stick with him back in the field.

As for Lily, she didn't have to worry anymore about him pushing her about the show or being concerned about her either. The score between them was even, and they'd both lost.

"You called her job?"

Doug frowned at his Nigerian friend. Matthew and his family had joined Doug and Father Patrick for dinner. When the guests had questioned Doug's silence, the priest had been more than happy to tell them about the whole disaster.

"It wasn't like that. I simply asked if she was doing all right and said I hoped she wasn't working too hard, because she looked a little . . . down."

Matthew's wife, Chioma, stopped chewing. "Did you actually say that? To her boss? Oh my. Have you ordered the first round of flowers yet? This is going to be a tough one."

Father Patrick laughed. "I offered to pay for the first bouquet myself. He won't hear of it. He thinks she overreacted too."

"She did. Another inch and that bowl of chili would have burned me," Doug said, though he wasn't sure anymore if the whole thing wasn't his own fault.

Matthew spooned up more of the leftover chili from the pot. It was a bit spicy for spring, but Father Patrick had grown to love it.

From Matthew's expression, he liked it too. "I've been in touch with the friends you told me about at the Enugu clinic, Doug. From what they tell me, you and Lily make a good couple. Sounds like you've thrown your share of dinners too." Matthew's eyes sparkled with humor, but there was a bit of rebuke in his tone.

Most people thought missionaries were so spiritual that they never got angry or made mistakes. Having grown up on the field, Doug knew better. He never tried to hide his emotional ups and downs from his friends, and they in turn never failed to correct him when he was wrong. They all shared a great respect for one another. Doug was so happy

179

that Matthew had talked to his friends that he even put Lily out of his mind for a while.

"Is everyone well there? What did they say?"

Matthew smiled. "Everyone on the team is in good health. In fact, Ifyangi is expecting another child. He says he hopes you will be back before the boy is walking."

Doug laughed out loud. Ifyangi had six daughters and spoke this way each time his wife was pregnant. Then when the girl came and wrapped him around her finger like the rest, he forgot all about having a son. Before such things had only been funny. Now Doug also felt a pang of remorse in his heart. Would he ever have a child of his own? A few days ago, he'd dared to hope so. Now he felt only doubt.

"I'll write him again tomorrow. That scoundrel. He probably knew before I left. Anything else?"

His guest's voice sobered. "The new doctor is doing well with the diabetes patients through diet and exercise, though much more help is needed. A hospital in England has donated more incubators for the twin nursery. Dialysis continues to be the current need. Unfortunately, Olufemi, your last kidney patient, has died."

Doug's fork clattered to the table. They had all known that Olufemi would probably die before equipment arrived, like so many others before him. Still, the reality of it was a blow. How could Doug be here eating chili and wondering about women when people were dying? He looked at Father Patrick.

"Do you see? I cannot stay here. They were counting on me. They still are. All this talk of walk and pace. God needs runners too."

Father Patrick looked around the table, and his eyes rested on Chioma, who usually spoke little but looked more than ready to speak now. She stood, rocking the baby in a cloth gathered around her shoulders.

"You have helped save many lives, including mine and my son's. Have you considered that perhaps we were part of your assignment as well? Do our lives mean nothing to the Lord?"

Doug looked around the table. All three faces, each of a different hue, looked back at him with equal kindness. No suitable response rose to his lips. Did one life mean more to God than another? Were the eyes of God, always looking, ever watching, somehow closed to his patients? No.

Though Doug might not understand it all, he knew that God had a plan in everything, both in life and in death. Ifyangi had been telling Doug for years that death and life were both necessary, but Doug had a hard time accepting it. Perhaps because his own death would mean the end of his father's line and his own.

Doug rested both elbows on the table, perching his chin on his fists. "I hear what you're saying, Chioma. It's still hard for me to think of so many people dying when dialysis is so readily available here. I will continue to try to secure funds for the equipment, but once more I must give the outcome to God."

Matthew took a sip of water. "Father Patrick tells me there have been numerous gifts from the church as well as the gift from the Nia Network. Though one life was lost, many more will be saved. I've also been talking to some friends from home around the city. I hope to have a check soon. Leave the fund-raising to me for a while and concentrate on making up with your lady friend."

Everyone laughed except Doug, whose mind was fixed on the memory of Lily's anger. The eyes he'd thought vacant had blazed in rage as she tossed that bowl. Trying to drum up support for the mission suddenly seemed a whole lot easier than quieting that woman's storm.

"It's good to see you, Miss Chau," the receptionist said.

Lily looked around the waiting room of Big Apple Medical, her HMO and the place where she'd met her former boyfriend. The woman facing her now had often connected her personal calls to Ken over the past few years, even calling Lily at Garments of Praise to leave messages from him. It seemed strange to be here now, but today was Ken's day off, and she'd switched doctors to Anne Lassiter, a spunky redhead with a British accent, not long after she and Ken had started dating.

Jean saw Anne for her appointments too and found something about the woman troubling, though she couldn't put her finger on it. Lily felt it too, but it wasn't an issue, since she didn't see her much anyway. The way Lily felt today, though, fingers and somethings didn't matter. Something within her had died and hardened like the stones on her desk. She wanted to be green again, to bend and stretch around life instead of snapping into jagged pieces every time things didn't go her way.

Lily needed help.

"Anne will take you now," the receptionist said just as Lily started to thumb through the stack of ancient *Better Homes and Gardens* magazines. The copies of *Sports Illustrated* were in Ken's office, no doubt, though he rarely took time to read them.

"Great," Lily said before her doctor exploded into the waiting area with a smile and an outstretched hand.

"There you are. Come on back."

Taken off guard by Anne's new perkiness, Lily followed

the doctor into the back, answering the usual bedside manner questions with as much enthusiasm as she could drum up. Anne seemed to realize Lily wasn't up for much talking, so the two women walked the short distance to the exam room with minimal chitchat.

Inside the room Lily started for the exam bed covered with tissue paper down the middle, as though germs didn't exist on the sides. She always made an effort to stay right in the center. Ken laughed at her for it, though he admitted germs were everywhere.

Anne waved Lily away from the bed altogether, offering her the chair instead. After a moment's pause, Lily sat, thinking that the only other time she took this seat was during her mother's checkups, one of which was coming up soon. Whether it would dispel the doubts Doug had placed in her about her mother's diagnosis, Lily wasn't sure, but wondering about it was definitely wearing on her. Sometimes she thought it'd be easy to make one of those fold-up predictors she'd loved to stick her fingers into in elementary school.

Mom has it.

Mom has it not.

I'm crazy.

I'm crazy not.

Deep down she already knew the answer, or at least she thought she did. She just wasn't ready to deal with it yet. Or with the man who'd suggested it.

"So it seems you've been a little blue lately?" The doctor wore her best smile, so wide that Lily wondered if she wouldn't produce a lollipop from behind her back. Or perhaps a sticker.

"Blue? Yes. That's one way to put it. Outbursts of anger, insomnia, loss of appetite, inability to focus at times. Yeah. Blue."

Lily pulled her skirt over her knees, trying to remember why she'd worn it. The wind had been vicious outside. The memory of the chill lingered on her skin.

Anne nodded. "That's a rather serious list of symptoms. Any changes in your schedule lately? Problems at home? You care for your mother, right? What about relationships? Seeing someone new?" The doctor's voice faltered.

Lily's eyes narrowed. Was that information in her file? She didn't remember sharing anything about her mother with Anne. They did both come to this practice, but still . . . Had Ken told her about their breakup? The details? She took a short breath, then a longer full one. If there was one thing about Ken, he was discreet and not exactly chummy with co-workers. The receptionist maybe? What did it matter? She was here to get help.

"Yes, there's been a lot going on with my mom. I've scheduled an appointment. They couldn't take us right away, it seems."

The doctor looked over Lily's past charts, then left the room. A nurse came in and took Lily's vitals. A few minutes later, Anne returned.

"I'm going to refer you to a psychologist for further evaluation, but in the meantime, I'm giving you a short-term prescription for Zoloft. I do see that there is a family history of mental illness in your chart—"

"What?" Lily sat back, no longer caring about the chill or the skirt easing over her knees. "May I see that, please?"

Anne's cheeks reddened. "I . . . you'll have to fill out a release form at the desk. They'll send you a copy. The nurse will come back shortly with your prescription. Call me if you have any problems. The receptionist will call you about the psychologist appointments. Don't worry about those. The doctor I'm sending you to is great. A friend of mine.

You'll see her once a week for as long as you're taking the antidepressant."

Lily heard the words but didn't even try to understand them. Anne's words were even, but her fumbling with the chart gave her away. Lily reached over and took the chart.

"Hey! You can't do that. The release form—"

"I'll be glad to sign it on the way out," Lily said, handing the chart back to her. As she'd suspected, next to the mental illness questions in her medical history, Ken had written, "Father, possibly bipolar." He'd also circled Alzheimer's under the illnesses on the maternal side. At worst, what he'd done was probably illegal, using things Lily had said in personal anecdotes in her medical file. At best, it felt like a slap in the face.

Was that the real reason he'd broken up with her, because he thought her to be some future mental case? Ken was the one with a problem, working sixty plus hours a week to save up for some imaginary retirement all by himself. Doug might overstep his bounds sometimes, but at least he said what he thought to her face.

The doctor tried to regain her composure. "One of the nurses will bring back your ticket for the front. I hope you feel better soon."

All Lily could do was nod. She hoped to feel better soon too. Already she felt worse. She climbed onto the exam table, lay down, and stared at the ceiling. Chenille had said to get help, but why didn't this feel like help? If anything, it depressed Lily more. As much as Doug got on her nerves worrying about her, a design session with him would probably do more good than anything this place had to offer.

Doug.

He was the real reason Lily was here. Her outbursts with Chenille bothered her, but the way she'd thrown that dish of chili across the room at the center? That was downright embarrassing. If nothing else, Lily had always prided herself on her restraint. Between Ken and her mother, she'd had to. Maybe priding herself on anything was the problem. Didn't pride always lead to a fall? And fall she had, head over heels, both into the darkness of anger and . . . dare she think it? Into the depths of love.

How Doug had managed to make her feel in a few weeks what Ken hadn't been able to manage in two years she wasn't sure, but it was true nonetheless. What would become of her and Doug Lily couldn't fathom. He'd probably be gone back to Africa before she pulled herself together, but she really hoped not. When she'd left Ken at the restaurant the night he broke things off, she'd walked away thinking she'd never care for anyone that way again—

The door swung open, but it wasn't the nurse.

"Anne? Here's the food—" Ken pulled upright at the sight of Lily. He almost dropped the Styrofoam container in his hand. A thin stream of reddish sauce and several pieces of meat slid out of the gaping carton and dropped onto the floor. "Lily?"

"Hello, Ken," Lily said as her mind worked quickly, putting together the puzzle she'd missed, fingering the something wrong with Anne, the something dripping all over the floor.

Orange beef.

"Doug? Is that really you?"

A smile spread across Doug's face as he approached the counter of the Man-O-Cure salon with open arms. "Yes, Stan, it's me."

Stan didn't hug him. He just stood there, staring. "I can't

believe it. They said you were dead. They were only half right."

Doug chuckled and raked a hand through his hair, realizing he wasn't going to get so much as a handshake in this condition. "I look a little wild, huh?"

The salon's manager shook his head. "A little wild? No. A little weird is more like it." He pressed every button on the intercom. "Lock and load, everybody. We've got an emergency."

Shrugging out of his jacket, Doug realized Stan wasn't joking. Funny how much difference a few years could make. He would have never been seen so much as going to his mailbox looking like this in the old days.

The manager took another long look at Doug and made a painful expression. He hit a few keys on the computer and pulled up Doug's file. "Ellis or Abboud?"

Doug sank into one of the overstuffed chairs, no longer amused. This was going to be a long day. "I'll let you pick."

"Thanks," Stan said. "I'll have to go with Abboud here, definitely for the tie. Still a 40 regular?"

"Probably. I haven't worn a suit in a few years."

Stan laughed. "That's obvious. What are those horrid things on your feet? Slip-ons? Flip-flops? With socks? They were right. You had a nervous breakdown. Well, never fear, we're here to help. If you keep your mouth shut, no one will ever know the difference."

Just then Doug broke out in a fit of laughter. This was just what he deserved for being so concerned about Lily when he was walking around looking like a middle-aged beatnik himself.

"All right, Stan, you make me look good, and I'll try to be on my best behavior."

"Good," Stan said, tossing Doug a trash bag. "Put those clothes in there and go to the sauna. You're going to need the head to toe treatment. Any preference on scent? I know you always liked vetiver."

"Let's stick with that. No mint, please. I have a feeling I'll be tingling enough when this is over."

Stan nodded. "You got that right." He turned to the salon's manicurist. "Matter of fact, Roxie, toss me that digital camera."

The camera sailed through the air, and Stan made a narrow catch. "Smile, you're going to look better in a minute. We promise."

Doug gave the camera a wide grin.

"Thanks, go on back. She should be ready for you at the first station." Stan paused and called one of the employees to the front. "Get this in three hundred dots per inch. Black and white, color, and sepia. And make sure you get those socks. And the shoes too. Don't cut those slides out of the shot whatever you do." He stared at Doug's feet again with a look of disdain.

An alarm rang inside Doug's head as the camera's flash went off. "What's all this with the picture? What are you going to do with it?"

Stan waved Doug to the back. "Come on, Mr. LaCroix, you know we can't let a moment like this pass. Your publicist would kill me. I still lunch with her, you know. This is going straight to the *Times*. If we hurry, we can still make the society page."

An attendant came and pulled Doug toward the dressing rooms.

He took off one of his slides and threw it at the reception desk. "Stan, do not send that to the *Times*, do you hear me? I mean it. If I come out of here and there is so much as one reporter in this place, I may do and say some things we'll both regret. Are you getting my meaning?"

"I hear you. Practice all those regrettable things while you're back there, okay? Maybe we'll get TV coverage too. Face it, Mr. LaCroix, the limelight is where you belong. Now let's get back there so you can start looking like it."

12

But whoever drinks the water I give him will
never thirst. Indeed, the water I give him will
become in him a spring of water welling up to
eternal life.

John 4:14

It was a good thing Doug hadn't chosen the mint
for his facial. After four hours of being scrubbed,
preened, and finally dressed in an impeccable suit
of clothes, he felt right at home and like a fish out
of water at the same time. Had he really dressed
like this every day?

Stan came into the back of the salon for a final
once-over. "Very nice. When we had to go for the
42 regular, I was a little worried you were going to
look paunchy, but you don't. You look very distinguished. And who knew that graying hair would
look so good with your eyes? I would have thrown
that blond dye out years ago if I'd known. You
could run for office in that suit. And that tie.
You have to hand it to Abboud. He always
comes through."

Doug had to agree. Though he'd balked

when Lily called him handsome, he'd have to say the word was almost fitting now, though he'd drawn the line at having makeup applied to cover his scar. "Mr. LaCroix. Please," the makeup artist had said. "I can blend it perfectly if you'll just let me."

He'd tried his best to explain that he had every confidence in her skills, he just wasn't interested in hiding his scar. Of course, he wasn't interested in talking about it either, except maybe with one person. And he wasn't so sure that person was even talking to him anymore. The least he could do was show up for her taping looking like a human being.

Doug shook Stan's hand. "Thanks, man. Thanks for everything. I mean it. I know I gave you a hard time."

Stan looked confused. "A hard time? You must forget how you used to cut up in here every week. We stayed prayed up for your arrival."

Doug's face went blank. "Was I that bad?"

Stan laughed. "Worse. Now come on. Folks are waiting for you."

Oh no.

"Tell me you didn't send that picture," Doug said as they walked to the front.

"If I told you that, I'd be lying. Now open that door."

Doing as he was told, Doug opened the door to the salon's reception area. A flash of cameras met him as he stepped into the room. Staff from every fashion paper from *W* to *Women's Wear Daily* lined the room. Folks from the *New York Times* whom he hadn't seen in the field in years shoved microphones up to his mouth.

"Is it true that you sold your company and gave all the proceeds to the victims of 9/11?"

These guys leave no stone unturned.

191

"I'd rather not discuss my personal finances, thank you," Doug fired back just as rapidly.

What was it about manicured nails and a good suit that brought it all flooding back? He was starting to hate himself already.

Just when he was about to cut and run for the door, his old publicist cut through the crowd in three-inch stilettos and a string of the biggest pearls he'd ever seen. She looked very, very glad to see him.

"I should kill you for not being dead," she whispered to him before turning to face the crowd.

"Thank you for coming to see Mr. LaCroix on his return to our fair city. I'll be arranging interviews for the next twenty-four hours. Please leave your card with contact information and preferred location with me after the press conference."

Press conference?

"What in the world—"

TV cameras from all the major networks wheeled in. The lighting in the reception area brightened. Despite Doug's efforts to stop it, it was showtime. He'd be lucky to make it to Lily's taping two days from now, let alone make it back to the center. He'd have to call Father Patrick and explain.

"Roll it!" someone shouted in front of him as a handsome young journalist stepped toward him with a microphone.

"We're live in a New York salon with Doug LaCroix, the famous designer who dropped out of sight a few months after the terrorist attacks of 2001. Mr. LaCroix, it's obvious that you're alive and well. Can you tell us a little about where you've been for the past few years? Some people speculated you were dead."

Doug paused, knowing he could still get up and walk out. He'd done it plenty of times before. But if somehow, some way God could use this too, like Chioma had said, he had no right to not follow through.

"What's your name, son? You'll have to give me a minute. Most of the people who used to interview me are either dead or retired."

Laughter echoed through the small room.

"Brad Haley, sir."

"Brad Haley. Good name. Nice suit too. One of mine, I see. Someone over there is really sharp."

More laughter.

"To answer your question, Brad, I'd have to say that some people had it half right." Doug paused and looked over at Stan. "I did die. I died to my old life and my old ways and returned to the faith I was taught as a child."

Brad pulled the microphone back a little. "So you went on a journey of spiritual discovery, a search for your inner self?"

Doug pulled the mic back to where it had been before, pulling Brad along with it. "No, son. Nothing that silly. I became a Christian. I thought I'd always been one, being the son of a missionary and all, but when those towers fell with so many of my friends . . . while I, who had a meeting there and was held up in traffic and couldn't make it, was spared, well, I knew I had to change—"

The young journalist looked worried and tried to tug the microphone, and the conversation, back in his direction. "Well, it doesn't look like you changed too much, sir. In fact, you look better than ever. We're glad you've worked through this guilt over the tragedy—"

Doug yanked the mic from the young man completely. "This is not the way I've looked for the past four years. In fact . . . Stan, where's that picture of me when I came in here today?"

The manager, being ever prepared, had already enlarged the photo into a poster and had it mounted onto a foam board. "Here you are, Mr. LaCroix."

"Thank you, Stan. This is Man-O-Cure Salon, by the way, people. Also home base for the Coming into Light Ministry to AIDS patients and their families. Just had to throw that in. Where were we, Brad? Oh yes, this." He held up the poster to the astonishment of the crowd.

"This is how I would still look if I didn't have a favor to do for a friend. Like I was trying to say before, I grew up hearing the Bible stories and the altar calls. I've folded the church programs and the gospel tracts. But somewhere I forgot that even the feet have to be washed in the blood of Christ, that even the hands have to be healed by his death. So that's where I've been, America, being the feet and the hands, joining into the suffering of Christ."

The cameraman directly in front of Doug wiped a tear from his eyes. Brad extended a hand for the microphone. Doug gladly handed it over. It'd be a madhouse from here, but at least he'd kept the main thing the main thing.

"Well, you heard it, folks. Famous fashion designer Doug LaCroix has been born again," the young journalist said, dragging out the last two words like an old-time revival preacher.

Doug's publicist kept her smile as the cameras shut down. She dug her nails into Doug's arm. "Are you crazy? What was that, another career suicide? You might as well have stayed in whatever desert you were in for all it's worth. Nobody will want to interview you now."

He pried her red lacquered nails from his arm. "I should be so lucky."

"It figures." Jean's scissors clacked at lightning speed around the edge of one of Lily's latest patterns. Lily watched with a pained expression as her friend's fingers made corrections here and there, fixing errors her own eyes hadn't seen. Again.

Following the psychologist's instructions, Lily lowered herself to the floor for a push-up, hoping her toes wouldn't roll off the body ball they were perched on. She wobbled but made it down. "One . . ." How did she used to do this every day?

"I mean, if Ken was seeing her, why couldn't he just say that and leave your mother out of it? Men. They want it both ways. I told you, when I went for my physical, that woman couldn't look me in the eye. I knew then something was wrong, but I thought she was just weird. Never thought it was Ken."

"Two . . ." Lily managed to make it back to horizontal with a little less effort this time, but too much effort for her to spare air on agreeing with Jean. That was the great thing about talking with Jean. If Lily didn't respond quickly enough, her friend would answer herself. And what was there to say anyway? "Three . . ." Lily fell this time, her face just missing the floor.

"Forget the ball. You'll have to work back up to it. Here, let me help you." Jean leaned over and helped slide the inflatable sphere from under Lily's outstretched legs.

Knowing that Jean could do body-ball push-ups one handed, Lily felt really silly to have to get down to the floor for a few reps. Admitting defeat to a woman more than ten years her senior didn't feel good, but Jean was no ordinary woman. Some twenty-year-olds wouldn't be able to hang with her either.

Not to mention that you're in love with someone her age.

195

"Thanks," Lily murmured, relieved to be back on the floor, where she quickly cranked out ten push-ups before rolling onto her back for sit-ups. It'd been a long time since she'd done them on the floor. It hurt. Her bones seemed to jab the floor from every angle.

The squats should have come next, but Lily just wasn't up to it. Instead, she extended one leg for a good stretch.

"You know the worst part? They called to tell me Mother's appointment is with Ken even after I requested someone else. Can you believe it? I even asked if Anne was available. It's just preliminary, of course. They'll have to refer her to a neurologist. You know how it goes—"

Jean chuckled. "No referral, no service. I know. It's a pain sometimes. I'm just thankful to be covered, really, the way people are going without care nowadays." She looked at the floor. "I remember when I wasn't covered."

Thankful? That was a new addition to Jean's vocabulary, perhaps because it didn't come out of Lily's mouth so often anymore. It was as if Jean didn't want certain words to be lost from their conversations, so she adopted them until Lily could take them back. *Thankful.* Though Lily needed it now more than ever, she couldn't seem to force it past her lips.

She settled on a quick assent. "I guess you're right."

The scissors started again. Lily forced herself to do a few squats. The psychologist had been right about the exercise. Lily had to push every repetition, but already she was starting to feel better. The rest of that blather the woman had said didn't make a bit of sense. She seemed to be looking for some childhood trauma, some family secret. There weren't any that Lily could think of. Didn't every family have mysteries?

That night when her father didn't come home and the space between her and her mother, the gap she couldn't ever seem to cross. Lily had told the doctor about these things in a flat voice while the woman scribbled notes. Staring at the clock now, Lily tried not to imagine how much the HMO had paid for that visit.

The scissor song halted. "So what about Doug? Are you through with him after that fight you had or what?"

"Why do you ask? You interested?"

Lily felt a twinge of jealousy at Jean's even mentioning Doug. So now she was paranoid too? What would be next, a full-blown nervous breakdown? Jean was closer to Doug's age than Lily's. That they'd been involved once didn't help either.

Look at me, acting jealous. Must be this thing with Ken.

Giggles floated from Jean's mouth like bubbles, very different from her usual hearty laughter. "Oh, please. Do you think I'm interested? Now, that would be funny. Doug La-Croix . . . and me. Honey, don't worry. He's all yours. And don't bother to answer about whether you're interested in him anymore. You cleared that right up."

Lily scratched her head. Her scalp was still sore from the many washings she'd given it after lying on that exam table at the doctor's office.

"I'm sorry. I know there's nothing between you and Doug," she said. "There may not be anything left between me and Doug either. He hasn't been at the center for a few days. It seems he only had to be there on clinic day. I guess I scared him off for the rest of the time. I'm going to have to catch up with him though. The cameramen are coming in to shoot us tomorrow."

"Maybe you did all this so your relationship wouldn't make you lose the contest. Not on purpose or anything. You know, subconsciously."

Lily respected Jean, but sometimes even she said stupid things. "Have you been watching Dr. Phil again? If so, cut it out. I have no idea what I'm doing consciously, subconsciously, or otherwise. You think you know everything about me. You don't. I don't even know everything about myself."

Jean laughed again. The old way. "I don't know everything about you, but I know your heart. And our work," she said, peeling Lily's pattern off the blue Lycra it'd been attached to. Instead of the usual steady shape that resulted after Jean's cutting, a lopsided mess fell to the floor. "When you got on that show, you traced straight. When Ken dumped you, you traced straight. But ever since that argument with Doug, you've been patterning like a first-year student with broken wrists."

Lily smiled. Jean had her there. She missed Doug's timeless eyes and his rugged voice. The phone rang across the hall in her own office before Lily could give it more thought.

"If I'm off the call before two, then—"

"I know," Jean snapped, not having thought or played much today. "If I don't see you before two, I'll see you tomorrow."

Lily nodded and caught the phone on the fifth ring. Ken's voice, uneven and apologetic, met her on the other side of the phone. "You don't need to come in for a visit with me. I went ahead and gave your mother her referral, though I have to say that I don't think the findings will be conclusive. They never are. I could just go ahead and give a preliminary diagnosis if you're uncomfortable about the tests."

At least they agreed on something. "I think so too, but I'm going to go ahead and do the tests just to be sure."

"Yes. With a diagnosis, you can get your mother some treatment. There are lots of great programs—"

"Programs? So you definitely think she has Alzheimer's?"

"Don't you? I just thought since you were getting the tests done . . . I'm sorry. I just called to let you know."

There was a crackling on the line. Candy wrapper, no doubt. Probably not a Mars bar, but still . . .

"Forget it. How are you? And Anne, of course." There was no reason to be juvenile. They'd been together for two years for goodness' sake. "And put that candy bar down. You'll be sick."

"Oh, Lily." He gasped the words as if he couldn't breathe.

That hurt a little, but she whisked it away. "Really, how are you? You know how I am. Crazy. Not surprising with a history of mental illness in my family. Maybe I have Alzheimer's too. It could happen."

"I am so sorry. That was totally out of line. I know you requested the chart. I'll deal with whatever consequences come my way. It was a stupid, cruel thing to do, but some of the things you told me about your father and the way you can get melancholy sometimes . . . I was wrong though. It's just your personality. Anne shouldn't have given you that prescription."

"It's helping."

If blah was good, that is. There wasn't much more than a dull grayness, but that was probably better than the vivid light show she'd had going on before.

"Maybe. I can't help thinking some of this is my fault. I didn't handle things very well between us."

His fault? Lily laughed. "Oh, so now it's all about you, huh? Why didn't I see that coming?"

The rap of Ken's knuckles sounded through the line. "I have to go. They're waving a patient back. I just wanted to tell you about your mother's referral and to say, well, that I'm sorry about everything and I hope you'll forgive me. For everything. And if it helps, I'm not seeing Anne anymore. It was just a crush from working together so much, I guess. Silly."

A forty-year-old man with a crush? Now, that seemed silly.

But hey, Lily was the resident loon, so what did she know? Why did even her thoughts seem so bitter, so angry? Ken had somehow managed to rouse her worst emotions from their graves.

"Sorry to hear you two aren't together."

Lily closed her eyes.

"I'm just plain sorry," he said finally. "About everything."

She opened her eyes, looked around. She realized she had cared for Ken and still did, but she no longer loved him. He could live his whole life and never understand what had gone wrong between them. That made her pity him a little and envy him a little too.

Ken sighed. "Good-bye, Li Li."

She stiffened at the sound of her Chinese name, then relaxed, trying not to laugh. Though Ken looked Chinese, the thought of him suddenly trying to be cultural struck Lily as sweet and ridiculous. It made her think of another man, the last man she'd heard speaking Mandarin across her kitchen table.

She bowed slightly. "Cheers."

She paused as her back straightened. Ken seemed frozen too, as if trying to place the phrase. Lily tried to place it too. It sounded . . . global. Where had she heard it?

Doug.

Ken spoke first. "Yes, well. Good day to you too."

Lily hung up the phone, knowing that the day wouldn't be good, that the fears she'd bottled so tightly—losing Ken, her mother really having Alzheimer's, falling in love with a stranger—were running down the sides of her heart and into her shoes.

She hadn't told Ken he was forgiven, partly because she wasn't sure if he'd done anything wrong besides having the sense to know what he could handle. She reached into her purse for the bottle of antidepressants, the imaginary bulge she thought everyone could see as she passed by. The failure jutting out of her pretenses.

Ken had known his limits, the borders of his faith, his relationships. Lily, evidently, had long since rambled past her own fences, maybe God's too. If only these pills could erase her feelings for Doug, maybe it'd all be worth it. She'd kept herself all these years, certain no man would want a loose woman. Now she was something worse than that.

A crazy woman.

Lily couldn't believe her eyes, but her nose didn't lie. The distinguished gentleman in front of her didn't look like Doug, but he sure smelled like him.

"Is that you?" she asked in a whisper as the camera crew entered Garments of Praise behind him.

"Unfortunately," he said, giving her a wink. "Sorry you haven't been able to reach me. It's a long story. Don't worry though. We'll do fine."

We? Lily wasn't worried about we. Doug didn't have to do a thing but stand there and look . . . stunning. She, on the other hand, wanted to run and hide. Her skirt was cute, and she'd borrowed a pair of Raya's platform boots, but she had no idea how she might react in front of a camera, especially with Doug looking like that. She'd thought there would be some time of training or preparation, but from the way the team was barreling toward her, on location meant just that.

Hart Nash whisked into the building wearing Lily's kimono and a big smile. "Here we are!" She paused to embrace Doug. "And you. Amazing. You look better the older you get. Isn't he amazing, Lily?"

Quite.

"Absolutely. Thanks for assigning him to me as a mentor. He's great."

"I'll bet."

What was that all about? Nash was acting like a woman with a secret. That made Lily even more nervous than she had been.

The taping passed slowly, with retakes from every angle and repetition of the same things over and over. Though her segment would be only a few minutes of the show, the crew would need to shoot hours of film to be sure they had everything they needed. As the day went on, Doug brightened and Lily wilted. Only when it was time for their off-camera consultation with Nash did Lily perk up.

Her heart raced as Doug closed the door to her office and sat beside her in the extra chair someone—probably Jean—had been thoughtful enough to place there.

Nash rubbed her hands together. "First of all, let me say that my instincts in choosing you were exactly on target. What you've come up with has been phenomenal. The thing I hadn't counted on is what may trip you up though."

Trip her up? What was that supposed to mean?

"I did everything you said to do with her," Doug said. "Are you saying there's a problem?"

"You tell me," Nash said, walking over to Lily's computer and slipping in a DVD. What flashed on the screen took Lily's breath away.

It was her.

And Doug.

The image of the two of them kissing blocked out what was said.

Doug howled like a wounded animal. "What did you do, bug the whole place? Come on, Hart. That's low. Really low."

It was low, but it got worse.

Next came the two of them at Lily's apartment, discussing the Fluid collection. Another kiss.

Lily started to cry. "You put a camera in my apartment? Are you crazy? My mother is there."

Nash folded her arms. "There's no camera at your apartment. We gave Doug a timer to take to all your work sessions to record how many hours you worked together."

"That little black thing?" Doug and Lily both said together.

"Yes, that little black stopwatch has a very powerful camera inside it."

Doug banged a fist on the table. "I want every copy of that. Now. Or I walk."

"You could probably do that. Both of you signed release forms with some language that is very, very subject to interpretation. A judge could go either way. Even with your little Jesus phase, Doug, I thought you'd have the sense to have a lawyer look over it at least. I got lucky there."

Lily felt faint. She didn't have money for a lawyer, and she couldn't speak for Doug, but something told her that his high times were a thing of the past as well, despite his dapper appearance today.

"So what are you saying?" Lily asked. "You're going to show this to the whole world, and there's nothing we can do about it?"

"Not exactly. This isn't *Jerry Springer*, okay? That footage will be used only in a total emergency."

Doug snorted. "Like what? The show being canceled for low ratings?"

Nash made a clucking noise with her teeth. "Exactly. For now we'll edit out all the love scenes and put Lily's best face forward. As for you, Doug, we have some of your only before-the-makeover footage, so that will probably be pruned out and spliced together as a highlight on the show."

He looked a little sick at the sound of that.

"You know what, Lily? I really want you to have a shot at this, but I might just have to bail. This show is headed in the totally wrong direction if what we've just seen and heard is any indication. Of course, that would mean you losing your shot and probably having your face plastered all over TV kissing an old man, but I don't think I can stick this one out."

Nash's eyes started to water. "Listen, Doug. Don't take the high road here, okay? I know you don't care about any of this, but for some of us, this is the last chance we've got. You can make a comeback a million times, because you really don't care. Sadly, I do. I don't like the way this was done either, but I need this gig. Lily needs it too. Will you please stay? I'll do everything I can to keep that footage off the air."

Lily stood up and opened the door to her office. "Ms. Nash, please leave and take your crew with you. Mr. LaCroix or I will be in touch with you in the next few days. Do you have the timer on you, Doug?"

He lifted his messenger bag off the doorknob. He came up with the timer the show had issued him and handed it to Nash.

"Here. I brought it to be sure we'd done everything correctly. I was even planning to tell you today that I'd probably need to take myself off the judges' panel since Lily and I are—or were—involved."

"So wait a minute. You two aren't seeing each other anymore?" Nash squinted at Lily. "It seems a shame to give up on him now. At least reap the fruit of your spoils. With that scar, he looks like a new James Bond."

Doug slapped his forehead. "Hart, please leave. Now I know why you and I never made it past the first date. You're a ninny."

Lily watched the woman go, not knowing whether to laugh or cry.

Doug shut the door and walked toward her. "I would hug you, but the whole nation might be watching."

She laughed. "I don't care. They've seen everything else."

"Not everything," Doug said, reaching down and sweeping Lily off her feet and into his arms. "I always save something for the big finish."

Their lips touched softly at first, then joined as old friends glad to see each other. The kiss was brief but sweet. Lily scrambled to her feet, almost falling over in Raya's platforms. She'd have to remember to wear her own shoes when people turned her world upside down. Any anger she'd felt toward him melted away.

"So what do you think we should do?" Lily asked, smoothing the edges of Doug's new short hair.

"Get married," Doug said.

"I mean about the show."

"Me too," Doug said, taking a few steps back to lock the door. "You might not win, but we'd certainly have nothing to be embarrassed about. Nobody wants to see married people in love anymore. It'd never make the screen."

Lily swallowed hard. Married? Was he serious? Fear shot through her again, racing from the soles of her feet, up her arms, and into her upturned palms, palms she squeezed shut.

"You're right. It probably wouldn't make the cut."

13

For they drank from the spiritual rock that accompanied them, and that rock was Christ.

1 Corinthians 10:4

"How is she? Really?" Pinkie whispered as Lily's mother stood at the end of the bed instead of walking closer to say hello.

Barbara got up and headed for the waiting room, though both Pinkie and Lily begged her to stay. "It's okay. Have a good time," she said. "I'll be back."

Lily patted her neighbor's shoulder. "Don't worry about Mom. She's okay. We're here to see you."

Pinkie smiled, pointing to all the new flowers that had replaced the near greenhouse filling the room on their last visit. "I'm fine too. God is good. I've had many prayers and visitors. I'll be going home with Barbara soon, though I'd rather go to my own place. She's been here with me though, right through it all. Strange how the hard times have a way of pulling people together."

Lily nodded. She and Barbara weren't

the best of friends, but they both believed in sticking by family, in seeing things to the end.

"Of course Barbara has been here. She loves you. I'm sorry I haven't been here every day like I wanted to be, but Mom is still getting used to the center, so I'm taking my days off again. For a while I was working straight through. I hope to get by here more."

With everything going on with that crazy TV show and Doug half convincing her to marry him, Pinkie's hospital room was probably one of the safest places for Lily to be. Having that camera planted in the timer had somehow made her more paranoid about everything, if that was possible. Her medicine helped, but it took something away too. For now, though, she was staying on it and following the doctor's directions. Time was passing quickly, and her prescription would be over before she knew it. Or at least she hoped so.

Lily took a deep breath, hearing Doug's voice again in her head.

Get married.

How could a proposal sound so romantic and so scary at the same time?

Pinkie shook her head. "Do you think I'm going to move into this place? No, no. I'll be going home this week, Lord willing."

"How wonderful," Lily said with a sigh. "I know it'll be good to be out of here, though it seems like they've taken great care of you here."

"That they have, Li Li. I can't complain. There's just something about going home though, you know? Right, Su?"

Lily's mother, far from the conversation at the end of the bed, nodded her head in agreement, then pointed at the flowers. "Pretty. Look nice on table."

"Yes, Su. I think so too. Maybe when I get home we'll go shopping for vases. Would you like that?"

Lily's mother nodded quickly. "Yes. Shop. Lots of shop."

They all laughed then, though pain mixed in with the humor. How long would it be, Lily wondered, before she was visiting her mother in a room like this? Or worse yet, before someone was visiting her? The past few weeks had been like a nervous breakdown in a takeout box.

Pinkie dug her fingers into Lily's arm, pulling her closer. "Really, how is it for her? Is she eating? Don't let them give her those powdered eggs. They give her a stomachache. And tomatoes. No tomatoes. Did you tell them?"

Lily sniffed back her tears. "Yes, I told them all of that, but thank you for caring. It's an adjustment for her, but she seems okay. Physically."

She added the last word with regret. Lily hated to admit it, but in the past few days of Doug's absence at the center, her mother had withdrawn a great deal. And someone had given her a powdered-egg omelet (who would make such a thing?) filled with tomatoes. She didn't think there was any need to bring it up to Pinkie now. Her mother seemed fine.

Pinkie nodded. "She slipping back in time a lot, huh? It probably helps that she sees me here, knows I'm okay. She might come on back around."

"Yeah," Lily said in a low voice, knowing, as Pinkie did, that it wasn't likely. Things were getting worse with her mother, not better. She'd thought it herself, and now Doug seemed convinced of it too.

"She has tests tomorrow for Alzheimer's."

Pinkie shook her head. "Where do they keep coming up with that?" Lily smiled at her mother's friend. "Oh, maybe it's best. Who can know? These minds that God made do all kinds of things . . . I hope that's not it though."

Barbara stuck her head in the door. "Pastor Gibbs is out here, Mama. And they brought half their church with them. Say they've come to sing to you."

Already taking her mother's hand, Lily shook her head when Pinkie tried to get her to stay. Pastor Gibbs headed up a small Haitian congregation where Pinkie sometimes taught English to the Creole-speaking children.

Lily's mother waved good-bye to her good friend. "Be careful. Too many people. They break your flowers."

Lily guided her mother out, thinking of all the times her mother had been worried for Pinkie when strangers showed up at her door asking for prayer after nightfall. Little had her mother known that just a few years later they'd have much bigger things to be scared of. Things that didn't knock before they came in.

They squeezed past the church group and into the hall and took the first elevator they came to. When it opened, Lily's mother pulled away from her and grabbed the elevator's only passenger.

Doug LaCroix.

"Li Li? Is that our doctor?"

"Yes," Doug and Lily both said at the same time.

Lily stepped into the elevator, careful not to let his body touch hers. She was still embarrassed about the way she'd kissed him in front of her mother and Pinkie the last time they'd all been here together.

Doug kept her mother's hand and took Lily's hand too. "I was coming to show Miss Pinkie that I still know how to get a haircut. I couldn't do anything about my eyes or my age, I'm afraid. I suppose a good haircut will have to do."

Lily looked him over. "Works for me."

Behind the locked doors of Lily's office, Doug had almost gotten Lily to agree to marry him, but she'd gathered the strength to turn him down in a good suit and Italian leather shoes. Something about him being water and her being fire and the two canceling each other out. Doug could have kicked himself for drawing that connection in the first place. Sure, they were different, but they had Christ in common and a whole lot of something else going on or they wouldn't be kissing so much.

Now, a few days later, he was back at the center with another Chau woman on his mind, Lily's mother. Today she'd have her tests done, and Doug planned to do all he could to help things run smoothly. It was his final day before the doctor returned from his vacation and a day when Lily would probably need him more than ever. Things were going fine until Doug hit a snag in his plan.

Dr. Ken Lee.

What is he doing here? Doug wondered as Ken buzzed his way into the center. As cocky now as he'd been the first time Doug had seen him, the guy flipped out a flimsy ID card from his job with the letters *MD* at the end of his name, almost as big as the photo.

Doug straightened. "Hello, Doctor. How may I help you?"

After dealing with those TV people, he was ready for just about anything. He and Lily still hadn't decided what to about that either. He was sticking with the marriage solution.

"Mrs. Chau. Is she here? I need to talk to her," Ken said.

Doug couldn't believe the guy's nerve. When he'd called to speed up Lily's mother's referral, Ken had treated him as anything but a peer. Now he expected to walk in here and have his way?

"I'm sorry, but I can't discuss any of our clients. You'll need to contact her daughter for permission and have her alert us. Or I could relay a message and get it back to you."

After a sharp look, Ken took a step toward Doug. "I can appreciate you trying to do your job, Mister Missionary, tailor, or whatever it is you are, but Mrs. Chau is my patient, and I'd like to be here for her once she comes back from her appointment."

Doug smiled. "How noble. You'd like to be here for her daughter too, of course."

As if their strained words had beckoned her, Lily dragged in, looking tired but beautiful. It was all Doug could do to keep from sweeping her off her feet the way he had their last time together. Instead, he went to the day room for the chicken soup he'd made for her the night before. He'd also scheduled a helper to go with her to the appointment this morning. He'd been surprised when Lily had accepted the help.

Lily's mother followed him next, pushed in a wheelchair by one of the aides from the center. Doug didn't know if that was good or bad. Certainly, if she'd needed immediate treatment, the hospital would have kept her. Regardless of the diagnosis, he wanted to be there for Lily. In fact, he insisted on it.

It seemed that Ken had the same idea.

The two men squared off, each standing by one of Lily's wilted hands.

Lily looked up at Ken in surprise but extended her hand to him. "What are you doing here?"

Ken smiled victoriously at Doug.

"I came to check on you and your mom. I know you and

I have been through a lot, but the past two years should count for something."

She smiled and pushed the soup away. "It does. Thank you for coming."

Ken pulled away and sat down beside Doug. Ken whispered under his breath. "One point for me."

Doug only smiled. The good doctor might have won the battle, but Doug would win the war.

He'd have to.

Turning away from Ken, Doug noticed a new glaze in Lily's eyes, a film he'd seen reflected back from his own face in the mirror when he'd changed prescriptions on his antidepressants. He'd hated the pills at first after the situation in Uganda, but he'd come to see them as what they were, medicine. He took them every day now without a second thought.

There were times, though, like during the last few weeks before he'd left Nigeria, when Doug needed to see all the colors, feel all the pain around him. With others hurting so much, he felt guilty sometimes about feeling better, or worse yet, feeling nothing. He wondered if Lily felt anything now.

Ken's face twitched slightly at the sight of Lily's mother. Doug thought about walking over and kicking the guy in his shins, but it didn't seem very missionary-like and probably wouldn't go too far in winning Lily's affections.

Although the way Lily was acting, she might not have noticed if Doug walked over and tap-danced on Ken's head. Maybe that blockhead was what she wanted. Like Ken had said, two years was quite an investment. Doug had had very few relationships that had lasted that long. Still, what he had with Lily felt just as strong as or stronger than those relationships. God made all the difference.

While he sorted through his conflicted feelings, Doug realized that this forced sabbatical had ended up being more work than he ever could have anticipated. He'd thought that going back to medicine was the best way to serve God, but after spending the past two days in interviews explaining his faith and the goal of the medical missions program, he wondered if he hadn't gotten that wrong too. Though he wanted to battle it out with Ken for Lily's affections, Doug went to the sanctuary to pray instead. Maybe this whole thing was another one of God's redirections.

He really, really hoped not.

Lily sat with her mother. Though she didn't invite him, Ken followed. The three sat quietly.

"Are you all right, Mother?" Lily asked.

Her mother didn't answer, but Ken shook his head as if Lily shouldn't be concerned. "Well, Lily. If your mother doesn't want to talk, perhaps you should sing to her. Lily's a good singer, right, Mom?"

More so than being the butt of Ken's joke, Lily resented his familiar tone. How easy to call her Mom now when he'd admitted he didn't want to be stuck with having her living in his home. Not that it mattered. Ken had been a big part of her life. That was over now. Trying to be friends probably wasn't the best idea.

Lily's mother turned her head slowly, scanning their faces. "Li Li? Sing?" she said, laughing softly.

Lily's shoulders slumped, but she pushed them back quickly, wishing she could touch her shoulder blades together like she'd once seen someone do on TV. These new bony shoulders had to come in handy for something. If Ken came any closer, she'd try to poke him at least. If he'd just kept quiet it would have been okay.

"You know what, Ken?" she said. "Thanks for coming, but

I really don't think I need your help. Doug is here. I'm sure you'll know the results before we do anyway."

"That's just it," Ken said. "The gerontologist called already. They'd like to have your mother come back for another test. They weren't sure if the HMO would pay at the time you were there, but it's been cleared now. I know it's a pain, but they'd like you to bring her back in."

Lily felt a pang of coldness sweep her mind. She'd taken only half a dose of her medicine today, wondering if she'd feel the difference. She did. Especially with Ken around. She settled back into her seat, trying to consider what this might mean.

Don't try to figure it out. Just flow.

"Okay, Ken. I'll call them. I'll do my best to get her back there today."

"Thanks," he said, standing to leave.

"Oh, and by the way, I know you never liked my voice, but God does. I hope Anne's singing is more to your liking."

He threw up his hands. "Hey, that's over. I told you that. It just wasn't working. Cultural differences."

Now, that was truly funny, since one of Ken's biggest beefs with Lily had been what he perceived as her over-emphasis on being Chinese. Seeing how she couldn't speak Chinese and ate with chopsticks like a two-year-old, Lily could hardly agree, but she knew that Ken needed everything in his life, including his girlfriend, to fit into his mold.

"Cultural differences, huh?" she said. "What culture would that be exactly?"

Too late Lily saw where Ken was really going with this whole thing. It wasn't about him and Anne at all. It was about Lily and Doug.

He must really be getting desperate now.

214

Ken must have thought he had her going, because he kept going too. "You know. Culture. Identity. You and I were good together. I shouldn't have listened to my mother. I don't want my children to have to choose between one culture and another the way I did." He touched Lily's shoulder.

Lily brushed Ken's hand aside despite how warm it felt against her skin. What a pack of lies. Though Ken probably had taken Anne through his "How would you raise our kids?" scenario. Lily's Chinese-American answers of wanting to teach their kids all the things she wanted to know herself about the food, language, and history of China had made no sense to Ken. ("What difference does it make? I didn't do any of that and it never hurt me any.") Perhaps Anne's answers hadn't quite passed muster either. Still, Lily knew that she and Doug were at the center of all this talk.

"That's the great thing about being a Christian. It trumps everything else. Thanks again for your support today. Talk to you soon."

Lily reached into her purse for her cell phone, thinking Ken would be gone when she lifted her head. He wasn't. "So what is it about him, huh? He's like what, fifty something? He's going gray, for goodness' sake."

"I know. I love it," Lily said, not thinking about who she was talking to. "It's nothing I can explain, Ken. What's between Doug and me just is. What was between us just isn't. Much of that was your choice, but looking back, I see we'd have run out of steam eventually. Maybe we already had."

Lily's mother was snoring now, her head back against the chair. It'd been a long day for her. And Lily too. She needed to get back to that soup Doug had made for her. Real soup too. Not the canned stuff. Those were the things she loved about him. He made simple things seem big. She never had to wonder if she mattered to him. Now, with Ken standing here muttering under his breath about nonsense, Lily wondered if she'd ever mattered to him at all.

Lily's mother gripped the edge of her blanket but kept her eyes closed. When she opened them, she seemed surprised to see Ken there.

"Where is the good doctor?" her mother asked as the breeze subsided. "I have something to tell him."

Ken looked pleased. "I'm here, Mom. Right here. What would you like to say? I'm all ears."

More like all mouth.

Lily's mother waved her hand as if to shoo Ken away. "Not you. The other one. The one from China."

Ken swallowed, then walked away without saying a word. Two years ago, when Lily's mother had her right mind, she would have never considered an American stranger to be one of her countrymen. She probably wouldn't have even allowed Lily to have Doug over for dinner. Though the long nights had been hard, whatever had taken her mother's good mind had taken some of the bad parts too. Perhaps going through it all with her mother would do the same for Lily. Lily grabbed the front of her blazer and wadded it into her fists to keep from crying.

She stopped an attendant who was passing by. "Can you get Dr. LaCroix for me? And the attendant for Mrs. Chau too? It looks like we're going to have to head back to the hospital."

When Doug started toward them a few minutes later, Lily's mother's face lit up as if seeing her own son. "There he is, Li Li. I knew he'd come."

Lily wiped her eyes. In this new, forgetful land, Doug was a friend who'd been some of the places her mother had been. Lily was the outsider who couldn't speak Chinese, while Doug, gifted with the fluency that comes only to those who absorb language at a young age, spoke the language with ease.

As he joined them and sank between Lily and her mother, kissing both of their cheeks, Lily wondered if he could translate the message of her heartbeat.

"I love you, Mr. LaCroix," she whispered in his hair as he kissed her mother.

"I know," he answered back, kissing her face again. "But it's nice to hear you say it. You won't marry me, so it's all I've got."

It was Thursday, Raya's day in the office, and her boys were running wild. Lily smiled at the sight of them. Despite the very different ways Jay and Ray had joined Raya and Flex's family, their resembling looks and rhyming names made most people none the wiser.

Jay walked into Lily's office and put a vase with a single white rose on the front corner of her desk, the spot where Ken's lush red roses had wilted until housekeeping threw them out.

"Thanks, Jay," Lily said, taking a sniff of the bud and cherishing its freshness, though she wondered at its color. "Where'd you get this?" She slid the bud back into the vase.

Jay pulled up a chair. His little brother giggled nearby, no doubt sending Raya in circles in the office next door. Jay smiled with the confidence of a much older man but the honesty of a boy.

"I got it from a funeral. The guy was a friend of mine from my old block."

Lily swallowed. He seemed so comfortable discussing the

funeral, as though it were a detention or an extra school assignment.

"Are you sure that's okay? The flower, I mean? And are you okay? Was it a close friend?" What a herd of questions.

His expression told her that her instincts about the number of questions had been correct.

"You sound like my mom. She asks me a million questions too. I'm okay. Sad, but okay. That's why I brought you that rose, I guess."

Lily's heart pounded. Her desk was covered with work, including the next set of sketches for *The Next Design Diva*. After a long talk at the hospital during her mother's extra test, she and Doug had decided to see the crazy show to the end. Though more and more she wondered if he was serious about his proposal and how long she'd be able to hold out before accepting if he was. She still couldn't figure out how their lives could come together in one place, but that hadn't stopped their hearts from coming together.

Jay waited patiently while Lily floated among her thoughts. She shouldn't even be sitting still, let alone talking to a teenager. Still, something kept her from turning him away. Something in her wanted to know what he meant.

"Why? Why me? That flower, I mean."

The boy stretched his long legs out across a stack of vintage *Vogue* magazines Lily had dug up from a trunk in her closet. He shifted his weight to one side. A pile of sketches and fabric took up most of the chair. She motioned to move it, but he shook his head.

"Forget it. This place looks like open air compared to Mom's office. I'm used to it. Now, about the flower. I brought it because I know your mom's all sick and that TV people are tripping on you.

"I just wanted to let you know that it's all good. Bad stuff happens. People die. Folks leave you. And it's okay to be sad. It bugs people out when you are, because if you're sad, then they might have to admit that everything ain't all super happy like they putting on, but don't sweat it, you know? I don't."

Warmth ran to Lily's eyes and turned to tears before she could think of anything to say. She'd spent hours with a psychologist and days drugged by pills, but Raya's son had summed it up. She was sad, but she was okay. Things would swing up again, just like they had for King David, who'd spent dark days in the cleft of a rock, under the wings of God. As she brushed her tears away, Jay held up a finger.

"Oh yeah," he said. "I got one more thing for you." He reached into his jeans pocket, which seemed to swallow his whole hand, and produced a smooth, flat stone. The light played over its green-black surface.

Jade.

"Where did you get this?"

"I found it in the subway on the way home. Somebody must have dropped it. I don't think it's real or nothing, but I thought you'd like it."

Lily swallowed hard, remembering a similar stone, one her father had kept in his pocket, one he'd worn smooth by screaming with his fingers instead of with words.

"It's real. I can tell. Thank you very much. You're growing into a great guy."

The baby made a sharp cry in the hall.

"Jay! Can you get him?" Raya's voice sounded nasal, like she was on a conference call or something.

Lily stood along with her young friend and walked him to the door. "Thanks, Jay. For the rose, for the rock, and for just being you."

Jay scooped up the baby and checked him over, talking to Lily without looking up. "I have a rock too. Onyx. Dad got it for me. It's my cornerstone, you know? When life rubs me wrong, I rub the rock. Or I just hold it. Hold on. Sometimes that's all I can do."

Unable to answer, Lily watched her teen psychologist disappear into an empty conference room down the hall to look after his brother. She thought about following, playing with the baby for a few minutes, but there was too much work to do. Just the thought of it knotted Lily's shoulders. Megan had forgotten to tell Lily about the diet she planned to go on after their last fitting, so the prototype had been too big. (Who told her to go on some fruit fast without telling anybody?) *The Next Design Diva* had sent Lily a tape of the first episode of the show, and all the other contestants' clothing lines seemed to hinge on making copies of the latest trend from every mall in America, only with triple the price tag. With everyone else so similar and Lily's work so different, her Beautiful One line had ended up looking either very strange or very wonderful. The viewers would have to decide which.

One after the other, work and worries weighted Lily's mind down until she reached for the piece of jade on her desk and whispered a broken psalm.

When her eyes finally opened, her fingers moved quickly again, only to the phone this time.

"Hey, babe." Doug had obviously checked caller ID this time or she wouldn't have gotten through. She'd finally seen his TV interviews last night and knew why he was always ignoring his phone when they were together. How she'd ended up with someone famous was beyond her, but for now things were what they were.

"I know you're busy, but I just wanted to hear your voice

and to say that I'm really glad you've been concerned about me lately, but I think I'm going to be okay."

"I know."

"You do?"

"Yep. It's me I'm worried about. I threw a shoe at somebody, did I tell you that? The day they shaved me down and dressed me up. I took off my shoe and just flung the thing."

Maybe Doug was the fire after all.

"Are you serious? Was anybody hurt?"

"Nope. It seems that I used to do much worse. It's all a blur, those times. I was just going through the motions."

Lily smiled, wishing they were in person instead of on the phone. "And now? Are you still going through the motions?"

"No. Now I'm alive, though still a bit confused. Your friend Ken implied that I need to figure out what to do with my life. If I recall, you said the same thing that day you tossed my chili."

Though Doug couldn't see her, Lily still covered her face. "Look, I was upset. I said a lot of things I didn't mean. As for Ken, he really can't give anybody any advice on knowing what they want to do with themselves. He's as wishy-washy as they come."

"Yeah, well. I don't know. Pray for me. I'm doing a lot of thinking. I'm glad you called. Call anytime."

"Oh, I'm on the secret hotline list?"

He laughed. "Absolutely. In the top slot."

"Okay, have a good day and don't throw those shoes at anybody else."

"I can't. They threw them away. Can you believe it? I paid twenty bucks for those things. They could have lasted another six months. I'm a little ticked about that."

"You are so funny, you know that?"

"I do. Now, you be good and don't behead anybody with Tupperware. Especially me. Just leave a note in my pocket and tell me to get lost. I'm kidding, of course."

Lily pinched her eyes shut, imagining Doug's dancing blue eyes. "I think your head is safe for now. Your heart? I can't make any promises there."

The phone went silent for a moment. "My heart was gone the moment I saw you."

14

He split the rocks in the desert and gave them
water as abundant as the seas.

Psalm 78:15

By the end of the day, most of Lily's work had disappeared from her desk along with her resolve to take
Doug up on his offer for dinner. The thought of eating
at Father Patrick's (or with Father Patrick, for that
matter) was a little scary after the way her mother
had flirted with the man the last time they were
there. Doug had reminded Lily that the priest hadn't
seemed to be bothered by the attention, but that
freaked Lily out even more. A mother who possibly
had Alzheimer's and a boyfriend who just happened
to be their priest would be a little too weird—even
for Lily and her mom.

What had started as a random call earlier today
had turned into a volley of calls, each one more
intense than the next. After the last call with
the dinner invitation, Lily was almost scared
to the see the man in person. Who knew
missionaries could flirt so well?

She found out quickly a few hours later, sitting in Father Patrick's candlelit kitchen while the priest chatted with her mother in the other room. Though still not totally herself, Lily's mother managed to talk a little and seemed to be having a good time.

There was no Thai chili or Chinese chow tonight, just steak, potatoes, salad, and candles everywhere. Big ones, little ones, skinny ones, fat ones. The candles lined the counter and made a centerpiece in the middle of the table. Though she'd enjoyed eating shepherd's pie with down-home Doug, this uptown Doug was pretty nice too. The simplicity of it made it that much more beautiful.

"This is gorgeous," Lily said as Doug sat beside her and laced his fingers in hers.

"Glad you think so," he said, pulling her into his arms. "You're gorgeous too."

Lily lost herself for a minute, burying her face in his shirt and trailing his scar with her finger. Then she remembered where she was and sat up straight.

"What if Father Patrick walks in?" she whispered.

"Say hello and offer him some dinner," Doug whispered back.

"You're a mess, you know that?" she said shaking her head.

"I'm quite aware of that fact, but thanks for the reminder. Keeps the head from swelling when nitwits say nice things about me."

After a few more rounds of laughter, they paused to pray over the meal. Doug cut some of the steak on his plate and offered it to Lily first.

"Delicious. What did you do to it?"

"Not much. Just olive oil, sea salt, and fresh pepper. You like it?" Doug said, offering her some more. "I think it's more fun watching you eat this than it will be to eat it myself, you know." He smiled, glad to see her eating so heartily.

"I guess so. I'm just eating it up, aren't I? Steak isn't usually my thing, but this is really tasty. The salad and potato are good too." She dipped a finger in the salad dressing.

Doug took one of her fingers and brought it to his lips. "It is good."

She sat back, staring at her fingers as he let them go. Doug had seemed so reserved during that taping for television, so in control. But with her he seemed relaxed, but excited at the same time. Sometimes that made Lily squirm in her chair. She never knew what he would do next. Not one to be outdone by his finger kissing, Lily touched the corners of Doug's eyes, feeling each line, something she'd wanted to do for days.

Doug closed his eyes and let her hand slide down his face and over the stubble of his evening shadow, another enticing development in his new look, which seemed to change daily. When Lily's fingers reached his lips, he kissed the heel of her hand.

Lily started to cry.

And he let her.

There were no questions asked or explanations given. Doug simply let her cry. Every now and then he touched her hand or kissed her finger. Those finger kisses only made her cry harder, and she finally hid her face in a napkin.

Doug pulled the cloth from Lily's face, rolling away the stone from her heart as he did. He stared at her with those furrowed, piercing eyes, now as wet as hers. He added laughter to his tears.

"Don't hide. Let me see you."

She gathered the napkin into her fists in front of her face, but Doug held on tight. With nowhere to hide, Lily shook her head.

"I don't want you to . . . to see me. I feel so ridiculous."

So he let her have the napkin too, even though he pulled it down from time to time to kiss her nose.

Once, his hair feathered against her cheek. "That tickles," Lily said, but she kept right on crying.

Doug sat back and draped his arm over her shoulders. "Do you need to go and lie down?"

She shook her head. "I needed to cry."

Doug nodded. "Tears are good. They cleanse the soul."

Tears are good.

Yes, sometimes they were. Good like white roses and pieces of jade. Good like Thai chili. As quickly as she'd started, Lily sat up and dried her eyes.

"This was so nice, this dinner. I really needed it. Next time I'll make you some roti, from Trinidad. Pinkie's recipe. Have you ever been to Trinidad?"

Doug closed his eyes. "Let's see, endless beauty. Deep water. A current that could suck me right in. I've been there." He kissed her forehead. "I am there."

Lily swallowed hard. She'd seen people like this, back in the dorms at college or in high school hallways. All that kissing had always looked ridiculous at best, nasty at worst. But this wonderful closeness was like nothing she'd ever felt. Her mysterious missionary with wrinkled eyes and shaggy hair had become a smooth-faced, well-dressed fashion designer, but what they felt for each other remained the same.

Doug was staring into her eyes when he looked as though he remembered something.

"Do you hear something?"

Lily listened. Was that music? No. "It's probably the TV,

but we should check on them." They stood, and they started out of the kitchen together. "You're nothing like I expected, you know."

He nodded. "I'm nothing like I expected either. I haven't kissed anybody over five years old in five years. I thought I'd forgotten how to do it."

Lily laughed. "You needn't have worried."

Doug lifted an eyebrow. "Doesn't seem so, does it?"

"Nope."

Lily stopped him at the door and touched his face. She was long ripe for a night like this, a love like this. A love she'd thought would never come. But how would she tell him about the mobile pharmacy in her purse? And what would happen when this prescription was over? She'd already decided against asking for another.

Crying might be fine tonight, but every night? Doug was kind, but he was also human. He'd probably be long gone by the time she pulled herself together, but for once Lily didn't care. Five minutes from now she'd be in the next room, lacing up her mother's shoes. Right now, just for this moment, she let herself be in love.

"I really do think that's music," Doug said as they pushed open the kitchen door.

Music it was.

Father Patrick and Lily's mother were cheek to cheek and hand to hand, enjoying an almost silent song on the priest's antique Victrola. The pair waved at Lily and Doug but kept dancing.

"Should we leave?" Doug whispered.

Lily nodded. "I think so. Sometimes there's only enough room on the dance floor for two."

New York wind touched Lily's cheek as she headed in to work the next day. As she entered the door of Garments of Praise, a breeze blew across the backs of her ankles. She smiled at that and at the love budding in her heart. It was pretty powerful, this love business. If they could bottle that, Zoloft would go out of business.

Opening her mid-calf raincoat as she headed for her office, Lily found herself humming "It Is Well with My Soul," the hymn she and Doug had sung together before parting last night. Well, before they'd parted in person—the phone had been ringing when she got home. Doug had told her to call him back when she got her mother settled. She had, and they'd talked for hours: about God, about her job, about Ken, and to Lily's surprise, even about her depression.

And Doug's too.

She'd started on the subject with a joke, but that had led to much more. "So what would you do if you fell in love with someone and then found out she was on anti-depressants?"

Doug had answered quickly. "Check to see if her prescription was the same as mine, and if it was, I'd see if we couldn't get a bulk discount on the fun pills."

"I'm serious, Doug."

"So am I."

She'd been shocked at first when Doug had begun to share, first about his own mental health struggles and, as the night stretched on, about his father's struggles with depression and bipolar disorder. As Lily had listened, she'd felt her heart opening like a flower.

"I was so worried about how you would react. You've been successful in so many areas . . ."

"Exactly, thus the need for said pills."

228

"Ken seemed freaked out that I actually filled the prescription, like I was admitting to some horrible secret something. He thinks the doctor diagnosed me too easily."

"And what do you think?"

"I think some people can live only in picture moments, the times when shirts are tucked in and pleats fall in the right places. When life comes untucked and people come undone, Ken and his kind can't handle it. What really irks me is that he said those things about the doctor, but he was dating her. He probably still is. Can you imagine?"

Evidently Doug could. "Don't worry about Ken. Or what he said," he'd told her. "Quick diagnoses don't happen often these days. Malpractice insurance is too high. Still, it happens sometimes, prescriptions written too easily, too fast, but from what you've told me, it doesn't sound like your doctor did that. She looked at your problem from all sides. Or at least she tried."

Lily agreed. If she wasn't pressing charges against Ken for writing things in her chart, he could cut Anne some slack. She'd told Ken as much when he emailed her asking her to sign an affidavit. That was the last she'd heard from him.

"You're overworked, stressed. That's all," Ken had said. Lily knew it was his notes on the chart that he was really worried about. He needn't have been. She didn't care about any of that. Not anymore.

She went to her sessions (with a Christian counselor now instead of the psychologist, but it sounded similar, just with Bible verses mixed in) and she took her pills, but it was something else, something that God alone was doing in the darkness of her heart—lighting a flame.

After talking to Doug long into the night, she'd stayed up with her prayer book, reciting the Lenten readings aloud and singing the psalms. Despite the morning's cold, Lily's heart was thawing, her hope breaking free.

Once in her office, Lily sat down and buzzed Jean's line. "Do you have any leather strips? Silver end caps, like for the ends of drawstring pants? Oh, and a drill. I need a drill."

Lily's request must have sounded really crazy, because Jean didn't say anything except that she'd be right over with whatever she could find. That meant she wanted to watch pretty bad, since Jean hated leaving her office first thing in the morning. She saved her wandering for the creative hour. The threshing floor, as Jean's space was called, kept her attention during the other hours of the day. Today, though, she'd rush around the place getting Lily's wish list, doing a favor for a friend.

Glancing through her emails (six from Megan alone) and phone messages, Lily smiled at the one scrawled in Chenille's script thirty minutes ago. "Roti tonight?" the words read in black marker with several happy faces below it. On the from line, she'd written "cute old guy." Lily shook her head. She'd have to stop them from calling him that.

Doug was a lot of things, but old wasn't one of them. He had an ability to listen to people and hear their hearts, draw out their stories, but that man was too hot to be called old . . . or was he? Why was aging something derogatory? Couldn't older people be beautiful too? Definitely, but he was still too young to qualify for the old group.

So am I.

Jean appeared a moment later in a tangerine St. John's knit suit and two-toned heels.

Lily's mouth hung open. "You look *good*. The gold on the shoes brings out the highlights in your hair."

"You think? This suit is definitely one of my favorites. I haven't been able to fit into it for a few years."

"Well, you're fitting into it now, that's for sure."

Jean smiled. "If you're fishing for paella points, you just earned a whole pot."

If Jean was the definition of old, Lily definitely didn't qualify. That was one good-looking broad, as Jean regularly referred to herself, despite the fact that Flex's office workout plan had whittled away any broadness she might have had.

"Here you go. It's Raya's," Jean said, plunking down a strip of black leather, a handful of sterling pieces, and a tiny pink drill.

Lily giggled. "That girl has all kinds of stuff in that office of hers. Thanks, Jean. And sorry for calling you away from your scissors. I didn't want to walk around here with a drill and scare you guys any more than I usually do. I know everybody probably thinks I'm crazy as it is."

A smile spread across Lily's face as the project she'd envisioned on the train came together in her mind.

Jean frowned. "We think no such thing. I didn't think you were going to mess up anything. I thought you'd given up on your Lent sacrifice. I hoped, even prayed, that you hadn't. You're doing so well."

"Not really. I just haven't had time to think about it."

"Maybe that's a gift too. Have you heard back from the show? Did you make the next round? You haven't mentioned it—" She stopped short at the sight of the white rose, not quite totally wilted but definitely deflated, at the edge of Lily's desk. "Where did you get that?" Jean asked in a faltering voice.

Lily followed her friend's eyes. "That? Jay brought it to me. From a friend's funeral. It was really quite comforting. We talked—well, he did—about sadness and how it's okay."

Lily pushed the silver pieces around on the desk in front of her: four end caps, six silver beads, and what looked like a clasp. She rummaged in her desk drawer for the wire cutters she sometimes used for small cuts. Perfect. She looked up at Jean, who was still staring at the flower. What was that about? "It's weird."

Jean shook her head. "It isn't weird at all. That boy is going to make a good husband someday. Speaking of husbands . . . you look a little too frisky this morning. You didn't do anything you'll regret, did you? Not trying to pass judgment or anything. Just with your religion and all . . ."

Lily put down the tools and pushed back from her desk, taking a longer look at her beautiful, elegant friend. Jean tried so hard to be cavalier about "the God thing," but the concern in her eyes was evident. Though she didn't necessarily want to follow God right now, she desperately wanted for someone to follow him, for some Christian to be authentic.

Lily hoped God would make up for all the times she'd already failed at that. She walked over and hugged her friend. "No, I didn't do anything I will regret, but thank you for caring. We ate and kissed and talked and kissed . . . and then we went home and talked some more on the phone. I don't think I've ever talked to or kissed anybody that much in my whole life, let alone one night. And guess what? Mom and the priest were slow dancing in the living room while we ate dinner. Can you believe it?"

"I sure can. Your mother is a beautiful woman."

"But—"

"No buts. Sometimes gifts come to us for no good reason. The job is opening our hands to receive them." Jean hugged Lily, speaking the words into her shoulder.

Jean rubbed Lily's back and squeezed her tight before letting go. Were those tears in her eyes? Yes, most definitely tears.

"I'm so proud of you, Lily. Really. As if you were my own daughter. I'm glad you've found someone who can make you as happy as you look this morning. I've missed that smile. Doug is the best I could have asked for you. Keep your faith in God. Men have their own minds."

Lily wiped her own eyes. Where was all this coming from in Jean? And all these tears in herself? She was turning into a fountain.

"Women have their own minds too, especially around here. Now, get back to work before I cry all over my patterns."

Jean shook her head. "I'm going to work in here today. I've been fighting Chenille on that afternoon creative time business. It seemed a waste to me to just do nothing, but Chenille counted up my hours and told me to use them today—or else. Which means she's just going to bug me to death if I don't . . . relax. So I'll stay in here with you. Hand me your design notes." She pushed her glasses up on her nose. "And when we're done with that, you're going to tell me what sort of foolishness you're making with that drill. Are you trying to tread in my territory and make a little jewelry?"

"I am. And I'm glad you're staying. I really have no idea what I'm doing. You and my mom are the ones good with this."

Lily slid her hand into her pocket and smoothed her fingers across the coolness weighting down the bottom. Her hope stone. She handed Jean the file containing her designs and notes for the show, hoping Jean's reaction wouldn't put a damper on her happy feelings.

Jean sat down with the file, then looked up over her glasses. "You'll do fine if the necklace turns out anything like these sketches. Though I see here that Doug made some notes on the second collection that you didn't incorporate."

Here we go.

"Yeah. Doug and I are going to meet about those notes if I make the cut. I held off because I didn't agree."

Jean rifled through the pages. "No need to be afraid. No time either. Anticipate success and do what's necessary to make it happen. I know this is a different kind of design for you, having to keep commercial concerns in mind as well as the artistic. It's a hard balance, but it can be done."

Jean sounded so much like Doug sometimes.

"I hope I can. My head knows how, but it's like my heart doesn't. And the only way I know how to create is from the heart. How can I just tear up everything and make it some assembly-line piece?"

Jean crossed her legs and took off her glasses. "I've worked for the best. Not everyone has it, not even some of the big names. What they do have is vision, good people working for them, and impeccable taste, even if they lack the artistry. Do you think Raya wanted to be here making uniforms? Or even doing the sportswear for Flex's line? You've seen her gowns. She was born for eveningwear, bred for bridal. And yet she's still here. One day she'll have her own firm. So will you. But that day is not today. Today you make the changes."

Eyes closed, Lily listened to the words, letting the truth of them spread over her mind. It ran down her back instead.

"I hear you, but I'm just not sure. What you see there is what I am. If they want me, they'll want that. I don't know how to be something else."

"I'll show you, then." Jean took the top sketch on the pile, a dress with a kimono shape and fluted hemline, and ripped it in two. "Send me the computer files and I'll mock this up—for you. It's beautiful, and if you had a name, it might be the buzz of anyone's fall collection. But again, that day ain't today. This business is hard. Cruel even. The wrong people sometimes make the right moves. The right people always seem to make the wrong ones. I'm not going to let it happen to you."

Lily wanted to cry, but she couldn't. Weeks of crying had left her dry. "I don't know if I want it that bad, Jean. It doesn't seem worth it. I was fine before . . ."

Jean smiled. "That's why I want you to have it, hon. Because you don't want it. Because when your time comes, you won't be afraid to make art, to shake things up. I wish I could say to let it go, give it up, but I won't say it. Vera Wang can't have all the fun. The women of America need you. I need you."

Jean was crying again, but she wouldn't let up. "You keep designing from your heart, being yourself. They'll decide how far they're willing to go. One of these times they'll let you go, and we'll rejoice. Don't betray your style or you won't be able to create at all. Still, remember that this show is looking for a design diva, so the look has to be universal. We knew from the first it'd be more trendy, which isn't really you, but you can make it work. Listen to Doug. He's steering you right."

Lily nodded, taking a deep breath and taking the folder back. The image and its correction were on another page in the file. In the few minutes they'd been talking, Jean had scrawled down some precise and helpful notes, ways to keep something of the original piece. It wouldn't be the same to Lily and wouldn't turn out to be anything she would want to wear, but Lily was thankful for the opportunity, for the experience, and for her friends.

Taking up another of Lily's files, the one with Megan's

name, Jean settled back into her chair. "Now, about this kissing business. Word has it that you've been busy on that front. Is it that good? Humor an old woman, would you?"

Lily hammered the last clasp in place and threaded her new necklace around her neck. She smiled at her friend. "Come on now, Jean, you know me better than that. I don't kiss and tell."

15

So this is what the Sovereign LORD says: "See,
I lay a stone in Zion, a tested stone, a precious
cornerstone for a sure foundation; the one who
trusts will never be dismayed."

Isaiah 28:16

"We've been at this for a while," Doug said, taking
in Lily's tired eyes. "Want to call it quits?"

She nodded, folding the swatches scattered over
her living room floor. "You know what I really need?
A walk. Would you mind putting this stuff up for
me and staying here with Mom while I go out for
a bit? I hate to ask . . ."

Doug stacked the fabric squares and slipped them
back into the tubs labeled "Fluid" and "Flint." "I'd
love to stay with your mom for a while. She probably won't even wake up while you're gone."

Lily beamed. "Thanks." She kissed the corner of his right eye. "I'll be back."

Changing quickly into a pair of sweat-
pants and a shirt and jacket, Lily waved

before heading out. "I have my cell in my pocket. Just in case."

Doug chuckled. "We won't need it. Go on."

He stacked the plastic bins on the couch and headed for the kitchen. Maybe he could whip up something quick for a late dinner. They'd been working for hours. The meager contents of the fridge didn't give him much to work with, but Doug managed to put together some salmon croquettes with béarnaise sauce and a nice salad. He was just setting the table when he heard the first scream.

"He is late!"

Doug clicked off the stovetop and headed down the hall into Lily's mother's room, where he found her tangled in a flowered bedspread and flinging her body as if having a night terror.

Doug sat on the edge of the bed, trying to soothe her, talk to her softly, but nothing helped. She just kept screaming.

"He is late! God help us. He is late!"

She swung her arms, knocking the glasses Doug sometimes wore for close-up work off his face. He picked them up and then held her frail but strong arms. She tore at his fingers. He hoisted her into his arms, ran for the phone, and punched the numbers for Lily's cell. He wasted no time trying to explain. "Come home. Now."

"I'm on my way!" Lily shouted.

Doug certainly hoped so. Lily's mother was trying to bite his wrists. He'd hate to have to restrain her, but this was out of control. Though he'd hoped not to have to, Doug dialed 911 and gave the operator a swift overview of the situation.

Lily and the ambulance arrived together.

The paramedic didn't hesitate to administer her restraints. "Sorry, folks. We've got to be able to transport her. We'll give her something to calm her down."

Lily clung to Doug's arm. "Can we ride along?"

The woman shook her head. "No room. Call her doctor and meet us there."

"Wait!" Lily said. "Can he go along? He's a doctor."

Doug fished into his pocket for his wallet and flashed his AMA card, but the paramedic looked doubtful.

The other ambulance attendant was still trying to get Lily's mother to swallow a sedative.

Doug had seen enough. He picked up Lily's mother and carried her to the ambulance. Once there, he climbed inside.

The paramedics looked irritated but slammed the door and drove away. Doug prayed as they went, knowing that Lily was depending on him to look out for her family.

His family too.

He touched Lily's mother's shoulder as she thrashed against the restraints and spoke quietly to her in Mandarin. "Well. All will be well."

She reeled at his touch. "Don't hurt me. Please . . . I am not Japanese, I told you. I am American, from China. Please . . ."

The terror in her voice broke Doug's heart and chilled his soul. He fingered the scar on his chin. He still had nightmares about the twelve-year-old Ugandan boy who'd attacked the medical team.

Later the two of them had become friends. Doug's scar served as his lifeline to the pain of the world, reminding him that somewhere a child was being forced to kill, a woman forced to starve.

The question was, what had happened to Lily's mother? Who had been late? And why did the memory of it send her into a screaming fit? Though she traveled from decade to decade most days, she had always been peaceful, forgetting Doug and then getting to know him all over again, playing mah-jongg and chatting over tea.

"Hold on, ma'am," the paramedic said. "We're almost there."

Lily's mother seemed to catch the woman's meaning. She closed her eyes. Doug did too.

As he bent forward in the ambulance, the thing that bothered him most was that something horrible seemed to have happened to Lily's mother, something that had to do with being or not being Chinese. Had the American dragon of racism, as his father had called it, had something to do with the memory ravaging this woman's mind? He hoped not but braced himself for the worst.

As if reading his mind, Lily's mother curled into a ball and covered her face with her hands. "Please don't. My husband has money!"

The female paramedic gave Doug a cautious glance. "I'm going to medicate her. This is ridiculous."

Doug watched as the man and woman did their jobs. Lily's mother stopped moving as the medicine took effect. Just then the doors swung open and the gurney rolled out into the hospital parking lot.

A group of nurses came to greet them. The whole group was moving fast. Someone pointed to Doug.

"Do you have her information?"

He nodded. "The basics. Her daughter is on the way. She's covered. Big Apple Medical."

"He's supposed to be a doctor or something," someone whispered.

"That guy? No way. He's a fashion designer. We watched him on TV, remember?"

Doug grabbed the clipboard someone pushed his way and ducked behind a potted plant to fill in the little he knew.

Lily ran in and almost tumbled over Doug's outstretched legs. "Where is she?"

"Right behind that curtain. Didn't they talk to you yet?"

"No. You talk to me. What happened?"

"I wish that I knew. She started screaming that someone was late and . . . Lily?"

She didn't try to hide her tears from him this time. "It's a flashback. She has it a lot. Never like this though. I'm not even sure what it all means. Why Dad being late would make her so upset. Did she say something? Give you a clue? What do you think it means?"

Doug pulled her close. His voice faded to just above a whisper. "You don't want to know what I think."

"There seems to be something triggering this memory, correct? Your father was late? Can you tell me about it?" The emergency room doctor seemed caring despite his obvious strain.

Lily closed her eyes. "I'm not sure what it was really all about, but I'll try to remember. My dad was always on time. Home at 5:42. Seated for dinner at 6:00 sharp. One Friday he just didn't show. My mom didn't really seem upset, but I was freaking out. When I woke up and he was still gone, I was thinking of calling the police and knowing Mother wouldn't let me when my father's key turned in the door. He walked in like nothing had happened, with no explanation. Though I'd heard her crying during the night, Mother said nothing to him then. Just slammed the dishes into the sink, some of her best china plates. She turned to stone in front of me, a statue. It'd seemed like such a big deal, an emergency, but they never spoke of it in front of me."

The ER doctor, a few years younger than Lily, listened to the story as though it were his favorite TV drama. "Definitely weird. And you never asked them anything?"

"Ask my parents for an explanation? No. It didn't work that way. It still doesn't. I should tell you she just recently had some scans done for Alzheimer's, but we haven't heard anything back yet. The doctor warned me that if she does have it, the disease can advance suddenly."

Lily stopped there, not wanting to repeat what else the specialist had said, that if her mother had the disease and it took a quick jump, it wouldn't be long before her mom wouldn't recognize her at all.

Lily had taken her full dose of her medicine the day she'd been given the rundown of the possibilities and hoped and prayed that the day when her mother drifted away from her forever would never come. Even now dread tightened around her as each second passed. Despite her hopes and best-laid plans, she might lose her mother after all. Maybe even tonight. That was too much for her to even think about. At least Doug was here to keep them both calm—

"Get away from me! You got what you wanted. Leave me alone. I'm no spy. Chinese. I am *Chinese*!" Lily's mother pummeled Doug's arm, then clawed his face before the ER doctor restrained her.

Lily wanted to scream too, but no sound came out. Doug tried to come back to the stretcher, but the doctor motioned for him to stay back.

Sobbing over the sight of her mother's tiny body thrashing so violently, Lily didn't know what to think. The quiet little woman whose hair she'd combed, whom she'd fed oatmeal to, became a lioness before her eyes. Only instead of protecting Lily, her mother was protecting herself from something horrible, something Lily wished would burrow back into her mother's memory and die.

"Let's take her on back," an orderly shouted.

Her mother's hand clutched at her arm as Lily walked

beside the stretcher. "You. You are Chinese. Have they hurt you too? Get a dress to cover yourself or your husband will see. They must not see. We must get back. We are late."

Tears poured from Lily's eyes and onto the camisole dress she'd been trying on in the store when Doug had called. She'd flipped the saleswoman two twenties even though the dress was on sale, and she'd run all the way back home. And now her mother thought she was wearing a slip. Even worse, her mother thought she was a stranger wearing a slip.

She doesn't recognize me.

"Mom . . ."

Doug, who'd caught up with them, shook his head at Lily. "Leave her where she is," he whispered.

Pretend? Act as though she were a stranger? Lily wasn't sure she could do it, but if it would help things any, she would try. "I'm here, Mom. I'm here."

"Mum? Is that your name?" her mother asked. Her eyes darted from Lily to the wall.

Lily clutched her mother's hand, perhaps trying to squeeze her back to reality, a reality where she was Lily's mother. Her necklace clanged against the stretcher.

"My name is . . . Jade."

"Jade." Her mother reached up and touched the stone, now threaded onto a strip of leather that hung around Lily's neck. "Can you walk? Can you help me? My dress is torn. The soldiers, they threw my purse somewhere over in the weeds. They're still close. We must hurry."

Doug nodded to Lily to continue, to play out the scene. She looked to him for assurance and was glad to find it on his face.

Unfortunately, her mother found Doug's face too. She shrieked. "Run! They are coming back. They have already ruined me. Go home and stay inside!"

The nurse pushed Lily aside and inserted a needle into her mother's arm. "Run," her mother whispered as sleep overtook her.

Lily stifled a scream of her own as Doug wrapped his arms around her. She wished she could run. Hide. But where could she go? This hurt would follow her wherever she went.

It had always been there.

In the next few hours, the last of Lily's composure slid away. Her mother slept while Ken and the specialist came and assessed the situation.

"Alzheimer's is my diagnosis," the specialist said. "The disease has advanced as I suggested it might. Who do you use for care currently? You might want to up your nursing schedule to around-the-clock care for a while."

She stared past the man, looking at nothing. Up her mother's nursing schedule? Go to around-the-clock care? They weren't even at half-the-clock care.

"She goes to an adult day care center at my church. The rest of the time I take care of her." She squeezed Doug's hands. "My friends help a lot."

The specialist looked at Ken, then back at Lily. "Do you work?"

She nodded.

"Then quit. Or hire a nursing service. You can't continue to care for her yourself. She needs to be watched around the clock, especially in a case like this where the patient has a traumatic and recurring memory that makes her want to escape."

Doug kissed Lily's hair, which seemed to aggravate Ken, but Lily was too tired and too grateful to have some support to care.

"Maybe it'd be best if you leave, Mr. LaCroix," Ken said. "Weren't you with Mrs. Chau when this started?"

"I was in the kitchen. I hardly think there's a connection." Doug's nostrils flared.

The specialist flipped through the chart. "Hmm . . . and she seemed to get upset when you were with her in triage a few minutes ago as well. Dr. Lee is right, sir. It may be best if you leave for now."

Lily narrowed her eyes at Ken. "Don't make this more difficult for me. Please. I need him here."

The specialist shook his head. "We can't take any chances. It's your mother we're most concerned about here, not you. Call some other friends."

Unsatisfied, Ken went further. "Mr. LaCroix has been working at the center Mrs. Chau attends and spends quite a bit of time at her home as well. What do you think about that, Doctor?"

The specialist seemed strained to his limits now. "No. None of that either. For now Mr. LaCroix needs to stay away. He's not your husband or anything, right?"

Doug's hand tightened around Lily's, gripping for assurance.

Her hand remained still. "No. We're not married."

Doug turned away, hands in his pockets, and headed for the door. Lily watched him from the corner of her eye, willing herself not to run after him, not to put herself first the way she'd been doing for weeks. Doug had always made clear his desire to return to Nigeria and finish his mission work. She had always made clear her desire to take care of her mother, even if she had to win that stupid reality show to do it. Although now that too would be just another broken dream.

It was best to admit to herself now that she might never

have a place in Doug's fluid, impromptu life. Waiting for Ken had driven her crazy, but suddenly she wasn't so sure about Doug's prayer-and-a-suitcase lifestyle either. A relationship with Doug came down to the same thing it'd come to with Ken—getting the guy or taking care of her mother. She wasn't the Jade her mother remembered, the one who would run away to save herself. She was Lily of the hope stone, the Rock of Ages.

Li Li of the promises.

If only I didn't love him so much.

Lily didn't know how long she'd been sleeping in the waiting room chair, but the dream of the past few minutes had been wonderful. Doug's arms had been curled around her, his fingers stroking her hair. It had even smelled like him.

"Good morning, beautiful."

She smudged the sleep from her eyes with the heel of her hand. This was no dream. It was better.

"You're here," she whispered in amazement.

"Where else would I be?"

"But the doctor—"

"Shhh . . ." Doug kissed her knuckles. "How is she? We'll figure out the rest later."

"Really out of it. We had a long night."

Doug gave her a squeeze. "Well, at least you know something of what happened. I'm so sorry."

Neither of them said anything, but their hands kept moving, their lips meeting.

Lily finally spoke. "There's more to the story, actually. Or at least I think so. She said some things last night . . ." Lily dabbed the corners of her eyes. "Let's just say I'm glad you weren't here. I almost wish I hadn't been here."

"No, babe. Like you said, this has always been here. You felt it. For some reason now is the time for it to come out. I've been praying all night, and I'll continue to pray. For your mother and for us. Not even Ken and his foolishness is going to confuse me. You're the one."

Lily's fingers slid into the neckline of Doug's shirt, seeking warmth. At the sound of his words, she felt herself relax, felt her body agree. She was the one for him. And he was the one for her. Yet the journey to this point had been so long, so perilous, that she wondered if she'd make it to becoming one. That seemed almost impossible now.

"I kept thinking about my father's part of the story, the version I saw. He was late, but Mom had been late first, a long time ago. Before I was born, I guess. There was another woman with her, maybe one who got away unharmed. My mother didn't.

"Mom could do a lot of things, but she couldn't get past my father with a torn and bloodied dress. Eventually she had to tell her husband the truth, that a group of drunken soldiers, wounded and sent home, had mistaken her for a 'Jap.' A spy. The enemy."

Doug trembled once as though a chill had run through him. "Are you sure? Did she say all that?"

Lily nodded. "Yes. She could remember only the one with the blue eyes. He had his name on his shirt. Maybe Dad got the name out of her somehow. In any case, Dad didn't come home until the next day, just like the day when I was in college. Only the first time he was bloodied and beaten when he took his tea . . ."

Doug scratched his chin. "Your dad just never got over it, I guess. He knew it wasn't her fault. But still . . ." His voice choked in his throat.

Lily's voice was crystal clear. It was all coming together

now. "Yes. That's why she asked me to promise to stay with her when he came in late. He never got over it."

Lily rocked back and forth in the waiting room chair, banging her sides on the hard plastic. Doug tried to stop her at first but soon let her go.

He leaned over and put his elbows on his knees. "There's more, isn't there? Something to do with me somehow. The reason I'm triggering her flashbacks. Just say it. Spit it out."

"It's your eyes. The man who did it . . . he had blue eyes."

Doug squeezed Lily's hand, no doubt wanting a promise of his own.

She clutched his hand back, though much more softly. "No matter what happens from here, I can go through life knowing what love really is, knowing that I've had more of it in a few weeks than some people have in a lifetime."

He let go of her hand. "Don't talk like that, Lily. We can make this work, you know we can."

Lily didn't answer. Not that it mattered. Doug probably didn't need words to sense her doubt. The resignation in Lily's shoulders could have told him everything. The laughing, loving woman who'd opened her heart to him as a flower, who'd talked to him like a friend, was retreating back into her stone fortress right before his eyes. And from his own defeated look, he didn't blame her a bit.

He sighed, wondering how he could turn the tide that seemed about to crash in on them. The wave that threatened to wipe the still-fresh traces of their love clean. To think of his own mother, his own losses, was tempting now, but he shoved the thoughts aside. Those days were gone. There was only now. Only Lily and her mother. Would he stay and join their family? Lily's presence begged the question. Unfortunately, he had no answer. He'd never considered asking Lily to come with him. He didn't dare entertain the thought now.

It would never work, this thing between the two of them, but somehow it had to. Doug was too used to singing a duet to go solo now.

16

His arms are rods of gold set with chrysolite.
His body is like polished ivory decorated with
sapphires.

Song of Songs 5:14

She'd kissed him anyway.

Lily had tried to convince herself to pull away from Doug, to make things easier, but like some action adventure heroine, she'd wanted to have her time with him, even if it might not last. Leaving her mother at the hospital hadn't been easy, but she knew she needed some rest to clear her head and figure out what to do next.

But when Doug had told the cab to go on and walked Lily to the door, she'd forgotten all her brave good-byes and clutched his face in her hands. He'd taken her mouth to his, begging her with each brush of his lips to say something, fix something, do something. Lily had kissed him back with pleas of her own, until they'd stopped, spent with questions and empty of answers.

Pinkie, who'd insisted on coming back to her apartment after a phone call from Lily at the hospital, had seen it all from her window.

"I didn't know you had love like that in you, girl. I'd hoped so, but I wasn't sure. Don't go downtown and get married on me though. I don't do courthouse weddings. Do it in a church. I'll be there."

"I'm not so sure there'll be a wedding, Pinkie. And I'm definitely not sure you're up to coming if there is one. Let alone Mom . . ."

How could Lily even be talking about such things, as if her mother were in the next room resting instead of at the hospital receiving fluids and under observation?

As she always did in these situations, Pinkie laughed and straightened the slipcover on the couch. "Nothing could keep me from coming. And the way you two were kissing on that porch, we need a preacher right now. Your mother would agree."

Pinkie's words made Lily smile. True enough, she and Doug had something special. Where it would go from here, though, was anyone's guess. Doug had already called to check into the around-the-clock nursing care her mother would require, but Lily knew she couldn't afford it. Doug had offered to help with that too, but right now Lily just wanted to sleep. Though no doubt a certain someone would be waiting in her dreams. He certainly wasn't what she'd expected a missionary to be like. Love wasn't what she'd expected either. It was better.

"Thanks for trying to cheer me up, Auntie. I appreciate it."

Pinkie fanned herself with a magazine from the table. "Your mom is going to be okay. We all will. I mean, look at you. Not long ago you were moping around here playing with rocks. Now you've got a new man and you're going on TV."

"The TV thing will probably be on hold for now. The man too." Lily plopped onto the couch.

"Oh, stop moping already. Your mother is going to be fine. Go on the show and marry the man. The way you two are going, you might squeak in two babies before your body closes up shop. Wouldn't that be something?"

Lily covered her face with a pillow. "My body has probably already closed up shop. In fact, it never opened. I might be too old for babies, I'm afraid."

"You're not too old yet any time you can go all over New York City in your underclothes," Pinkie said, pointing at Lily's camisole dress. "Oh, and Jean left something on the table for you."

Lily stood and walked to the table. The scent of Jean's yellow rice and beans had somehow escaped her distracted mind. There was a note too, saying Jean had sent in the last of Lily's sketches to the show and explained the situation. "It's in their hands now," her friend had scribbled at the bottom of the note. Calling her friends had been hard, but she was glad she'd done it.

The show. Lily couldn't even think about that now. Last night she'd left her mother with Doug to take a walk and think over her collections and had ended up at a trendy store trying on a dress that had the shape of something she had in mind for the Fluid collection. Now all that seemed a million miles away. Lily left the food on the table and put the note back in its envelope.

"Barbara is going to pick me up soon. I just came over to pick up the place before you get a nurse in here. Su would have preferred it. I packed her a bag too. You take it up to the hospital."

"Thank you. And thank Barbara too for bringing you over. You really shouldn't have come though."

Lily turned on her side, thinking of what friendship really boiled down to sometimes—a bowl of rice and a clean pair of underwear.

Seated in the recliner now, her neighbor put her legs up on the footrest. Strains of her seldom present accent broke through her speech. "I had to come. She's my friend. So she never told you, then? Not any of it? I told her she should have. I thought maybe she had. You seemed to know something."

So Pinkie did know what had happened. "She didn't tell me really. I pieced it together last night, listening to her scream. I wish she would have told me, but I can see that she couldn't. I sort of wish Dad were here now that I know, but I know he wouldn't have wanted to talk about it."

Pinkie ran a hand along the fabric of Lily's father's chair. "No, he wouldn't. Never did. He hated that I knew. Thought I would tell Johannan or something."

"Did you?"

"Of course not. He always knew there was something though. The Lord often gave him dreams about Su."

The two women rested quietly, remembering both men. Lily saw her father's guarded face in a different way now, shaded by the secrets he'd kept. He wouldn't have been pleased for so many people to know those secrets now, not even Lily. He wouldn't have been happy to know that his daughter had to swallow a pill to get through the day either.

"He would have been proud of you."

Lily tried not to cry. "I've always thought of you as Mom's friend, even maybe been a little jealous at times of how close you were. Today I see that you're my friend too. Thank you for that. Thank you for helping my mother carry the burden of her secret. I wish she'd felt like she could tell me, but I'm glad she could tell you."

Lily stood and walked to the recliner. "How are things at Barbara's? I called a few times since you've been home, and sent a card, but I got the idea she wanted me to stay away."

Pinkie snorted. "That girl would turn away Jesus himself. She's taking good care of me though, I can't lie on that. I should have done more with her when she was young. I'm not sure what, but something. Maybe it will work out with the grandkids. Sometimes you just have to ask God for mercy and move on."

"Yeah." It was all Lily could think of to say. Mercy. Movement. She needed both. But where to go? She suddenly felt like there was no room for even her heart in her chest, like her mother's secret had shoved everything out of the way. And there were still some things she wanted, needed, to know for sure.

"So there's more than Dad's fight with the soldier?"

"Yes," Pinkie said.

Lily waited for her to add more. She didn't.

It seemed she was going to have pry the rest of this story out of Pinkie. She'd never be able to discuss this with her mother, even if her mind was in the right place.

"And Dad hurt the man?"

"Yes."

"The man hurt Dad too?"

"Yes. Very much."

Tears came now, as Lily couldn't ask anything more. Of course the man had hurt her father, even before the first punch had been landed. Lily fought back the bitterness rising in her throat. Whoever had hurt her mother was probably long dead or had long forgotten the incident, yet the pain remained a generation later.

Verses and hymns rushed through Lily's mind, but her heart felt numb.

Pinkie patted Lily's hand. "Just let it go, honey. You have to. Your daddy never did. Hard things can poison you, make you lose faith in everybody, everything. Even in the bad places, there are mercies."

Mercies? Pinkie's words took Lily's breath as a memory skirted across her mind. She was in the park again with her father, folding paper cranes. The warm breeze had made Lily's hair dance, tickling her father's face. He'd laughed and kissed her cheek. "You are a mercy to me," he'd said, and though her little mind hadn't understood completely, she remembered knowing that meant something good.

"Yes," Pinkie said. "Your birth, your life, was a mercy to your father. Your mother too."

"I don't know if I made them happy, but I tried."

Pinkie nodded. "Yes, you did. I talked with your father quite a bit that last week before he died. He was very, very proud of you."

With no tears left to spare, Lily simply stood and walked to the recliner. She bent down to kiss her neighbor's cheek, taking in the smell of care in the woman's clothes, baby lotion and fabric softener.

"You've been a mercy to me, Pinkie. To us. I thank you."

Pinkie's generous bosom rose and fell. "Nothing to thank me for, baby. Thank the Lord. He said people will know us by our love. It doesn't always work that way, but we have to try, especially for our friends. And Su is a good friend. She was a mercy to me too. Us old folks all have stories, you know."

More secrets? Lily didn't want to imagine. Her parents had expected so much of her that it had never occurred to her that they weren't perfect too. And Pinkie? All Lily's life Pinkie had served God and man without complaint. What skeletons had Lily's mother helped this woman bury?

Lord, I thank you for my friends. Help us hold together through whatever may come our way.

Raya, Jean, and Chenille had called her cell and left messages, but she wasn't ready to talk. She'd struggled to discuss her mother's pain from the past with Doug. Pinkie was the closest thing to family Lily had, and still she'd run out of words. She needed some time . . . with God.

"I'm going to get on this couch and take a nap. Would you like to go and lie down in my bed until Barbara comes?"

Pinkie nodded. "I may do just that. Barbara took the children to the library. I told her not to rush back."

"Okay, you rest here, and I'll put a set of the rose sheets on for you. I know you like those better. Let me know when you're hungry, and I'll heat up some of that rice. Do you need water for your medicine?"

"Yes. Thanks for reminding me."

Lily stood and went to the sink for a glass of water.

Lily returned quickly with the glass to find Pinkie holding an assortment of pills in her hand.

The older woman smiled. "Thank you, Lily. You're a good girl. You made up for everything. Even that blue-eyed baby boy."

Lily's glass shattered on the floor.

17

The bows of the warriors are broken, but those who stumbled are armed with strength.

1 Samuel 2:4

"There was a baby? Your brother?" Doug could hardly believe it.

"Yes. My brother. She carried him to term, but he was stillborn."

Was that too a mercy? It seemed cruel to think so.

Doug stared past her, through her. "How could they have kept that in all those years? Amazing. That generation was so different though . . . I don't know what to say. I guess it would have been extremely difficult on your parents if the child had lived, but I can't help feeling sad. I mean, he was your brother."

Lily nodded, thankful to have someone explain the mixture of anger and grief that had wracked her. She stood and pushed back the only part of Doug's hair that still had any length, the silver locks now veiling his eyes.

He pushed the hair aside for her and

sat down on the floor beside her amid the boxes and piles of pebbles strewn about her office.

"Something told me I'd find you here," he said, helping her slide a stack of magazines into a box. "Are you taking everything?"

Lily shrugged. "I don't know. I can't make sense of anything, where to go, what to keep. Megan's pattern is done, and the show says they'll call if I make the next round. Like I care about that anymore."

Doug pushed the box away and traced Lily's lips with his fingertip before kissing her gently. "There's something to keep, okay? In fact, why not just leave this stuff here. You don't have to make any decisions right now. I know it's hard after juggling so much for so long, but just let the balls drop, Lil. They'll bounce back when they're ready."

"But will I?" she asked.

"Yes. You will. We will. God is faithful. Here's something else to keep," he said, standing and pulling Lily up to her feet. He pulled a slim cell phone from his pocket and placed it in Lily's hand.

"I already have a phone, but thanks."

"This is a hotline for the nurses. You can call them, and they'll pick up because they see this number. And you'll know when this phone rings that it's something about your mom."

Her heart melted. "Thank you. Sort of like that Bat phone, but not."

Doug stared blankly, then nodded. "Oh yeah. Batman. I grew up in Asia. Sometimes such things escape me."

She wrapped her arms around him. "That's okay. You catch on to the stuff that counts."

Head on his chest, she listened to Doug's heart, knowing that it was his love she really wanted to pack away in a box where she'd know it couldn't be broken or lost. In all of this, he was her something to keep.

"Speaking of keeping . . . ," Doug said. "I know you're going through some hard things right now and making changes, getting rid of things. I hope my name isn't on that list. I'm ashamed to say it with all that's going on, but I want you more than ever."

Though she knew Doug was sincere and trying to be serious, his words struck Lily as funny, especially his puppy-dog look. She covered her mouth.

He took a deep breath. "So that's funny? Man. See what I get for the whole trying to communicate thing? I'll stick to grunting. Or Morse code."

Laughter forced its way through Lily's fingers, her first in many days.

Doug shook his head. "The line between hysteria and despair is pretty thin, I see."

Lily nodded, allowing this gentle joy to cleanse some of the wounds in her heart before reality sank in again. She let go of Doug's hand and sat back down on the floor. Tears poured down her face.

"I can't do this."

He crouched low beside her. "You can't do what?"

"Love you. Marry you. I don't know what's going to happen to my mother. To my life."

He took her hand. "It's okay."

"It isn't. We're not married. I can't depend on you to get me through this. I mean, you're already paying for the nurses and that phone . . . oh, I just don't know."

"You don't have to know, okay? I shouldn't have said anything. You don't have to worry about me right now. You've had a lot of hard blows."

Lily wiped a tear tickling her chin. "And what's the next

hard blow? When you go back out to the mission field? Or when you decide to travel the world again doing fashion shows? As wonderful as our time together has been, I just don't see you putting down roots anywhere. You're fluid, remember? I'm flint. Stone."

Doug sat on the floor. He pulled Lily toward him. "God spoke to the rock, and water flowed out of it. In every stream there are stones marking and remembering what God has done. I know things are hard right now, but don't make permanent decisions in this temporary circumstance."

She hung her head. "I hate to say it, Doug, but the only temporary circumstance in my life right now is you. This stuff with my mother has been going on for years. I knew it would come to this at some point. I just didn't know the details."

Why are you pushing him away?

Her eyes almost blinded with tears, Lily rose and removed an autographed Sugar Hill Gang album sleeve from the wall. She handed it to Doug, but he wouldn't take it. Her eyes caught a dried hydrangea that had long ago lost its color. After tossing that out, she tried to focus on something else. She paced the room only to pivot sharply and run into Doug's chest.

"Stop. Just leave the stuff."

Lily turned away from him, knocking her goody jar of pebbles, beads, and buttons onto the floor. She bent down to pick them up.

"I just need to find something I can do now. Not something I could have done in the past or something I can do in the future. Just something. Now."

Doug grabbed her hands. "I'm here. Now. And I have something you can do. Kiss me."

Lily stopped gathering the baubles and sat down in the

chair next to her desk. Since their first kiss in the conference room, she'd kissed Doug many times, but this time there was something in his voice, in his tone, that made her almost afraid to reply. After living so many years trying to keep a promise, she knew one when she heard it.

Doug sat down beside her. He leaned his head back and closed his eyes. She needed a promise too.

When she turned to kiss him, Doug was already there. Unlike their kiss earlier, this time his lips were hungry but trembling. Afraid. She covered his mouth with her own, tasting a mint he'd eaten somehow without her seeing him.

She lifted her head. "Awfully minty in there. You just knew you were going to get some more kisses, huh?"

He smiled. "I hoped so. And I'm going to leave it at that. I know there's a lot going on inside you right now. To be honest, there's a lot going on inside me. Even though that was a long time ago and I know from experience that people do terrible things in wartime . . ."

She closed her eyes. "I know."

Doug held her hand. "So I'm sorry if I got insecure at the hospital. I felt like Ken was trying put some space between us, some kind of cultural wall. Don't think it doesn't hurt me that when your mother looks into my eyes, she sees pain. Someone who hurt her."

"Not all the time. She had a great time with you. And I think she'll be fine about it. It's me I'm worried about."

His eyebrows furrowed. "I wondered. Come on. Let's have it, then. Do you look at me and see a rapist too? A dead baby? Are you questioning what people really see when they look at you?"

Lily tilted her head back. Her necklace, her hope stone, hung askew at her neck. "I don't know. When I look at you, I see someone who loves me, but I do feel like my faith in mankind, in goodness, is a little shaken. I read about the Japanese internment camps in books. People called me names growing up. I felt what it was to be different, but it didn't feel like this.

"Now I feel myself questioning everything. If I make it to the next round on the show, will it be because I'm good enough or because they needed a Chinese girl? If I have any chance to win, should I just sell out and do whatever will win so that another Asian woman will be represented? Or do I just pretend none of it matters? It's complicated." She'd have to thank Jean for that phrase. It was very handy.

Doug rammed a knuckle into his mouth, then snatched it away. "Complicated. Yes. That's a good word. Anything worth having usually is. I think you're worth having, Lily Chau. The same blood runs through us. The blood of the world. The blood of Jesus. Don't let messed-up people mess you up."

She nodded. "Okay. It's just hard. Confusing."

"I know. And I'm afraid what I have to say might not help. I have a confession to make."

"What?" Lily backed up into the desk. Sheer terror passed through her. Was this some sort of reality show too? Was a camera going to drop from the ceiling showing Doug's real family—a wife, two kids, and a dog?

"Whoa. Don't look at me all crazy like that. It's just that the phone I gave you isn't just your hotline to your mom. It may be our hotline too for a while. Matthew Oyobo has raised the funds for a dialysis machine. I'm going to go to England and fly it over to Nigeria. Make sure it arrives safely."

Lily's skin started to itch. "When do you leave?"

Doug squinted. "Tomorrow."

The day blurred greens and blues, a rainbow of sorrows. Today Lily's mother had come home . . . and her love was leaving. Yet as in her favorite hymn, all was somehow well with Lily's soul.

Stroking the almost translucent skin of her mother's forehead, she sang the tune softly, then smiled as a faint smile curled her mother's lips. They hadn't been home long, but already Father Patrick had come, Pinkie and her daughter had called, and Jean's basket of provolone and apples, a strange combination Lily had been addicted to last year and hadn't eaten since, was unwrapped and on the kitchen table.

Lily wondered where Doug was, how far he'd gone on his journey away from her.

Lily headed for the couch, bringing her mother along. The phone rang.

"Hello?"

"Did you get the basket? Protein. It's good for the brain. And work out when you're ready. Endorphins are good medicine."

"Thanks," Lily said, checking the vase of orchids on the table in front of her. She reached into the sewing bag on the side of the couch and produced a pair of shears. With a few snips of the stalks, she rearranged the flowers, transforming the tight cluster into a loose bouquet.

Though Jean usually filled in the gaps in conversation, this time she stayed quiet.

Lily did too. She fixed her eyes on the orchids, considering the seed from which their beauty had sprung. The past few months had stretched Lily, prepared her for the birth of a change. And now that it was here, she had nothing to wrap it in, not even one raggedy prayer.

"Look in the bottom of the basket. Under the cheese. That should cheer you up. Call me tomorrow. And just a hint for the record, my rule is no man chasing, but today I might make an exception—"

"Jean . . ."

"Okay, okay. Again I've said too much. See you later."

Her mother's eyes had closed, but Lily knew she could probably still hear everything she'd said. Lily went to the table and probed the basket, digging under the tissue. Her fingers hit something cold and round. A lot of somethings, like a string of pearls. Lily pulled it up and looked at it. Jade prayer beads.

A Post-it was taped to it.

I only ask that you include me in your prayers.

Lily ran her hands across the beads, admiring the masterful detail. These were not strung together with odds and ends as her necklace had been, but they had the same hardiness to them. Beautiful but not breakable. Good. She had a lot of praying ahead of her.

The day nurse, who'd called earlier to meet Lily, arrived for her shift.

At the sight of Lily, she broke out into giggles. "It's you! From the TV show. I knew you were Lily, but not that Lily."

Huh?

"Come in, and yes, I was on a pilot—"

"*The Next Design Diva*! I voted for you. I mean, who couldn't? Those kisses with you and Mr. LaCroix? Hot, hot, hot!"

Lily crumpled into one of the dining room chairs.

"What, you didn't know?"

"I didn't. With my mom and everything . . ."

The stone-cut oatmeal and blueberries Lily had eaten for breakfast tumbled in her stomach as the nurse took her mother away. Hart Nash had left several messages in the past two days, but Lily hadn't been able to catch her and wasn't interested in hearing any more about the show.

264

Now millions of people knew about her and Doug. Her mother had Alzheimer's. Doug was out of the country . . .

In acceptance, lieth peace.

Lily stood, fingering her organza blouse and black velvet pants, touching her hair, washed in rosewater in case she somehow managed to see Doug today. She'd left two messages already. There was someone else she needed to talk to, however. Hart Nash. She grabbed her cell and punched the numbers.

"Hart speaking." The words snapped from the receiver before Lily was ready.

"Hello. It's Lily Chau. Is there something you'd like to tell me?"

A flutter of paper—or birds—sounded through the line. "Lily Chau! I've been trying to get you everywhere. They said you had a family emergency, but your cell was off . . . never mind. Look, you're a hit! The designs are a hit. So much so that I need more. Can you add some pieces? Same feel, of course. I'd need them in seventy-two hours."

"No." Lily's voice sounded beautiful in her ears. She'd expected to say yes, especially now when she so desperately needed the money. But this time her heart spoke first.

"Excuse me? Did you say no? Let me rephrase. I need more pieces. Now. Otherwise, your line won't make the next cut for TV . . . or anywhere else. Ever."

Lily took a deep breath and checked the clock. It was 12:17. Doug was probably already checking in at the airport. Possibly checking out of her life. Though Doug said he'd be coming back to New York, Lily knew he probably wouldn't be able to leave Nigeria.

"Okay. It's been nice working with you. I wish you all the best—"

"What are you, crazy? You're going to throw your career

265

away before it starts? And we showed you on TV with Doug LaCroix. Don't you care what people will think?"

"Not really."

Lily's mother wandered into the living room wearing her favorite skirt. She walked to the kitchen and began to clean. The nurse followed behind, waving to Lily to keep talking. "She's fine," the woman mouthed. Lily nodded. She'd been thinking the same thing. She looked at her mother's clear expression, as if the past several days of confusion had never happened.

The phone shook in Lily's hands. "I understand, Ms. Nash. But I'm not sure if you do. I'm tired. I've worked so hard to make a life that I haven't had time to live one."

"Okay, look. I understand that you're going through some things. I'll give you some more time. You got so many votes that if we don't slot you, there'll be an uproar. When things settle down, give me a call."

Lily's mother looked up from wiping the fridge. "Where is the doctor?" her mother said softly.

Lily looked at the clock. "He's at the airport. Waiting to go to Nigeria."

"So why aren't you there too?" her mother asked.

Tears sprang to Lily's eyes. "Mom? You know who Doug is?" The doctor had said not to expect much too soon. This was more than she could handle.

"Of course I do. What a silly question. Now go and get him before he leaves us. Why are you here, anyway?"

She patted her mother's arm. "I'm here because you are here, Mother. Where else would I go?"

Lily's mother straightened. "Me? Is that why you're here?"

Lily's face was wet with tears now. "Mom, come back to bed. Rest. I promised to take care of you, and I will. Let's get you back to your room—"

Her mother gripped her hand. "Li Li, any promise you made to me was fulfilled long ago."

"Mom, come to bed."

At the Cana wedding, Jesus brought them wine. He fulfilled their desires. Was this is what she had done for her mother?

Now will you do it for me?

Swallowing, Lily found her voice as the nurse disappeared down the hall. "Yes."

Go to the airport and turn Doug's water into wine.

Lily wiped her eyes. "Mom, I think I'm going out."

The nurse appeared again, with her keys in hand. "I'll drive!"

The traffic to JFK airport rose like a wall in front of them, only a shade taller than Lily's fears. What she would say to Doug she wasn't sure, but she couldn't let him leave without knowing that he'd be back, that they'd be together.

Forever.

"You have cell phone?" Her mother asked with a clarity Lily hadn't seen in over a year.

Lily looked out the window at what seemed an endless row of cars. "Yes, Mom. I have my cell. Should I call him?"

Lily's mother reached across her and grabbed the door handle. "No, call us when you find him. Get out."

"What?"

The nurse agreed. "We'll be fine. Go on—"

Lily eased her mother's hand off the door handle. Maybe she needed to let Doug go like she'd planned. Maybe. She closed her eyes. No, for all the peace of acceptance, she couldn't let this go. Love came easy for some, tumbling care-lessly down every street they turned down. Not for Lily. This was the one. The fulfillment.

She opened her phone and checked the time. She'd never make it. He was already in the air. To her surprise, that didn't change anything. She dialed Doug's number, hoping he would answer and wondering what she'd do if he didn't.

He did. "Lily?" He sounded breathless, like he'd run a marathon. "Where are you?"

She gripped her mother's hand. "On my way to JFK. I don't think I'll make it though. Are you in your terminal already?"

Doug laughed. "No. I'm sitting on the steps in front of your apartment. I was going to try the hospital next."

She covered her mouth. "But your flight . . . the machine."

"Someone else is taking it. I needed to stay here, with you and your mom. With my family."

Lily's mother stared straight ahead, having heard Doug's words through the phone. A single tear slid down her face. She turned to her daughter and smiled.

He makes good wine.

Everyone from work showed up for the final episode of *The Next Design Diva*. Lily had spent many hours working on her outfits, ranging from sky blue silk to slate gray wool. Lily's pieces, now transformed on the bodies of models from around the world, graced their wearers with a look blended from across the world's shores and across one man's heart. Lily, in a crushed silk gown, and Doug, in a suit embellished with Chinese brocade, were a pair no other contestants could match. And no one dared try, since the two walked forward to claim first prize. Father Patrick sat in the front row beneath a giant sewing needle, looking up every few minutes.

The host took center stage. "This one was difficult, as some people thought Lily had an edge because of her little love thing with her mentor, but we didn't have anything about that in our rules. Since it's clear from the tapes that she did the work, and since Mr. LaCroix exempted himself from voting, we're going to let the decision of the people stand," Hart Nash said with a smile. "Everyone please welcome, Lily Chau, your next design diva!"

As the $100,000 check was placed in her hands, Lily stared at Jean in the front row, and she started to cry. Raya's family sat three rows back, next to Chenille and Lyle. Jay sat the end of the row. He held up a white rose, a hybrid with splashes of pink. His mother had probably had a hand in that. At the last minute, Raya's dad had offered to fly them all out.

"I want to thank all of you for coming, for voting for me," Lily said. "Last year I made a Christmas gift for someone I loved and dreamed of having my own line of clothes. Today I stand here receiving a wonderful gift." She looked at Doug. "And a man meant just for me."

Doug squeezed Lily's hand and blew a kiss at her mother. "I'd kiss her, but I'm sure you're all tired of watching that." The crowd swelled with laughter.

Father Patrick rose from his seat with a Bible tucked under his arm. He climbed the stage and took Nash's place at the podium.

Lily turned toward Doug. "You told me once that the best way to win this contest was to marry you. Did you mean it?"

He pressed his lips together and nodded. "I did."

"Good. You're getting a double feature tonight, America. I'm getting married!"

The audience went wild as Raya, Jean, Chenille, and even Pinkie and Lily's mother climbed the stage. Father Patrick made quick work of the nuptials, praying over them both as he went.

When the ceremony was done, Lily could see only Doug's eyes and the wonderful lines creasing them.

"You may kiss the bride."

"Gladly." Doug swept Lily into his arms and pulled her to him. He kissed her neck, then touched the stone that hung from it. "Make sure you take that off tonight," he whispered. "I'd hate to break it."

Lily laughed and closed her eyes, flattening her face against his chest as they exited the stage.

"My necklace will be fine, husband. You just worry about yourself," she said, releasing thoughts of everything but this moment. There was no going back to the past or staring into the future now.

Tonight was for love.

Acknowledgments

This book was definitely a team effort. Thanks to everyone for their patience with me while discovering Lily's story.

Special thanks to Jennifer Leep for believing in this book and in me; to Kelley Meyne for catching so many of my "nonsensicals"; and to the great proofreaders at Revell.

To the art department, you are all the best. You've made some wonderful covers for this series. Thanks so much.

Karen Steele, Aaron Carriere, and LaVenia LaVelle, thanks for getting the word out about this series and believing in it.

To the catalog staff and the folks who write the cover copy, thank you! You make my books sound so good I want to read them!

Lonnie Hull DuPont, thanks for being you. Your enthusiasm and professionalism are an inspiration.

To Claudia, Jessica, Amy, Jen, and Staci. Thanks for reading this, even when I didn't know what it would be yet. I'm honored to have you as friends.

To Camy Tang, thanks for answering my endless questions about Asian culture and for being a great friend.

To Heather, Bonnie, and all my friends in the blogosphere, thanks for the encouragement.

To my family, thanks for putting up with me this year. I love you guys.

To my husband, you are my fire, water, flint, and stone. I couldn't do this without you.

To Jesus, thank you. You did it again.

Dear Reader,

I hope you enjoyed Lily and Doug's story. I had a hard time writing it because parts of it spoke to me so strongly it was scary to know what I'd be learning next! It was great though, because as I learned about these characters, I learned about the Lord. As usual, there were some glorious surprises along the way. Look out for Jean's story soon!

Blessings,

Marilynn

Discussion Questions

The questions below are intended to enhance your personal or group reading of this book. We hope you have enjoyed this story of strength in weakness, dreams fulfilled, family, love, and faith.

1. Jade is a story about a Chinese-American named Lily. How do you see Lily's ethnicity play into the story? How is ethnicity portrayed through the other characters (Lily's parents, friends, Ken, Doug)?
2. Early in the story, Lily is offered the opportunity of a lifetime but has a hard time accepting the offer. Why?
3. Lily's circle of friends is a multicultural array of women. Is this a blessing for her? How so? Do you have similar friendships? If not, how can you broaden your circle of women friends to include other women of color?
4. "Everyone needed friends, people who sought to accept more than to understand." How are Lily's friendships developed throughout the story?

5. How are Lily's friends different? The same? Does Chenille's character support and/or challenge Lily differently than Raya, Jean, or Pinkie?

6. Jean's character seems to be searching for something. What? Does she find it? Is Lily searching too?

7. Secrets are woven throughout the story. Lily admits to having stuffed parts of her life in a drawer. How have these secrets shaped her? Have you had secrets? If so, how have you dealt with them?

8. What other characters have secrets? How have their secrets shaped them?

9. Throughout the story, Lily pushes herself to do all and be all for the people who need her. How does she come to terms with her struggle to uphold all her responsibilities? How did Lily learn to take time for herself? Can you relate to Lily's struggle?

10. The story includes characters of all ages. How does Lily's age play into the story? Where else do you see age play into the plotline?

11. In the middle of the story Lily talks to Raya's son, Jay. What does he say to Lily? How does it affect her?

12. What do you think initially attracted Lily to Ken? Was it the same when she met Doug? How did her feelings toward both change as the story progressed?

13. How is Lily's relationship with Doug different than her relationships with Ken? Are they in any way similar? Why or why not?

14. How are Lily's relationships with men different than her relationships with women? Do you think the relationship she had with her father influenced her relationships with other men? With Ken? With Doug?

15. While Lily held tight to her relationship with Ken, she

at first seemed hesitant in her relationship with Doug. Did something change for Lily? What? When?

16. In the beginning, Doug couldn't wait to get back to the mission field. How and when did his outlook change? Why?

17. Lily's faith is a big part of the story. How was her faith challenged? Have you experienced similar challenges?

18. Compare and contrast Lily at the beginning of the story and the Lily who emerges at the end. Does she change? Do people ever truly change? Why or why not?

19. What do you think is the most important lesson for Lily? For Doug?

20. What do you predict will happen to the characters you met in Jade?

Marilynn Griffith is a freelance writer who lives in Florida with her husband and seven children. When not chasing toddlers, helping with homework, or trying to find her husband a clean shirt, she writes novels and scribbles in her blog. She also speaks to women at conferences and prayer gatherings. To book speaking engagements or just say hello, drop her a note at marilynngriffith@gmail.com.

Fashion meets **faith** in the Big Apple!

shades of style

marilynn griffith

PiNK

Don't miss book 1 in the Shades of Style series by Marilynn Griffith

Revell
www.revellbooks.com